# KILLING CARTER

COLIN WELDON

To the little broken souls
still looking at the stars.

# 1985

# Thomas

It's cold in the basement. It always is. The flame from the candle has gone out, and I can't reach it. Not that it matters, I don't have any matches. It's now pitch black and cold, and I can't read my book anymore, which is annoying because I was really enjoying it. It's my favourite. The Twits, by Roald Dahl. When the lights go out, there's not much I can do but lie on the mattress and think about the story I'm writing myself. I've lived in my imagination for as long as I can remember. It's like my brain knows it's gonna be alone for a while, so it just starts to entertain itself before the door at the top of the wooden stairs is opened. I lay quietly and wonder what time it is. I think I've been down here for a few days now, as I've managed to get through two books, and that's how I keep track of the time.

My wrist is hurting a little bit. Sometimes I can fit a bit of my sweater sleeve under the metal, but not this time, which is annoying. I remember the first time they put me down here. I thought it was a little game like hide and seek, but by the time they found me, it had been over two days. There were no books back then, no mattress, only the heater and a bucket. She was the one who insisted that I at least have something to sleep on.

I close my eyes and start to think about the story I'm working on in my notebook. It's hidden somewhere safe for now. Somewhere, they'll never find it. I'm just about to drift off when I hear a creak in the door upstairs.

Light flows down the steps like a river as the shadow descends. It's her.

'Oh no, the light is gone again,' she whispers, from the top of the stairs.

There's the flick of a switch, and the only light bulb down here reluctantly glows to life. She descends gently down the wooden steps. One of them is half broken, so she has to skip that one, we all do. It's actually my fault that it's like that. I fell down the steps when I was much younger, and my leg went straight through it. At least, I think I fell down. I might have been pushed, but I don't remember.

She flows down like some sort of ghost. Her feet don't seem to touch the steps. Her face is white, lit from above now by the dirty light bulb. She's holding a tray with a bowl and drink on it. I move my back against the heater. It's just a reflex action. She leans over and places the tray on the little wooden table beside my mattress. She looks at me with strange, vacant eyes and gives me something that looks like a smile or a good imitation of one. She reaches one of her thin fingers over and runs it through my hair. I always freeze inside when she does that.

'Big day for you today,' she says.

I don't know what she's talking about. She leans down. I flinch a little backwards towards the heater. There's a little clinking sound. She leans down and places the tray on the floor before moving off and lighting the candle again. She returns and kneels down by the mattress. I can see there's a bowl of soup, some juice, and a card balancing on the bowl. She hands it to me.

'Open it,' she says.

I take the card—there's no envelope—and look down. It has a picture of a red bike on the front of it and large yellow letters that say, '11 today!'

Is it my birthday?

She smiles at me again, but her eyelids seem to close for a second, as if she's falling asleep, before they raise again. She's not really looking at me or anything else.

I open the card. There's just a strange-looking X that's kind of squiggly at the bottom. I look up to her.

'Thanks,' I say.

I've learned not to say much when I'm down here. She raises a hand and rubs it a little too hard through my hair.

'You're such a good boy, only a few hours left,' she says, smiling, 'and for being such a good boy, I don't think you need these anymore.'

She reaches inside a pocket of her long black dress and takes out a key. She reaches over to my wrist and unlocks the handcuff. It flops down to the heater with a clunk. There's a slight sting in my wrist, and I rub it a little. It sometimes helps.

Her eyes drift off to the side for a moment, as if she's gone somewhere else. I close the card and put it back on the tray. There's a silence between us. Her head is sort of swaying from side to side before she looks me dead in the eyes and puts her finger up to her lips. She looks up to the top of the stairs as the sound of keys in a door filters down.

'Remember,' she whispers to me, looking back, 'just be quiet. Only a few days to go.'

She reaches down and picks up my book, handing it to me before standing and making her way back up the wooden stairs. The door closes gently, and the key turns.

I hear muffled sounds upstairs, which means he's home, but the soundproofing is so good that there's no point in trying to make out what they're saying. Besides, I don't care. I lean back against the wall and pick up my book, taking a small piece of bread in my fingers.

I look into the candlelight and begin to find myself lost in the pages again. I really don't mind it down here sometimes.

He doesn't come for me down here.

# CONTENTS

Chapter One ..................................................................... 1

Chapter Two ..................................................................... 9

Chapter Three ................................................................. 16

Chapter Four .................................................................. 24

Chapter Five ................................................................... 27

Chapter Six .................................................................... 31

Chapter Seven ................................................................ 33

Chapter Seven ................................................................ 37

Chapter Nine .................................................................. 41

Chapter Ten ................................................................... 46

Chapter Eleven ............................................................... 55

Chapter Twelve ............................................................... 58

Chapter Thirteen ............................................................. 68

Chapter Fourteen ............................................................ 74

Chapter Fifteen ............................................................... 82

Chapter Sixteen .............................................................. 92

Chapter Seventeen .......................................................... 96

Chapter Eighteen .......................................................... 114

Chapter Nineteen .......................................................... 118

Chapter Twenty ............................................................. 125

Chapter Twenty-One ...................................................... 129

Chapter Twenty-Two ...................................................... 136

Chapter Twenty-Three .................................................................. 142

Chapter Twenty-Four .................................................................... 148

Chapter Twenty-Five ..................................................................... 156

Chapter Twenty-Six ....................................................................... 160

Chapter Twenty-Seven .................................................................. 166

Chapter Twenty-Eight ................................................................... 173

Chapter Twenty-Nine .................................................................... 184

Chapter Thirty ............................................................................... 191

Chapter Thirty-One ...................................................................... 199

Chapter Thirty-Two ...................................................................... 207

Chapter Thirty-Three .................................................................... 214

Chapter Thirty-Four ..................................................................... 220

Chapter Thirty-Five ...................................................................... 231

Chapter Thirty-Six ........................................................................ 242

Chapter Thirty-Seven .................................................................... 251

Chapter Thirty-Eight .................................................................... 262

Chapter Thirty-Nine ..................................................................... 267

Chapter Forty ................................................................................ 271

Chapter Forty-One ....................................................................... 276

Chapter Forty-Two ....................................................................... 280

Chapter Forty-Three ..................................................................... 291

Chapter Forty-Four ...................................................................... 301

Chapter Forty-Five ........................................................................ 308

# Chapter ONE

## 2021

### Carter

I've never viewed love as a tangible thing, and I have to admit that apart from being a completely chemical response to procreate, it's served no particular role in my life. That's not to say I've never felt passion, or that I'm incapable of feeling; nor, according to my psychiatrist, am I psychotic or sociopathic. I guess it's just something I don't get. I'm looking through the tinted glass windows of my corner office, which looks out at the Manhattan skyline. The leaves are turning a nice brown this time of year. I look down at my feet, clothed in two-thousand-dollar shoes. I straighten the cuff of my perfectly tailored suit and examine the reflection of my face, one that most consider handsome. A dismissive voice somewhere in the back of my mind tells me my tie is crooked, so I fix it. I turn away from the window as the sun begins to rise through the cold yet beautiful sky of New York. I move to my desk and look at the carved wooden clock on my wall. A gift from an artist called Leah Cairns, whom I discovered and launched after seeing her carve wood on 32nd Street. Beside the ornate work is the contrast of the cold brand of my company, BMX Holdings. The logo is a simple gathering of the letters in bright red relief, surrounded by a yellow rope. I've never told anyone about the yellow rope, and I never will. I stare at the screen of my computer and fold my hands neatly in front of me. I move the cursor of the mouse and click the unread message, already knowing what's inside. I try to breathe normally. I unhook my watch and place it on the desk. I check the email address again out of habit.

From: Claireauthor@gmail.com.

The subject line reads, 'I'm sorry.'

I begin to move my eyes along the text:

'My Dearest Carter, I think that in some ways, looking at you was like looking into the sun. I know why you lied. I get it. Trust me. I tried to get past it, but everything in my physical being is telling me that I just can't. I guess the cracks in both our hearts were just too great to fill with love alone. We're like two broken pieces of separate puzzles that will never fit together. I can never give you what you want from me, and because of that, I have to let you go. You've meant the world to me, but my healing and yours are on two different paths. You are the most gorgeous man. I hope you'll at least miss me as much as I will. I hope you find those missing pieces that cause you to push the people you love so far away. I hope that I do too. Thank you for being the man you are and at least trying. I owe you that much. Take care of yourself. Be kind. Be happy.' C XX

I look at the email, allowing the feeling of panic and agony to wash over me and take me back to that place. A warm baseline of familiarity. I feel my chest contract and relish in the pain. I remind myself that this is what I deserve, that this is home, and that this is what I know. I highlight the email and press delete. I then coldly search for every email we ever sent or received from each other over the last three years. There are hundreds. I highlight them all, then pause for a moment before I press delete. It only takes a second for the history of our life together to vanish. I then move to the trash folder and highlight them again.

Delete permanently.

I calmly remove my phone from my pocket. I search for her contact details, selecting and deleting them. There's a folder I kept of all our photos on all our trips in the cloud. I go to it, briefly flicking through them all. The walks we took on the beaches around the world, the little stops at coffee places, restaurants, skiing. The hugs and smiles and little intimate moments that make up the memories we choose to keep as couples. I select the whole folder and click delete again. In less than two minutes, it's like she never existed. I then remove her email address from my contacts list. I stand from my desk, move over to the conference table, and sit in the chair. I undo my tie and break down.

I allow the dark storm to overwhelm me. I can't breathe, again. The pain subsides. I clear my blurry vision and take long, deep breaths. I begin to berate myself, the usual. Calling myself every name under the sun. You're useless. You're an idiot. You've humiliated yourself. She saw you for the worthless piece of shit you are. Everything you do is wrong. Everything you believe is wrong. You're a stupid child and you'll be alone forever. You're pathetic. This continues for several minutes until the intercom bleeps. I gather myself, safe now in the pain. My baseline restored. I straighten my tie again before moving to the intercom and pressing the button.

'Mr. Page, your 8 O'Clock is waiting for you in reception,' says Marge, my receptionist.

'Thank you,' I reply, 'Give me five minutes.'

I click off the intercom and move to my personal bathroom. I wash my face, comb my hair, and move back to my desk. I click the intercom.

'Send them in.'

## Two weeks later

I'm in the back of a limo on my morning commute to the BMX building. I go over the latest proposal for a new augmented reality system that the company is licensing on my laptop. It's an impressive product, allowing people to communicate in real time using bio-holographic technology that scans the person using it and projects them into your field of view using lenses. It's one of thousands of patents my company holds in new technology, pharmacology, construction, and some government military contracts. I close my laptop, having gone over the project specifications several times today. It's raining out today, and traffic is heavy. I roll the window down a half-inch and let some of the droplets catch me in the face. Rows and rows of suits holding umbrellas pass by the car. A steam vent is sending white plumes down an alleyway. Streams of water run down a fire escape, creating a misshapen puddle on the ground beneath.

I cross my legs and listen to the city. My eyes catch the soaked form of a homeless man sitting under a cardboard sign. I always pay attention to them. They were me, and I was them. The sound of the rain on the metal roof of the car brings the moment back for only a second. My bare teenage feet running down the sidewalk, carrying only a handful of loose clothes. My distraught eyes, struggling to see through tears, and my face and clothes covered in blood. My exploding heart was ordering me not to stop for anything and that no matter what, I was not to look back at the darkness pursuing me. The soles of my feet are cut and bleeding, but it doesn't matter. I have to go, fast. I grab hold of the memory like a cowboy wrangling a steer and whip it back into the dark place where it's kept. I close my eyes for a second and employ a 2-minute deep breathing meditation to get my heart rate back under control. This is the third time this week that memory has reared its ugly head, and I don't understand why. The mind is a curious thing. It defends and attacks seemingly without any pattern or regard for its own self-preservation. Its little mystery will be why it would choose to bring back a flash of terror from 23 years ago at this very moment. However, it's doing it for a reason. It's making links and patterns that its user, me, has now got to spend a few thousand dollars talking to a psychiatrist about. Someone who, at the heart of it, knows very little about the real me.

'We're having a bad day of it, sir,' says Roger, my driver. I nod, flicking my eyes to him in the rear-view mirror, and smiling.

'Don't worry about it, Roger. I love the rain,' I say.

'Is that right, sir?' Roger says, gazing at me.

I very rarely put up the divider screen. I like Roger; he's nearly seventy, a former marine, and recipient of the Medal of Honor. He's an ear to the ground sort of guy. He's been my driver for over seven years and knows everything about everyone. We have a strange and unlikely bond, Roger and I. I guess some people are just in tune. He's loyal, has a dry wit, and I have a feeling he knows more about me than he lets on. Not in a threatening way, mind you. Not in a way that would make me fire someone. In the same way that when you meet certain souls while travelling through the world, it's as if you've met before, on another plane of existence. You can't quite put your finger on why these people are important in your life, but you both know that for whatever reason they need to be there, they're vital for your survival. He has a missing finger on his left hand from the morning of the incident in Iraq. He's also got a prosthetic on his right leg below the knee. When he started working for me, it wasn't a very sophisticated job, so I arranged for him to be fitted out with the latest biotech option as a Christmas gift one year. It's an impressive piece of equipment with a full range of motion and sensory input. He tells me it's changed his life. He doesn't talk much about his military days, other than what happened that day, and even then, he doesn't like to talk about it much. Something I somehow understood better than most. Some dark things aren't meant to be seen again. He was a sniper and always told me that it didn't matter a damn how many fingers he lost on his left hand as long as he never lost the trigger finger. That was the peacemaker, the silencer of life, and the reason he was still alive.

'I hate the damn rain,' Roger says, 'My knees hurt.'

I smile at him.

'I know, Roger,' I reply.

'Everything all right, sir? You seem a little off, if you don't mind me saying so,' he says.

I lean my head back against my headrest.

'I don't know, Roger,' I reply. 'That's lady trouble,' he says.

The response elicits a genuine laugh. It feels good.

'What makes you say that?' I say.

'Only damn thing that can pop a man's balloon,' he says.

'You think my balloon is popped?' I say.

'Your balloon's been popped for two weeks,' he says.

I smile at him. He gives a caring smile back. My chest releases, I can feel the damn crack. I pull it back, seal it up, fast. Back to baseline.

'What's the word on the street?' I say.

'Oh, I wouldn't know, sir,' he says.

'I see,' I say.

'Must be lonely at the top,' Roger says.

'You think I'm at the top, Roger?'

'Well, you ain't on the street no more, that's for damn sure,' he says.

'Can't argue with that,' I say, my smile dropping. My gaze moves outside once again. We've gone a few feet up the road. The rain is coming down hard now. Through the distorted flow of the droplets down the glass, I see the homeless man again. There's a pair of red sandals on top of his cardboard box. I lean up and roll down the window to get a better look, but when I do, the sandals are gone. Rain blasts into the car for a moment before I can manage to get the window back up again. I lean back in the chair and wipe my face.

'There's a towel in the compartment on the floor, sir,' Roger says calmly.

I take it out and wipe my face. I look back at him. He smiles. He knows the reaction when old ghosts come thundering into our real world. He sees them himself. I wonder whether he put that towel there this morning just for me, knowing that this morning, I'd be seeing ghosts. I can't be sure, but deep down, I think that maybe he did too.

## Chapter
# TWO

Roger parks the car in the underground garage, and I exit the building again and head across the street to Jessie's Coffee Place. It's a little hole in the wall that serves the best coffee in the city. It's run by Jessie Kensington, an aspiring singer songwriter from Hoboken. Her father left her the start-up money in his will when he died a few years earlier from an aggressive form of leukaemia. She opened up the little hut right next to the BMX building. I don't think it was a coincidence. I queue up next to a woman holding the hand of a little girl wearing a red coat with yellow buttons. She has a white bow placed neatly in her short brown hair. Her mother is looking at the menu. The little girl looks up at me and stares, the way children do at people they don't know. There's something in the way that children look at me. They see something buried within mine that seems to resonate.

She gives me a smile. I smile back. Her mother turns, seeing the interaction, and politely nods before looking back and ordering from the booth. I glance down at how she's gripping the hand of the little girl. It looks a little too tight for comfort. I catch the eyes of the little girl, and, for a moment, I see something inside them. The polished and controlled exterior gives way allowing a sadness to seep through, as if she's crying out for help for something she doesn't understand is wrong with her yet. I wonder whether she asked for the bow to be placed in her hair this morning or whether it was placed there regardless. Her mother takes her order from Jessie, and they move away. I'm drawn to the little shoes the girl is wearing as they shuffle off down the street, a pair of little red sandals.

'Morning, Mr. Page,' says Jessie, bringing my attention back to hatch.

I smile at her. Jessie has a blue bandana wrapped around her curly, Irish red hair. She has soft brown eyes and freckles across her nose.

'I keep telling you not to call me that, Jessie,' I say, lightheartedly.

'I can't call you by your first name, it's not professional,' she says smiling.

I like Jessie, not in a romantic way, although there has been a hint of flirtatious interaction between us in the past. It abated quickly when I knew what she wanted to do professionally, and I never allowed myself to cross that line. It gives false hope and almost instantly removes the notion that a woman can see past the large building behind me. Jessie is talented. There's no doubt about it. She had slipped her demo into my hand with the sort of gumption and self-belief that were commonplace.

She'd made no apology for it, and I respected her for it. I'd listened to it in my office some morning a year or so ago. It wasn't ready for me to pass on to the music division, and I'd been honest with her about it. I'd broken her heart that morning. I'd seen it, but while talent was one thing, breakout talent was another. I told her, in no uncertain terms, to never give up on the dream and, when she was ready, to slip another song in with my next coffee. It had been a year, and still no demo.

'Usual brew?' she says.

I nod. She goes to make two tall Americanos, no sugar with an extra shot. I lean on the counter as a cool breeze takes my attention down the street. There's an early basketball game going on in the court on the corner. I can hear the sound of the ball as it hits the rim. There's a calmness about the moment.

'Eight fifty,' says Jessie.

I turn back to her and clear my throat. I glance down at the cups in their holder and then back up at her. She tilts her head slightly, a puzzled look on her face.

'No demo?' I say to her.

'It's not ready,' she says.

I raise an eyebrow at her.

'I know, I know,' she says, 'it's almost there, and when it is, it's going to blow your socks off.'

I smile at her and pay.

'I know that, Jessie,' I say, handing her a five and taking the cup, 'I believe in you.'

She mock salutes me.

'You better believe it; have a good one,' she says, looking behind me at a man I hadn't even noticed.

I move away from the booth and cross the street, taking one more look towards the basketball court. I move up the long stone steps to the glass doors of the BMX building. The doors open automatically, and I step through into the main foyer.

'Morning, Mr. Page,' says Marge, head of operations.

Marge, like Roger, has been with me since the start. She's a force of nature, a fifty-one-year-old African American widower to three teenage boys. Nobody messes with Marge, myself included. I approach the desk. Marge runs the place like a military operation.

'Morning, mama bear,' I say to her.

'Ya'll drink too much coffee,' she says, in that southern Georgia twang.

I give her the other Americano I got for her, removing it from the holder.

'No demo?' she says. I smile at her.

'Not today,' I say.

'That girl better get her head out of the clouds and get to damn work on them things or she's going to be left for dust,' Marge says.

'People chase at their own speed,' I say to her, leaning the counter.

'People spend too much time chasin and not enough time doin,' she says.

'I don't know what you mean,' I say.

'Sure, you do,' she says, lifting the lid off the cup and inhaling the aroma.

'Sweet blood of life,' she says, 'you know it's Friday, right?'

'I know,' I say, 'no calls from 9 to 10.' Marge nods.

'Give her a hug from me,' she says.

'I always do.' I lean back and go to move away when Marge looks at me.

'You know, there was a pretty woman in here yesterday from Warner, single, from what I can tell.

'She met Hamland in marketing,' she says with a raised eyebrow. I know what she's getting at.

'And this concerns me because?' I say.

'I'm just saying, she seemed nice, is all,' Marge says.

There's a warmth in her tone. It's kind, yet completely alien. I bottle it away. Rather than making me feel good, I can feel my heart rate pick up. The little tendrils of panic begin to swirl.

'Nothing gets past you, huh mama bear?' I say.

'Not a goddamn thing,' she says.

'I don't think love is meant for men like me, Marge,' I say, leaning in just a little closer in case anyone hears me.

I'm not sure why I say it to her like that. I'm not sure why I say it to her at all. Her eyes widen, a genuine sadness suddenly crossing them.

'No disrespect, Mr. Page, but you wouldn't know it if it hit you in the damn ass,' she says, smiling.

'Is that right?' I say.

'Oh sure, you've been with the most beautiful women that God's art department has churned out,' she says.

'And that's a bad thing?' I say.

'I'm just saying, you gotta see past the paint,' she says.

She wraps her hands around her coffee and leans back in her chair, there's an odd silence. I shouldn't be still at the desk, I'm already late.

'Does anyone know?' I say.

'I had it for twenty-nine years,' she says softly.

'Lucky you,' I say.

'Well, mostly,' she says, 'he was a damn ass.'

I smile at her.

'But he was all mine,' she says.

'I'll see you later, mama bear,' I say, smiling as I turn towards the elevator.

I step inside, and the doors shut. My slightly distorted reflection greets me. The dividing line of the doors seems to split me in half. There's a man in a suit looking back on the right and a little boy in blue shorts on the left. I reach my office on the top floor and seal the door behind me. It's 8:58 a.m., or nearly 2 p.m. in the United Kingdom. I reach my desk and open up my computer, activating the camera, and wait for the call. She's never late. The screen pops up, and in that instant, the world and everything in it falls away. I was wrong about love. It is real. I know it's real because the thirteen-year-old face staring back at me tells me so. It's a familiar face. All but one of its mannerisms are a carbon copy. She's happy. She smiles at me and wraps me in a blanket of contentment. Maybe this is enough. Maybe this is all I can do in this life. She opens her mouth to speak in her London accent.

'Morning Daddy!'

## Chapter
# THREE

Kimberly was born during a two-year marriage to my first wife, Olivia. We met in London and had one of those whirlwind affairs that have pretty much made up the entirety of my adult life. Olivia was and still is stunning. She has long black hair, the most captivating hazel eyes, and is incredibly kind. She has a wonderful family and sings in a local church near Buckinghamshire, England. A good soul who truly loved me. Pretty much the whole package, making it doomed from the outset. I was enamoured by her when we'd met by chance in a bar in central London, and it was full steam ahead. We got engaged within six weeks and were married three months later on the paradise island of Fulhadhoo, in the Maldives. Kimberly was conceived there, on the shores of a calm and peaceful evening under a billion stars.

I remember staring at my reflection in the airport bathroom on the way home. Playing with the weight of the wedding ring on my finger. A black hole opening in my chest. I remember despising my reflection and vowing to myself that I would not go down the same path again, that I would make it work no matter what. Kimberly was born nine months later. Nine months after that, I broke Olivia's heart. I remember the morning she moved back to London, taking Kimberly with her. It was late January in New York and we lived in a modest little condo, this was before BMX stuck oil on the first of my tech deals. I don't remember much about the day I said goodbye to her. I know it was warm and overcast out. They were all packed and ready for the airport when I went into the bedroom where Kimberly was asleep in her little wooden crib and placed my hand on her tiny chest.

She was wide awake and flailing her arms about, presumably waiting for the connection that a father is supposed to give his child. I recall feeling numb at the time. My hands were shaking. I felt something break in my chest, as if an irreplaceable piece had just shattered off. I looked into her little eyes and told her I was sorry, that someday she'd understand, that someday she'd be angry, but that it didn't matter where on Earth she lived—I'd be there. The irony wasn't lost in the moment, she knew she was leaving on an plane, but it didn't matter. I couldn't explain to myself, why I had made the choice, but I knew it was the right one, for her sake. I'd have lost her forever if she'd grown up knowing who her father was. This way, at least, there was a chance. A slim chance that I could have something in the world unspoiled. Somehow, she could lead a happy life, and what had come before could never be repeated again, even if there was a remote chance. I took her little fingers in mine and pledged a lifetime of protection.

The rest of the day was filled with darkness, screams, hidden tears, and a hole from which I didn't emerge for nearly a year. I became ruthless, bitter, and filled with a seething rage towards the world. I found it led to the type of success in the business world only really known by those with similar personalities, and I hated them for it. All of them. I flew to London once a week for the first three years of Kimberly's life. At that stage BMX was barely off the ground and I hadn't gotten much money then, but I did what I could for them financially.

Those first few years were hard work. There was so much anger, so much resentment, so much hardship and pain, but through it all, there was Kimberly. That unknowing little face that looked so much like mine, steering two damaged ships across an unforgiving ocean. Olivia remarried Ben, a schoolteacher, and they had a son two years later. He was a stable guy, a good father, and amazing to Kimberly. I was happy for them, but more than that, I was glad that Kim was able to have a chance at a normal life. She was staring out at me now from the screen. Her long blond hair flicked over her left shoulder.

'What's new in the big blue?' I say.

'Well,' she says, 'today, my friend Teddy told me that he fancies me.'

There's a part of me that doesn't mind that she moved back to London; her accent is the cutest thing ever.

'Who's Teddy?' I say. 'Oh for god's sake Daddy, you've met him like a gazillion times,' she says.

'Is he the one with the thick round glasses that look like jam jars?' I say, suddenly recalling the very boy in question.

Like a mixture of Harry Potter and a Barn Owl.

'They're not that thick, and he only needs them for reading anyway,' she says. A pout is forming on her face.

'Sorry Kim, I'm only kidding, so Barn Ow... I mean Teddy, fancies you then?' I say.

She tilts her head and squints.

'Well, I don't know if it's true or not but he's acting really weird around me,' she says. I look away for a moment to my diary to see quickly what appointments I have coming up. I look back up at Kim, who seems to be doing the same thing. It's an odd moment of synchronicity, but there are certain little habits that she has that could have been pulled directly from my DNA.

'Give me an example,' I request.

'He won't look at me when he's talking to me,' she says, 'it's so annoying.'

'Is he wearing his glasses?' I say, trying not to laugh.

'That's not funny,' she says.

'Yeah, he fancies you,' I say.

'What!?,' she screeches. I can't help but laugh. It feels good. I don't think I've laughed in two weeks.

'I'm just saying, Kim, that's what boys do,' I say.

'That's crazy!' she says, 'they ignore you?'

'What age is he?' I say.

'He's an older man, he's 14,' she says, flicking her fringe as if she's some sort of player.

'Well, you know the rules,' I say.

She frowns.

'I know, I know,' she says, 'be kind to his heart.'

'Well, actually no kissing, but yeah, that too,' I say.

'OMG, gross, as If, that's so disgusting!' she says.

I beam at her innocence and wonder how long it'll last.

'Can't wait to see you,' I say.

'Three weeks,' she says.

'Did you get my surprise?' I say.

Her eyes light up.

'No?' she says, 'Ah, what is it?' she inquires.

I raise an eyebrow.

"Oh, come on, just tell me once," she says.

'Absolutely not,' I say.

'Secrets make you lonely,' she says, echoing something I've been telling her for years.

*She's right. They do.*

'It's not a secret, it's a surprise. There's a difference,' I say.

She sighs and folds her arms. Huffing her face away from the camera. It's my favourite expression because I know she's going to love it. It's a saxophone.

'Fine,' she says.

'How's mum?' I inquire.

'She's good. She's downstairs making lunch for tomorrow,' she says.

The normality of their routine is soothing. I wonder what it must be like for her. 'How have you been since that whole girl thing?' she inquires.

I never keep secrets with Kim about my life and who's in it. She may be young, but I find it easy to talk to her about the women in my life because she seems to enjoy it and it means that I'm not a completely blank slate to her. She not at an age yet where I can tell her everything, not yet, but I hope to be able to someday.

'I'm fine; it wasn't meant to be,' I explain.

'You always say that, it wasn't meant to be,' she says trying to do a bad impression of me. I smile at it.

'Well, there's really no other way to put it, is there? If something's meant to be it will, if it's not it's not.'

'You didn't let her in did you?' she says.

'Kimmy,' I say, softly sighing.

'Don't you sigh at me young man,' she says, pointing at the screen.

That elicits a chuckle from me and I rest my head on my hand. I love it when she makes me laugh. Although we only spend a few minutes talking in the mornings, I could live in it for the rest of my life and be truly happy.

'No, I didn't let her in,' I say, giving her a resigned expression that lets her know she's right about everything.

'Well, then, it wasn't meant to be was it,' she says, 'until you do that, it'll never be meant to be.'

'Thank you, Dr. Freud,' I say.

'Who?' she says.

'Oh, for god's sake,' I say.

I can see her tapping on the computer, Googling him.

'Eh what?' she says, 'I am not an old man with a beard!'

'Well, you sound like one,' I say.

'This is why you're single,' she says.

I look down at the time and see who I have to speak to next. It's Tom Kent. This isn't going to be pretty.

'Kimmy, I gotta go. I'll call you tomorrow yeah?' I say.

'Tell me what my present is!' she roars in playful frustration.

'Nope,' I say, 'kisses.'

'Ugh,' she says, 'fine.' She leans in and kisses the camera.

I put my finger on the screen.

'Love you,' I say.

'Love you,' she says back, without hesitation.

Maybe all I need is this. I keep telling myself. Then the screen goes black and that darkness returns. Maybe it's not. I dial Marge.

'Is he there?' I say.

'He's waiting, yes,' Marge says.

I take a deep breath.

'Send him up,' I say.

I get up from the desk and move over to the side table, where there's a fresh bottle of spring water with lemon slices in it. I pour myself a glass and move in front of my desk. I gently sip the water as the sound of a helicopter somewhere off in the distance fills the silence. After a minute or so there's a knock on my door. 'Come in Tom,' I say loudly. Tom Kent enters. He's dressed in a tan suit and shirt that are struggling to contain the girth of a man whose pain has made its way into his stomach. He nods at me as if there's nothing wrong. I watch him closely. Tom has been the head of international events for six years. He's the best in the business. He has three kids and a devoted wife. He's well paid, and he's a friend. I say was, because in about three minutes, all of that's about to change.

'Morning, big guy,' he says casually, as he pulls out a chair and takes a seat.

I keep a fairly informal style with the people who work for me. With Tom, that informality had possibly been stretched further than it should have. We had worked very closely together, played golf together, had drinks together, and I'd let him past the first wall I kept very much in place for most people I met. So, he knew more about me than most, which in and of itself is not all that much but more than he should have. He leans back on his chair, his tie is poorly tied around his neck, and the knot is too small. What Tom lacks in style, he makes up for in dogged determination and smarts. I take a breath, finish my water, and put it on my desk. I look back at him and fold my arms.

'Tom, you're fired.'

## Chapter
# FOUR

It's the end of the day, and I'm walking past the concierge desk of my apartment building. Alberto, the head concierge, is sitting there dressed in a tailored black suit. He's an Italian man in his forties with thick dark hair. I don't know much about him, other than to say that anything I need, he gets without question. He's not one for talking much, which is unusual for a concierge, but it suits me down to the ground. At the end of a day, all I want to do is nod and go up.

I live in the penthouse on the top floor. A ten thousand square foot space spanning three floors with a rooftop garden. When you get off the lift, you're greeted with plush red carpets that lead up to mahogany double doors that open up into a vast and modern space. I installed floor to ceiling Georgian style windows that cast light everywhere among the minimalist and clean design. I hate this place. I'm not under any illusion as to how lucky I am to have such a magnificent home, nor am I complaining about it based on anything real or tangible. It's something else. I tell myself that it's not really mine.

It's something solid to leave behind for Kimberly so that, in some way, she won't grow up believing I was a complete failure as a father. It's opulent, well above anything my wildest dreams could have imagined, but it's never felt like home. It feels like an empty train station watching over a solitary passenger as he tries to figure out where to go. The sound of my shoes on the wooden floors reverberates around the empty walls. I move over to the drinks tray next to one of the long windows. The sun is going down, and the soft orange light across the city sends me back for a moment to Mulholland Drive. To the three months I spent living in my car in my early twenties. It was a beat-up old Chrysler that leaked, but it saved my life. Something about the colour of the haze being cast between the buildings. It's not quite the same, the LA haze has a somewhat violet tinge to it in the evenings, but it's close enough for my mind to ping a memory. I pour myself a measure of whisky and take off my suit jacket, flinging it on the piano that's placed in the corner of the living room between the windows. I lean my hand against the window and watch the sun go down. I think about the nights spent in that car in the hills of LA.

The only clothes I had were neatly folded on the back seat, and I had ten bucks to last the rest of the day. I wonder if people really know what it means to be truly free. To be a forgotten soul. It was the most peaceful I had ever been. It hadn't lasted. As I gaze out over the New York skyline, I think of Tom Kent. I think about his eyes. I imagine him going home to his wonderful family and telling them about my betrayal, despair, and sheer, unbelievable shock.

I think about them cursing me and wishing me harm. I think about all the unpleasant things that are being said about me. The hatred being spewed across the city up to my window as if carried by a hail of lethal bullets. One of them is hoping it hits its intended target. Right between the eyes. I'm the bad guy now. I feel a sickness in my stomach, and I drop my glass on the floor. It smashes into small pieces as I run to the marble floored downstairs bathroom. I barely make it to the bowl as I vomit. The surge of emotion is overwhelming. I begin to cry—more vomit, retching, and tears.

I don't know what it is inside me. What the hell is this blackness that wants to force itself out of every single pore. I've ruined a man today. A good man. And for what? I fall next to the toilet, my shirt covered in puke. I grab some toilet roll and try and clear my face. The tears won't stop. I whisper to nobody. 'I'm sorry.' I ruined a man to ruin myself. To isolate myself again. To hurt someone good, someone kind, someone with virtue so that somewhere in the world someone else can share a sliver of what's wrong with me. Maybe to pass along the darkness from one person to another like a virus and it makes me ashamed to be alive. I peer out of the doorway into my vast living area and see a little boy, perched on the piano stool, his back turned to me. His little legs too small to reach the pedals. He starts to play the keys. He turns his head and smiles at me, and I begin to feel better. I return to the bathroom and wash myself off before going out and pouring myself another drink. The little boy is gone as I sink into a chair and watch the last of the light disappear across the city.

## Chapter
# FIVE

I wake up screaming in the middle of the night. I jolt upwards. My face and hair are dripping with sweat. I'm disoriented and, for a brief moment, have no idea where I am. My heart is pounding.

'Lights,' I croak, my voice getting caught in the back of my throat.

The bedroom lights flicker on. I don't remember dreaming at all. I remember some sort of snapping sound, a flash of light, and then a sensation of heat and terror. I look over at my phone and activate the screen.

It's 4:13am. I wipe the sweat from my face. My mouth is dry. I flip open the covers and get up. I enter the bathroom and switch on the light. I pour myself a glass of water before catching my reflection in the mirror. I don't recognise the person staring back. I never do. I've always had a strange disconnect with my physical appearance, as if this face belongs to someone else. The face staring back has red eyes. He's been crying recently. I don't know why.

I take off my pyjamas and enter the stone and tiled shower. I turn on the hot water and try to wash off whatever has just happened. I place my hands on the wall and let the warm water flow over me as I try to remember anything from the night's events. Is it just guilt? A physical reaction to a cruel and senseless act? Am I going insane? I stand there for what seems like an age before the sensations of fear and shock fade. I hear my phone ring in the bedroom as I step out and wrap a towel around me. I walk out of the steam filled bathroom and over to my phone. I've been in there for thirty minutes. There are three missed calls.

I'd only heard the last one. The number is from the UK. It's Olivia's brother, Colin. He never calls me. It's at this point that I can sense a veil of anxiety in my stomach. I put the phone down, saying to myself that I'd return the call in the morning, that maybe he was just drunk again and wanted to tell me what a bastard I was. It wouldn't be the first time. He's hated me since the split and has never let me forget about what he sees as the most cruel act anyone has ever done in their lives, my abandonment of his sister and her child. I open a drawer, pull out a fresh pair of bottoms, and put them on. I flip the bedspread over and get in. I lay my head on the pillow.

The phone is always on the side table. Something is screaming at me to dial the number back. Before I have a chance to decide, it rings again. I lean over and pick it up. I move the answer bar closer to my ear. It's Colin. He's bawling his eyes out. I go numb. My mind disconnects from reality as the words come spilling out of his mouth. It takes him a minute or so to say it he's so distraught. I try to put it all together, but all I can do is grab onto disjointed words. Driving home. Drunk driver. Both dead. I lay there, unresponsive. My eyes are wide open, and I'm staring up at the light fixture. Directly into its brightest point. Little flecks of light dance around as I try to focus on anything but what I'm being told.

Through his tears, he hasn't told me what I'm too terrified to ask, but somehow it makes it out. I whisper.

'Was Kimberly in the car?'

I hear shallow panicked breathing and feel my world shattering. I am filled with rage, which explodes down the phone.

'Was Kimberly in the fucking car!'

He answers quickly.

'No,' he says, 'she's okay. She was staying at our place. It was supposed to be a night off for Olivia.'

*She's alive.*

He breaks down again, sobbing uncontrollably on the phone.

'I'm sorry, Colin, I didn't mean to lose my temper. Can I talk to her?' I say softly, trying with all my might to contain the beast in my chest.

'Hang on,' Colin says.

I hear shuffling as he moves around his house. I sit up in bed and close my eyes. I'm sorry, Olivia. I'm so sorry that I let you down. I killed you. This is all my fault. I did this. I hear little tears on the other end of the line. My eyes well up. I feel her heartbreak as if she's reached inside my body and connected her soul to mine. Tears fall again. They come from a darker place. A familiar place. I know how she feels. I know at this precise moment exactly how she feels. I need to grab hold of her. I need to take her little hand and hold on tight because I know what happens next. It's the most important moment in her life, and if there's no-one there to catch her, she'll turn out just like me, and I can't allow that. I don't know what to say. She's just sobbing down the phone, so I say the only thing I can.

'I've got you, Kimmy,' I say, 'you hear me?' I take a breath, 'I've got you.'

I look into the open door of my bathroom. Steam is still pouring out. There's a silhouetted figure of a little boy standing in the doorway.

## Chapter

# SIX

It's twenty-four hours later, and I'm sitting on BA2334 enroute to London. There's an empty champagne glass on the arm rest of my first-class recliner. We're at ten thousand feet and descending. I can see the lights of the city in the distance, cutting through the darkness of the night. I thought I was prepared for the triple blow, but not this. Light turbulence is accompanied by the seat belt sign. I never take mine off. It's strange when the mind suddenly decides to create fear about something. Raindrops begin to form on the window as the sound of soft, barefoot steps running in the night can be heard somewhere in the darkness. I keep my gaze fixed on the window. Accepting the fear that won't leave my side as I take slow, controlled breaths. Maybe it's what's waiting for me on the ground.

I walk through the immigration section, pausing just after the security booth. I walk through the airport and through the large arrivals security doors. She's the first person I see. She's standing behind a barrier, her little face propped up on her folded arms. I see her eyes light up. I can see that's she's been crying. I see Colin standing next to her. She darts under the barrier and comes running towards me. My suitcase falls to the ground as she thrusts herself into my midsection, wrapping her arms around me so tight as if her life depended on it, which now it does. I wrap my arms around her and lay my face on the top of her head. We don't speak. I can feel her letting go as she just cries against me. I look up to Colin, can see he's barely holding it together. She looks up at me, and I smile down at her.

'We'll be okay,' I say. I think she's trying to say something, but her voice is caught up with a million things converging into nothing. I pull her hair away from her face and wipe away her tears.

'Come on,' I say, 'we'll get through it.' 'How?' she manages to say back.

I don't have an answer.

# Chapter
# SEVEN

It's three weeks after Olivia's funeral. I'm back in New York and standing over my kitchen island counter, filling a large white bowl with cereal. I take almond milk from the fridge and pour it in. Kimmy is allergic to dairy. I look up to see her slumped over the dining table, scribbling something in a notebook with a pencil adorned with a fuzzy pink top. It's quiet in the house. The morning sun is coming in through the huge windows, but the shadows the light is casting seem cold and hard. She didn't sleep last night, and neither did I. The last month has been a blur of tears, anger, numbing pain, legal wrangling, bitterness, resentment, and fear. She didn't want to stay in England, didn't want to stay with her uncles, her friends, or her grandparents.

She wanted out. I couldn't blame her. I couldn't turn down her request to come with me to New York. I had taken on the role I had willingly given up all those years before without hesitation. It was only now, as she sat in the emptiness of my enormous space, that I somehow felt more alone than ever.

What did I know about raising a bereaved teenager? Nothing. I had failed as a father already. I failed in taking on the challenge of giving all I had to someone who would look to me for guidance, and direction. I was a hollow, directionless nothing, and those to whom I gave my all invariably left me anyway. She would too, it was only a matter of time before she found out who I really was. I wasn't ready for this. Wasn't able for it. I place the bowl next to her head and glance at what she's doing in her notebook. I stop for a moment; her drawing seems familiar. They're just simple concentric circles, one over the other, over and over again. She doesn't look up as I take my seat and begin cutting into my eggs. I press down on my coffee maker a little too hard. Some of it spills out onto the table.

'Shit,' I say, grabbing a napkin and wiping it up. Kim turns her eyes, normally I would at least get a smile, but not today.

'You want some more juice?' I ask softly.

She shakes her head gently.

'Come on, you have to eat something,' I say.

'I'm not that hungry,' she says.

'You will be,' I say.

'So what?' she says.

She wants a fight. I know she does. She wants to jump up, run across the table, and tear me limb from limb. I can feel the rage inside her, trying to figure out any way to lash out, no matter how small the provocation is. She won't. I know that much.

'Kim,' I say softly to her. She turns her head.

'Please eat something,' I say. She lifts her head and sighs. Sadness has a way of paralysing the expression on a person's face like no other feeling. It's as if the soul is being sucked out. What's left is just a shadow, an empty vessel with a blackness inside it that wants to take over. She raises the spoon and takes a mouthful. Placing it back in the bowl and leaning her head back down on her arm. She starts to doodle again. I lean over and place my hand on the table.

'I don't know what to do,' I say to her.

'What?' she says. I stop talking, reach over, and pour myself a coffee. Not the best thing to drink when your heart is already racing, but I need to do something with my hands.

'Forget it,' I say.

'I shouldn't have come here,' she says suddenly, getting up from the table and running to her room.

The abrupt exit shocks me. The urgency of it, the sudden break and abandonment of it. My chest begins to contract in panic. What the hell is wrong with me? I let her go. The door slams on the second floor, loud enough to make her point. I'm left alone again in this cold, large place near the clouds. A strangely comforting feeling washes over me. I finish my breakfast and put on my suit jacket before moving to the front door. I stop and look back upstairs. I can't leave, not like this. I move upstairs to her bedroom door and gently knock at it.

'What,' comes a soft reply full of tears.

'Can I come in for a second?' I say.

She doesn't answer, but I open the door anyway. She's lying on her bed. The walls are a soft pink, with butterflies and other decals on them. I had decorators come in before I brought her back to try and make it more comfortable. The room is full of things I think she'll like. There's an antique writing desk in one corner, a keyboard in the other. I step inside.

'I have an idea,' I say, not really thinking it through.

She's facing away from me, gripping onto a large teddy bear. She turns to look at me.

'Why don't you come to the office with me today? You've never seen it, and it beats the hell out of sitting around here all day?' I say.

I expect her to say no, but she pauses, looking around the room.

She turns and smiles at me.

'Okay,' she says. I'm a little surprised, but I manage a smile.

'What will I wear?' she says, ' I don't own a business suit?'

I actually laugh.

'You don't have to wear a business suit,' I say.

'What, like, jeans?' she says.

'You can wear whatever you want,' I say, 'but I'm leaving in twenty minutes.'

## Chapter
# EIGHT

A half-hour later, we're in the back of the limo. Kim is wearing a pair of blue jeans, a blue shirt, and a smart looking jacket. She's wearing a pair of black Converse I bought her a few days earlier. She's staring out the window at the passersby as I catch Roger's smiling face in the rearview. He looks over at her as she takes her phone out and begins messing with it. Who needs parents nowadays when kids are raised by fucking Tic Tok?

'You're looking like a real professional, little missy,' Roger says.

Roger's been kind to her since we got back. He's taken her shopping a few times and has generally been a rock through all of this. I think about all the people closest to me in my life, of which there are barely a handful, and I wonder what I'd do without him. Kim likes Roger a lot. He's the grandparent I couldn't give her. She looks up from her phone.

'Thank you, Roger,' she says.

She's on autopilot. Her responses have no real sincerity to them, Roger's eyes meet mine in the mirror. He smiles at me, and I nod back in thanks for trying to engage. Kim's eyes move back down to her phone. At that moment, my own phone rings. I look at the screen. It reads 'Pit Bull'. Daniel Foster is five feet three. He's my head of acquisitions and one of the fiercest negotiators I've ever met in my life. He's obese, balding, and unassuming. He's the kind of guy people look past at parties to see who's actually worth speaking to. He likes it that way. He's like a deep-sea shark, circling hundreds of feet below his prey while they go about their business. He moves slowly until he has to move, and they never, ever see him coming.

He has one of the keenest intellects and the ability to cut down the most aggressive people in the business. He's turning the Ivy Leaguers into mincemeat with glee. It would be easy to put it down to the "chip" someone like him gets growing up. The chip of always being the guy picked on in school because of the way he looks, but with Daniel it was different. His confidence in himself is resolute. I'd met him on a street curb one night after a party. He had a shiner and cuts on his hand. I sat down and asked him if he okay, and to this day, I'll never forget what he said to me.

'I loved every minute of it,' he'd replied, laughing, with blood oozing from his mouth. I answered the call.

'Danny,' I say.

'Carter, we have a situation here. 'Jean is on his way,' he says.

'Oh shit,' I say, looking at Kim. Today was not the day to bring her to the office. 'Yeah,' he says.

'Can you stall her?' I say.

'Stall Jean?' he says.

'You'll think of something,' I say.

'She hates me,' he says.

'Everyone hates you,' I say.

'One of these days I'm going to start taking that personally,' he says.

'I'll be there in thirty minutes,' I say, 'pull the Glomax merger file and just be nice to her when she's there.'

There's silence on the phone for a moment.

'She just arrived,' he says.

'What?' I say.

'She just walked past me,' he says, 'she's on her way to your office.'

I put my head in my hand.

'Screw it, just entertain her,' I say.

'I hate to reiterate this, but she hates me,' he says, 'but I'll take it for the team.' 'You're a good man,' I say.

I hear him muffle something under his breath before hanging up.

'That didn't sound good,' Kim says. I look at her.

'This may not be a great time for you to...' I can't finish the sentence.

Her eyes begin to widen with the rejection I'm about to lay on her shoulders, and I feel like a piece of shit. She looks down, and I see that face I left behind all those years ago, still in her bassinet.

'Never mind,' I say, looking up at Roger's eyes, which are boring into mine. 'Let's stop off and get some muffins. How about that?' I say to her.

'Okay,' she replies. I think I see an uptick in her lips, almost forming a smile. I meet Roger's eye.

'Jean coming in?' he says.

'Yes, Sir,' I reply.

'Battle stations,' he replies. I nod.

'I'd offer to throw myself on the grenade, but having done that already, I'll let you take this one,' he says, looking back to the road.

## Chapter
# NINE

Jean Rose was the CEO of Pink Pepper Books. She started her first store from a shed in her parents' backyard thirty years ago in a small town called Bemidji in Minnesota. The same town is now famous as the backdrop of a TV show called Fargo. We merged six years ago, as her humble beginnings spread across the country and into twelve countries around the world. I'd had an affinity for brick-and mortar bookstores. Now they were losing money, and as much as the board was pleading with me to do so, I just didn't have the heart to cut them from the portfolio. I was still looking for that one story, that one story that would change everything, so I'd covered some of the costs out of my own pocket to appease the bean counters. Jean was very much aware of the financial situation. She wasn't aware that I was the only person keeping them alive. That would complicate things. As far as she was concerned, I was the bad guy. Jean believed in them. So did I, and while I assured her over the years that I'd never let them go, she still saw me as just a moneyed suit. Jean was bullheaded and passionate, and while there had always been a line of respect that she'd been forced to convey to me, she was always prepared for me to pull the trigger on them and had kept me at arm's length throughout our partnership. Of all the people who feared me the least, she was one of them. These meetings were always tense.

I had Roger pull up outside Jessie's coffee shop, something I never liked to do because it came across as arrogant, but today I didn't care. I signal to Kim to get out, which she reluctantly did, and we walked across the street. There was no question this morning, so we walked straight up to the counter. Jessie emerges and looks down at Kim.

'Well, hello there!' she says jovially, 'and who might you be?'

'This is my little girl, Kimberly,' I say, looking at her. Kim looks up at me and frowns.

'Sorry, my completely adult daughter, who's definitely not a little girl, Kimberly,' I say, smiling to Jessie.

'Well, it's an absolute pleasure, aren't you just beautiful,' she says, 'I just adore your shoes, those are fire.'

'Thanks,' says Kim, 'my dad got them for me.'

She wiggles her feet and crosses one leg over the other.

'Cool accent,' says Jessie, 'I love, love, love the English accent, it's so sophisticated.'

'Dad says it's always used for the bad guys in movies,' Kim says.

Jessie laughs and looks at me.

'That's not always true,' Jessie says, 'what about Colin Firth?'

'He's the exception,' Kim says, raising an eyebrow and smiling.

'You're damn right,' Jessie says, raising a hand and giving her a high five. 'Yeah, or Kate Beckinsale,' I say to both of them.

'As if!' Kim says, 'she's so far out of your league you might as well be playing different sports.'

Jessie bursts into laughter.

'I like her,' Jessie says to me.

I give Kim a fake scowl.

'Yeah, I'm on the fence about that,' I say.

'What can I get you guys?' Jessie says.

'The usual for me and...' I look at Kim, who shrugs.

'You like strawberries?' Jessie asks her.

Kim nods.

'I'll make you my strawberry surprise, you're going to love it,' she says.

'I'll get a couple of your famous muffins as well,' I say. She moves away from the counter. I look down at Kim. She's staring at her feet.

'We should get Roger a muffin,' she says.

'Totally,' I say to her. Jessie comes back with our order and hands down a clear container with something pink. The ice in the cup clinks as Kim takes it and tries a sip.

'Pretty, huh?' she says as she hands me my two coffees in the holder and a little brown bag with muffins. I take a cursory glance into the coffee cup holder and smile back at Jessie.

'Almost,' she says. I pay before taking Kimberly back to the car. She hands Roger the bag of muffins through the window.

'Life saver,' he says to her, 'you try and enjoy yourself today, and if he gives you any hassle, you call me and we'll go to the park.'

'Okay,' Kim says. We walk the rest of the way to the office and leave Roger to park the car. Upon entering the lobby, I see Marge at the desk. She has a stuffed toy on the counter. Marge was the first person I told about Olivia. She's already standing up and moving around the table.

'Get over here right now and give this old woman a hug,' she says to Kimberly. They embrace warmly. Marge reaches behind her and grabs the teddy. It's a little pink unicorn. She hands it to Kim.

'Thanks,' Kim says.

'His name is Bob,' Marge says.

Kim laughs, and it fills the world with joy.

'Bob?' she says, looking surprised at Marge.

'Sure thing, why not?' Marge says.

Kim plays with the unicorn's ears.

'Okay then,' she says.

'Now what in the name of Sam, did your father bring you into this boring place today?' she says, looking at me.

'I thought she might help me out for the day,' I say.

'You know who's waiting for you in your office, right?' Marge says.

'I do,' I say.

Marge looks at Kim.

'You ain't going in there, are you?' she says.

'Who's in his office?' Kim says.

'Maybe it's best if you stay with Marge for an hour?' I say.

That face turns again, and at this point, I'm done caring.

'Never mind. She'll be fine, maybe the unicorn will calm her down,' I say to Marge.

'Well, this should be interesting,' Marge says.

'I'll see you later on, don't worry, little missy; she doesn't bite, and even when she tries to bite you, you bite right back.' Kim is still playing with her stuffed animal as we walk away.

'Who's she talking about?' she asks as we enter the elevator. I turn to her. 'You're about to find out.'

'What did you do?' she asks, 'maybe I shouldn't have come.'

'Don't be silly,' I say, 'might be fun to see your old man get his ass handed to him by someone else. Then maybe you won't be so hard on me.'

'That's not fair,' she says.

'Look, I promised you a day in the office, and this is what it's going to be, warts and all,' I say.

'Is it wrong that I'm kind of excited to see this?' she says. I can't help but laugh.

'Not at all, I'm sort of excited too.'

## Chapter
# TEN

We exit the elevator, and Daniel is just standing there, like a guard dog, leaning against the wall with his arms folded. He glares at Kimberly, seemingly biting his tongue at something profane that was about to spill out. I move outside and look towards the door to my office, it's shut.

'Well?' I say to Daniel.

'Well, she just walked in,' he says.

'So, it's that bad?' I say.

Daniel looks at Kimberly and raises his hand.

He gives me a look that asks, 'What the hell am I doing?'

'Hey,' he says to Kim.

Kim waves. I look towards my door.

'Okay, let's see what hell has in store for us today, huh?' I say to her as I turn to head to the office.

Daniel looks perplexed. There's a strange apathy surrounding me. Or, to be more accurate, a nonchalant wish for someone stupid enough to pick a fight with me today. We walk towards the office door, and I open it. Jean is waiting on the sofa next to the wall. A large TV screen is mounted above her head. She's reading one of my magazines, it's a National Geographic from ten years ago. I have a thing about whales. Jean is wearing a dark, fitted suit. She's tall, has long, dark hair, pristine black Louboutin shoes, and a crisp white shirt open at the neck. Jean's gorgeous, but she never uses it on me. She doesn't need to. She's got a keen intellect and is one of the fiercest businesswomen I've ever known. We have a strange relationship if you can call it that. I bought her company because I've got a love of books.

She'd overextended herself. When the crash of 2008 tore through the world, it was either sink or swim. I paid pennies on the dollar for it, but I saw something in her. She almost let it sink rather than give up control. I admired her passion and saw in the numbers that she knew what she was doing. She'd brought the company back from the brink with the BMX investments.

I bought her company five years ago with the understanding that she would remain as director of the literary division. She gives me a look like she's about to chew me out, but her eyes dart straight at Kimberly. She looks back at me, and her eyes soften. She uncrosses her legs and puts the magazine down on the table.

'Hello Jean,' I say, 'make yourself at home.'

I motion to Kim. '

Kim, this is Jean Rose,' I say.

Kim's mouth wraps around the straw of her drink. Jean's face turns to hers. Whatever she was about to hit me with appears to have vanished. There's a softness in her look. Kim gives her a little wave. Jean waves back.

'Hello, Kim,' Jean greets, 'it's a pleasure to meet you, cool trainers.'

'Thanks,' says Kim.

I think I hear a crack in Jean's voice. It's strange. I informed her via email of a personal tragedy a few weeks ago and asked her to handle some of the outstanding affairs we had scheduled. I didn't specify what that tragedy was in the mail, but news travels fast around here, especially with Marge in the building. She would have warned her to watch her step. Jean keeps her emotions very close to her chest. Other than when she's pissed off with me, as for empathy or connection in terms of friendship, it's always business. It's one of the things I like most about her. She's detached, like me. But there's something there now, in her eyes, that seems so familiar, and it looks like she doesn't know what to do with it.

She turns to me.

'I'd like to speak to you privately,' she says.

I turn to her, and smile at Kim.

'Let's get it, Jean, Kim's here to learn the intricacies of my day; if that means being chewed out by you, so be it,' I say, smiling at her.

I look at Kim.

'Take note, Kimmy,' I say, leaning against my desk.

Jean actually smiles at me and then looks at Kim.

'Sorry about this,' she says.

Kim seems amused by it all. Jean turns back to me.

'You cut my marketing by 30%, you son of a bitch,' she says, folding her arms, 'without so much as a reach around.'

She turns to Kim.

'Sorry,' she says.

'I don't know what that means,' Kim says softly, taking more of her drink.

'You also fired Tom Kent!' she says, 'are you out of your mind?' I take a breath.

I was out of my mind, totally and completely.

'If you going to sell off my company piece by piece, just get rid of me now, you don't think I have options?' she says, this time injecting fury into her voice.

She means it too. She came in here to tell me what's what, possibly get fired, and then tell me to go fuck myself.

'I'm not doing that, Jean,' I say.

'Then what the hell, Carter?!' she says, sitting back down on the sofa.

Silence descends in the room. Kim is looking at me.

'See?' I say to her.

I take a breath and pick up my coffee, taking a sip of it and move around my desk. There's an awkward silence swirling in the room as I think about what to say next. Jean fills in the empty space by looking at Kim.

'Do you like to read?' she says calmly.

Kim nods.

'You know they call me the demon around here?' she says.

'I do nothing of the sort,' I say.

'Of course, you do,' Jean says.

She turns back to Kim.

'What's your favourite book?' she says.

'I read the Lord of the Rings before Christmas, it was my mom's favourite book,' Kim says, her eyes gravitating towards the floor.

My eyes meet Jean's. I see a flicker of resonant sadness in them.

'I loved that book,' Jean says, 'you know, Tolkien actually made up his very own language for it. The imagination is amazing, isn't it?' Kim nods, she fiddles with her stuffed toy.

'I'm not offloading Pink Pepper,' I say, breaking a moment that is beginning to become uncomfortable.

Jean turns to me.

'You know what's happening in brick and mortar, and I need to make up the shortfall from last year's Christine Waits debacle,' I say.

Jean takes a deep breath and sinks into the sofa.

'That's not fair,' she says.

'I'm not blaming you,' I say.

'Yes, you are,' she says, 'you've never forgiven me for that, and now you're putting me up against a firing squad for it.'

Christine Waits was Jean's call. In her defense, it was legal who dropped the ball on it, and the board wanted her gone because of it. Waits was an author who Pink Pepper had signed for a seven-figure deal, the biggest in the company's history. Her book was brilliant, insightful, and, in truth, a masterpiece in literature, and it was about to rock the world. The problem, in the end, was that she didn't write it. She'd been a student at Princeton and had found an archived manuscript after hacking into the college servers. She turned out to be a better programmer than a writer. She'd found a twenty-year-old story from a student named Sarah Paulson who'd died tragically in a car accident and had simply taken it, hidden the file under an unbreakable encryption, and pawned it off as her own work. Only with the fortitude of Paulson's steely-eyed grandparent, who'd been her de facto mother and knew her writing and story well enough to recite entire sections, had she been discovered. It cost BMX a fortune in litigation and tarnished Pink Pepper with a stain it was still digging itself out of. Something new caught my attention on my desk.

There's an envelope next to my diary with my name handwritten in black ink across the front. I paused for a moment before picking up on Jean's comment. I pick up a silver letter opener, a gift from Marge on my birthday last year, and I slip it under the seal.

'Let's everyone just take a breath,' I say calmly as I open the envelope.

There's a yellowing piece of paper inside. I remove it and look at it. It looks like a page from a book. I check the envelope, there's nothing else inside. This is odd. I look at the page and begin reading it. I stop breathing. My office and everyone in it fall away as I suddenly find myself in a dark place, a chasm of nothingness. I don't know how long I'm here. I continue to read the page from the book I know all too well. Somewhere in the darkness, I hear a voice. My heart is pounding. I'm losing it. I hear the voice again. It sounds so familiar. I look up through the darkness and see Kim standing in my office.

'Daddy, are you alright?' she says, 'you've gone terribly pale.'

I glance to my left, to the mirror on the wall. My face has gone an ashen white. I crumple up the page and put it in my pocket. I clear my throat, try to focus.

'Give me a moment,' I say, my voice sounding shaky.

I need to regain control as soon as possible. I struggle to get the words out.

'You don't look well Carter,' Jean says softly.

'I'm fine,' I say, 'legal bills have that effect on me.' I smile at her, moving to the cabinet and pouring myself a glass of water.

I gulp it down.

'Bastards charge you for breathing,' I say.

*It can't be.*

I look out at the skyline and see a pair of eyes in the sky looking back like the Cheshire Cat. A ghostly grin forms in the clouds before disappearing. I want to run, as fast as I can towards the rising sun. To cast off my clothes and dive into the sea until I vanish into nothing. I can feel sweat on my brow and try desperately to compose myself.

'Even vultures have to eat,' Jean says, 'I get it.'

I pull myself back to reality by gritting my teeth and screaming into my mind to reveal nothing.

'I'll try not to take that personally,' I say to her, my voice slightly cracking.

I glare into her eyes again. There's no way she could know anything. No way anyone could. Whoever has placed that envelope on my desk isn't in this room. Are you sure? Says the voice of the little boy. He appears on the sofa, swinging his little legs. I ignore him. I turn to Jean and take a breath.

'I had no choice in firing Tom Kent. I can't go into details, but trust me on that,' I say.

She folds her arms.

'Bring me some projections for Q2 with the new endorsements, and I'll take another look at the budget, okay?' I speak far more softly than I'm used to.

She picks up on it and seems taken aback by the sudden, almost fearful way I'm speaking to her. She looks at Kim, then back at me.

'Okay then,' she says softly, 'maybe we can go over the numbers at lunch later in the week?' she says.

I nod.

'Sure thing, let's do that,' I say, stiffening up my body and shutting down my emotions, hoping she'll take the hint to get the hell out of my office. She does.

'It was really nice to meet you, and don't believe what they say about me, I'm really not all that bad,' she says.

'I believe you,' Kim says, smiling at her.

Jean gives her an earnest wink. There's something very attractive about it, which is an odd reaction for me to have as I've never looked at Jean that way, despite what everyone in the company thinks. She nods and leaves. Kim looks at me.

'She likes you,' she says as soon as the door is closed.

'What?' I say, still reeling from what's inside my pocket.

I move back around my desk and pick up the phone.

'I said she likes you,' Kim repeats.

I'm already connected to Marge and ignore her.

'Has anyone else been in my office this morning or late last night?' I say to her. 'Not that I'm aware of, is there a problem?' she says.

'Can you pull the camera feeds of the building for the last twenty-four hours? I want to have a look,' I say.

'Of course,' Marge replies with her usual sharp professionalism. I hang up the phone and sit down. Kim is looking at me. The little boy has vanished.

'Okay, you're acting really weird,' she says.

'Sorry about that,' I say.

'She was pissed,' Kim says. I smiled at her.

'Believe me, that was a light morning,' I say.

I can feel the weight in my pocket like a lead brick.

## Chapter
# ELEVEN

It's lunchtime, and me and Kim are sitting in Central Park eating frozen yogurt. It's a beautiful, sunny day. Kim is staring at the branches of a tree. There's a small robin darting about among the leaves. It should be a moment of serenity, but my eyes are scanning the faces of people passing by. I've had threats before. It's nothing new when your profile is well known. There are a lot of sick people out there who never had a chance., who don't fit into the system or have been so beaten by it that their minds just crack. I could have been one of those people. I should have been one of those people, but I guess I just figured out how to survive. The piece of paper in my pocket is no normal threat. Part of me is trying to remember is it something I actually did myself years ago and forgot about? Did I keep it? Put it in an envelope and leave it in my safe? Was I looking at it yesterday? I don't know. I don't think so. I turn back to Kim, feeling an urge to protect her from what's to come.

'You bored yet?' I say.

'Huh?' she says.

'It's not exciting being in an office all day, is it?" I say.

Kim is still grieving, and she needs strength. We both do. Kim suddenly bursts into tears. She drops her ice cream in the grass and buries her head in her hands. I move towards her as instinct takes over and place my arms around her.

'Oh, hun,' I say, 'It's okay.'

She shrugs me off.

'It's not okay!' she growls.

I'd been expecting this. She'd been unusually quiet all day, just sitting on my sofa in the office, doodling and watching TV. Numb. The body will only tolerate this for so long before reintroducing all of its chemicals in an attempt to reset the baseline.

She shrugs off my attempt at comfort and stands up.

'I don't know what the fuck I'm doing here!' she shouts at me.

She's never spoken to me like this. She suddenly seems to be directing all of her rage towards me. I see heads turn as her eyes burn. It's like I'm looking at a complete stranger, and I'm not equipped to deal with it. I react.

'Don't speak to me like that!' I snap back with far more anger in my tone than was intended.

It's more out of shock and fear than anything else. There's a button that's been pushed. Her anger has found a hole in my guilt at being her father. Her face drops, she turns and begins to run away from me.

I turn to see judgemental stares.

'Shit,' I say, 'Kimmy wait!' I say, dropping my ice cream and running after her.

It's now a full-blown scene in the middle of the park. I don't care. Something inside of me is shattered because of her abrupt departure. She's leaving me, rejecting me, and it's like a little supernova is going off in my chest. I run to her, run in front of her, and put my hands on her shoulders.

'Stop,' I say softly, 'please just stop. Talk to me.'

She glares at me with sad eyes.

'I hate you,' she says softly.

My heart cracks.

'Why?' I say back.

She looks away from me, somewhere off into the distance. She sits back down on the grass and folds her legs.

'I don't know,' she says, as her tears flow down her cheeks.

I look to the skyline, see the top of my building, where my office is located, and see the sun flicker in the glass. I take my phone out and text Marge.

'Cancel the rest of my day.'

A few seconds later, I get a response.

'Done'

I move down to Kim's level, we're both quiet. She just sits there and cries. I take the only action I know how to take. Change the view.

'Want to go for a walk? I'd like to show you something,' I say.

She looks up at me. I smile at her kindly, begging her with my eyes to give me a chance. She nods.

## Chapter
# TWELVE

On the south side of the Brooklyn Bridge, next to Empire Fulton Ferry Park, is where Jane's Carousel is. I decide to take the subway, as the distraction of the city might help take our minds off the park. We don't talk much on the way down. Kim's feet sort of shuffle along the pavement as we arrive at the carousel. It's old-fashioned and beautifully decorated with 48 hand carved wooden horses.

'This thing was built in the 20's' I say to her, smiling, 'pretty cool, huh?'

She looks up at me and nods.

'I guess,' she says.

Her voice has the same tone that I remember having as a child when you don't know how to apologise to a parent.

'Want to give it a go?' I say to her.

'Can we just watch?' she says.

My heart sinks a little, she seems disappointed, not so much in the destination as in me.

'Sure,' I say.

We walk over to an empty bench, and I motion for her to sit.

'Let me go get some fresh ice cream,' I say.

'Okay,' she says.

I come back a few minutes later, and we sit, watching a small number of families, couples, and tourists as they mount the carousel and take their slow trips down their own childhood memory lanes. They seem happy. I wonder what it is about going around in circles that people seem to enjoy so much. We don't talk for what seems like an hour. My mind is locked on the piece of paper lodged in my pocket. We just sit and watch. It's Kim who eventually speaks first.

'I don't know who you are,' she says softly, looking down at her teddy.

'What?' I say, looking at her.

'I don't, though,' she says.

'Of course, you do,' I say, realising that she's absolutely right.

She has no idea who I am. For years, I had been practising a speech in my head. I'd have to give her a speech about what happened between me and her mother someday.

Why I left.

'No, I don't,' she says.

'Okay,' I say, sighing, 'that's fair enough.'

I lean forward, leaning my chin on my hand.

'I'm not mad at you,' she says.

'Yeah, you are, and it's okay to be, really,' I say to her.

We are silent again as I try to contain the sheer terror of having this conversation. I'd rather be facing down a hundred Wall Street bulls in a boardroom than this right now. At least I know what I'm dealing with. Nothing prepares you for this.

'What do you want to know?' I say to her.

'Only what you want to tell me,' she says.

I smile at her.

'You'd make a good CEO, you know that?' I say.

'I don't care about money,' she says.

'Well, you should,' I say.

'Why?' she says.

'Because it's the world we live in,' I say.

'Does it make you happy?' she says.

*Nothing makes me happy*

'You make me happy,' I say to her.

She gives me an honest, joyful look that just melts my heart. I can feel tears beginning to well in my eyes. I clear my throat and take a breath, forcing them back to baseline before she can see them.

I can't do this. Not now.

*Who the fuck put that page on my desk?*

'That's not answering my question,' she says.

'You're very observant,' I say.

'Mom used to put little notes in my lunch box every day,' she says.

'Oh yeah?' I say.

'She drew these little hearts around a smiley face,' she says, 'it was supposed to be her face, but she couldn't draw very well, and it looked weird.'

I laugh.

'She was the best,' I say.

'You didn't,' she says.

It's as if I can actually hear a crack in my chest. It's difficult to put into words the loss of being a father, but you know you weren't prepared for it.

'I know,' I say.

'Don't get me wrong,' she says, 'you do really nice things for me and buy me stuff, and we talk loads more than other dads who aren't...'

She trails off.

'Aren't there?' I say

'Sort of,' she says.

I take a long breath and stand up suddenly.

'Okay,' I say, pacing away from her for a second.

I turn back and grit my teeth.

'Let's do this,' I say with affirmation.

'What are you doing?' she says.

I look away for a moment before moving back to the bench and taking a seat.

'Ask me anything you want to know about me, and I'll tell you anything, but...'

I extend my little finger.

'You have to promise me that anything we say between each other is just for you and me,' I say.

She extends her hand, and we lock little fingers.

'Agreed,' she says.

I lean back and fold my arms.

'Go,' I say.

'Why did you leave mum?' she says.

I throw my head back.

'Jesus Christ, hitting me with the hard stuff first, huh?' I say, smiling at her.

She doesn't smile back.

'Sorry,' I say.

'It's okay,' she says.

'Well,' I say, pausing for what seems like a year, 'where do I start?'

'Was it because of me?' she says.

'What?' I say, leaning up, 'No! Never, ever, ever think that.'

'Okay,' she says.

'Kimmy, you had nothing to do with it,' I say.

Did she? Did I run away like a coward?

'It was complicated why it didn't work out between the two of us,' I say.

'Why?' she says.

'Okay,' I say, "your mom and Ben were really happy, weren't they?'

She nods, and tears fall.

'Are you sure you want to talk about this?' I say.

She nods.

'Please,' she says.

'I know what it's like to grow up in a house where there's no love,' I say, 'I know what it's like knowing that your parents hate each other. I know that when that happens, they take it out on you.'

'You hated mom?' She says.

'No, that's not what I'm saying,' I say, 'but I knew that I wasn't the right man for her, I couldn't give her what she wanted, and she would have ended up miserable. I know what it's like to grow up in a house like that. I know what it does to people. I didn't want that for you.'

'I don't understand,' she says.

'That's why it was the best decision I've ever made. I was despised for it, but I knew what lay ahead; I knew because of who I'd become.

She looks up at me with those crystal-clear eyes. It's so hard not to take her in my arms and never let go.

'Kim,' I say, 'the truth about me is this.'

I pause and look back at the carrousel.

'I'm a complete fuckup," I say.

I feel a strange sense of release at the admission. As if the dam's bottom had suddenly weakened.

'No, you're not,' she says, wiping away more tears.

I can't even look at her.

'You're like a gazillionaire or something,' she says.

'I thought you said you don't care about money?'

'I don't, but I know how hard it is to get, you have to be super smart, successful, and hard working.'

'Well, that's not always true,' I say, 'but that's not what I'm talking about.'

'Okay, so you didn't want me to grow up in a miserable house. I get it. I'm not stupid. My friends' parents recently divorced.

'Okay, and how are they doing?' I say.

She pauses for a second.

'Okay, I think I get it,' she says, 'but that's not you being a fuckup.'

'Language,' I say.

'What?' she says, 'you're allowed to say it an I'm not?'

I sigh.

'Yeah, pretty much,' I say.

She shakes her head.

'My friends' parents at least tried,' she says.

That one hurts.

'I did try,' I say, 'some people just aren't meant to be together, and sometimes you're going to have to make the toughest choice to bring it all down for the greater good.'

'So, it was my fault,' she says.

'Oh god,' I say, putting my head in my hands.

The music from the carousel drifts in the wind. I look up to the gorgeous sight of the Brooklyn Bridge as it stretches across the Hudson.

'No, Kim, it wasn't. Let me ask you this,' I say her.

'Okay?'

'Did you ever feel trapped?' I say.

'Trapped?'

Yeah, as if you couldn't leave your room for fear of being yelled at or…I trail off.

'No,' she replies.

'Did you ever feel like you weren't safe?' I ask.

'No,' she says.

'Did you ever feel like you couldn't speak?' I say.

'No,' she says.

'That's why I left,' I say, meeting her eyes for a moment and holding them.

'I didn't do it because of you, I did it FOR you,' I say.

She looks away and down at her feet, then out to the water. She looks back at me.

'I still don't get it,' she says.

I can't help but sigh and laugh half-heartedly.

'You need a few relationships under your belt, kid, then you will. Just trust me on this one, okay?' I say.

'Okay, so you're telling me that in all these years, every single woman you've had as girlfriends, you'd end up in some sort of weird house where nobody could speak?' she says.

That one kind of stumps me.

'No,' I say a little hesitantly.

'So I call it bullshit,' she says, 'there's something else.'

I smile at her and shake my head.

'I'm not easy to get along with,' I say.

'Yes, you are,' she says.

'Thanks,' I reply, nudging her shoulder with mine.

'It's a long story, Kim,' I say.

'You told me you'd tell me the truth,' she says.

Not this one.

'I did, yes,' I say, 'it's not like I haven't been married, Kim. I've had good people in my life.'

'Yeah, and every time you bail. What's to stop you from bailing on me again?' she says.

There it is. The one question impossible to defend against.

'Ah Kim,' I say looking at her, 'that's never going to happen, and you know it.'

'Yeah, well,' she says.

'Look at me,' I say.

She does.

'I'm not going anywhere, ever, do you understand?' I say.

She just nods.

'I promise you,' I say.

My phone vibrates in my pocket. I remove it, it's a text from Marge.

Sorry to interrupt, the security footage seems to have been corrupted or something, it's not there.

My anxiety begins creeping into my chest. I look at the message again before catching Kim's annoyed eyes. I put the phone away.

'I'm sorry,' I say.

'Whatever,' she says, 'you're a busy man.'

We sit in silence. She gets up suddenly and walks towards the carousel. I fucked up, again. She gets on one of the horses and begins going around. I sit there and watch. My mind begins to drift.

## Chapter
# THIRTEEN

### 1987
### Thomas

I rub my fingers over the glass beaded eye of a very old teddy bear. I named him Snuggle when I was younger. It's hard to see him in the dark. The only source of light down here is the crack beneath the landing door. It creeps down the wooden stairs into the basement as if reaching an arm down to grab me. It isn't long enough to get all the way there. I can see my pale reflection in Snuggle's eye. I've got bags under my eyes because it's hard to sleep on the mattress down here. It's too old, and the springs are broken. It's also hard to move when they handcuff my wrist to the radiator. They don't always do that, only when they're really mad at me. It's weird though this time, I don't really know what I did, but boy, oh boy, did she let me have it. At least the cuff isn't too tight this time, and the skin has healed enough that it doesn't hurt that much.

It's just hard to sleep because it's about a foot off the ground and my arm keeps going numb. I've propped up the only pillow I have against the radiator, and I try to sleep sitting up. It seems to be the only way. The good thing is that at least I'm not hungry. I have plenty of food. They never let me go hungry, far from it. I have snacks and treats, and she brings me three meals a day, as well as homemade desserts that are delicious. For all her faults, she can cook. I'll be down here for seven days. I'm on day three. It's always seven days. That's the punishment, seven days in the dark, sometimes cuffed to the radiator. The walls of the basement are custom made by him.

He's an engineer, and the soundproofing on the walls is pretty much airtight. There's no point in shouting or screaming. There's a baby monitor thing in the corner so that they can listen to me if I need anything, but calling for help will only get me another seven days. That was a tough lesson I learned from my younger self. There's a hum coming from the corner of the basement where the gas boiler is located. It comes on and off through the day and night. It doesn't bother me that much, but sometimes there's a funny smell, which gives me a headache.

The thing about being afraid is that it comes in waves. I have weird feelings in my chest when she brings me food. My heart beats really fast, and I can feel my forehead begin to sweat. It's only when I'm left alone down here that the feelings begin to go away. I'm allowed a small flashlight that I use to read my books. It's really like a second bedroom, except that the mattress in the one upstairs is much more comfortable.

There's a well-stocked bookshelf down here, and I read a lot. I love reading about all sorts of things. It takes my mind away from the darkness and fear and lets me travel and be whoever I want, which is cool. The only thing I don't have down here is a clock or a watch, so I don't really know what time it is. I'm told what day it is when I wake up, so that's how I keep track. I try to sleep if I can when I'm tired, but I never seem to be able to feel fully rested.

My hair has been annoying me lately. It's getting really long, and my fringe is covering my eyes. I hate that feeling. I've asked her if she would allow me to get a haircut because it's hard for me to see, but it's always up to her. Right now, she's not allowing it. She tells me that my hair is her favourite feature and that I should stop complaining about it. I don't really want another seven days, so I stay quiet about it.

My stomach is rumbling at the moment, so I know, at least, that it must be nearly lunch time. I had blueberry pancakes this morning, which were delicious. The plate is still on the concrete ground next to the bed. She'll pick it up when she brings me my lunch.

I spilled some chocolate on the cream carpet in the living room. That's why I'm down here. It was only a tiny bit, and had I noticed before she got home, I would have cleaned up right away. She's always inspecting the carpet, always vacuuming it, sometimes up to three times a day. It has to be spotless all the time. I hate the sound of the vacuum cleaner. I find it hard to breathe when she turns it on. Normally I'll just go to my room if I can make it up the stairs without being chastised.

I was careless this time, and a tiny spot of chocolate landed on the carpet. I was no bigger than a small fingernail, but she'd made me get on my knees, burying my face in the stain like you would a dog. Five minutes later, I was down here.

I know this may sound strange, but down here, I feel safe. Yes, I'm alone in the dark, but she only comes down three times a day. She's not orbiting me like a wolf in a forest. She's so angry, all the time, especially when he leaves town on business once a month. That's when things get really bad. I hear her in the kitchen late at night talking to herself, crying, and banging cupboard doors, pots, and pans. If she's going to be awake, she makes sure I am too.

I notice a sudden break in the light from the door up the wooden stairs. I sit up straight, my back placed firmly against the radiator. I hear the key turn, a dark silhouetted figure appears, and she makes her way slowly down the wooden steps, carrying a candle so she can see.

Her face is lit from underneath, but she's wearing a kind smile. There's always been something strange about her eyes. They're bright blue, but there doesn't seem to be anything behind them. They're cold, they've always been cold. She smiles warmly at me. She's in a good mood. Or else she's trying to pretend that she is. Her eyes tell a different story. It's like looking at a shark.

She's holding a tray with a bowl on it. There's a plate with toasted bread. It must be soup. It still smells good, though. She comes over to me and kneels.

'Hello Thomas. How's my little man doing?' she says.

'I'm okay,' I say, looking away from her for a moment.

She places the tray on the ground, offloading the bowl of soup and toast. There's a large glass of orange juice as well as a small piece of apple pie. She looks at me and runs her finger over my forehead, brushing the hair away from my face.

'Perhaps you were right,' she muffles, 'we'll go get you a haircut this weekend. Does that sound like fun?'

She rests her hand on the side of my face. I feel connected to her. I was ashamed of myself for letting her down again, angry and not knowing how to be good.

'Yeah, I'd like that,' I say, flinching a little at the metal cuff around my wrist.

It's starting to hurt a little. She looks at it.

'Tell you what,' she says, reaching into her pocket and taking out a small key, 'you've been really quiet. How about you spend the rest of your time with two arms?'

She laughs at me, as if it's a little game. I nod at her, making eye contact. She seems soft, I think I heard her slur that last sentence. She reaches over and removes the handcuffs. My arm swings free.

'Your Daddy is coming home today, a whole day early. Isn't that super news?' she says, tilting her head.

It somehow sounds like a threat.

I nod my head.

'Yes, that's wonderful news,' I say.

She places her hand on my face again.

'Such a gorgeous boy,' she says, standing up, turning, and moving back up the stairs.

I watch the candlelight cast a shadow of her body on the wooden stairs as she glides back up. The door to the basement slams shut, causing me to jump. My heart is pounding as I'm left in the dark again. The aroma of the food is the only thing I concentrate on as I take both hands and begin to eat.

It's not wonderful news that he's coming back a day early. Not wonderful news at all.

## Chapter
# FOURTEEN

### 2021
### Carter

It's the evening, and we're back in the penthouse eating dinner. I've tried my hand at her favourite, beef lasagne. It's my first time making it. While I'm able to cook, it's not something I do often. I don't like being in the kitchen. I've moved the table over to be beside the window because I thought she might look out over the city as we eat. We haven't spoken much throughout the day. We came back after the carousel, and Kim went to bed for the afternoon to take a nap. I don't think she slept, though, because I could hear whimpering through the corridor. I gave up and tried to take a nap myself, but all I did was lie there staring at my suit jacket hanging on my door.

I haven't taken the piece of paper out of it all day.

I lay down the dish in front of Kim, whose feet are propped up on the chair. She's leaning her chin on her knee.

She looks at it, and I get my first smile since the afternoon from her.

'That's a nice job,' she says.

'Thank you,' I say, 'not bad for a novice.'

We tuck in, glancing out at the setting sun.

'So, what happened with the last one?' she says.

My eyes flick to her.

'The last one?' I say.

'Yeah, what's her face,' she says.

I chuckle.

'Claire,' I say.

The mere mentioning of her name sends memories of our whirlwind romance thundering through my mind. I loved her. That's what I call it. It's not really love, though. Not in the sense that you might be familiar with.

'So, what happened?' she says.

'We broke up,' I say.

'We?' she says.

I smile.

'She broke up with me,' I say.

'What did you do this time?' she says.

I can't help but laugh. It's a hearty laugh that comes from somewhere deep inside. She joins in.

'What? I'm just asking,' she says.

'Why do you think I did anything?,' I say.

'Dad!' she says, 'you can't be this incompatible with every beautiful woman you meet.'

I lean back and laugh again.

The laughter subsides, and a sadness follows. I look at her. She must see something in my face because she gives me this concerned look.

'I lied to her,' I say.

'About what?' she says.

I pause and look out at the orange hues of the setting sun. I bring my hand up and rub the side of my face. I lift my glass of Malbec and take a sip.

'Everything,' I say.

'What, like, everything?' she says.

'Everything,' I say.

'Did you at least tell her your real name?' she says.

I smile at her.

'Of course, I did,' I say.

'Well, then you didn't lie about everything,' she says, 'so what did you lie about?'

'Kim, relationships aren't easy,' I say.

'Seemed easy for Mom and Ben,' she says.

'That's different,' I say.

'Why?'

'Because some people are normal,' I say, 'I am not.'

Kim turns her head and looks around the vast living space.

'No shit,' she says, motioning to the inside of the room.

I grin.

'That's not what I mean,' I say.

'I don't get it,' she says.

'It's not important, Kimmy, what's important is that I lied to her, she found out, and that was that,' I say.

She puts her fork down and gets up to leave the table.

'Where are you going?' I say.

She turns back.

'You said I could ask you anything and you would tell me the truth! You pinky swore it,' she says.

I sigh.

'Okay, you're right, sit down, Jesus Christ,' I say.

She moves back to the table slowly and takes her seat.

'She asked if I was taking any medication,' I explain.

'Medication?' she says.

'Yeah, I was on antidepressants until a few months ago,' I admit.

'What?' she says.

'It's not a big deal, Kim, I'm under a lot of pressure, and there's things about me that are hard to deal with sometimes,' I say.

'Okay,' she says, looking at me like a crazy person.

'I'm not on them anymore, they sucked,' I say.

'She dumped you because of that?' She says.

'Well,' I pause, 'no, not just that.'

She calmly looks on.

'I have this thing, where I lie about little things,' I say.

'Like what?' she says.

'Little things,' I say.

'This is becoming painful to listen to,' she says.

'All right, let me give you an example,' I say. 'Say you're on your way to your friends' house, and they ask how long you'll be there, and you say 30 minutes, KNOWING it'll take you at least an hour. Have you ever done something like that?'

'All the time,' she says.

'Well, that's what I mean about little things, except I do it about everything,' I say, 'when I'm with someone, these little white lies become big white lies. I don't know why I do it, I just do.'

Her face drops.

'How many times have you lied to me today?' she says.

'I've never lied to you,' I say.

'Is that a lie?' she says.

I can't help but laugh, but instantly my brain goes into overdrive as I think back. I can't help but come clean.

'Yes,' I say.

'What?' she says

Her face is now deadly serious.

'How many little lies have you told me?' she says.

I lean back and rub my face.

'I don't know,' I say, my heart is beginning to race, there's a black hole opening up to a thousand chats we've had, and all of a sudden, I feel more exposed than I've ever felt in my life. There's a sudden look of fear in her eyes. As if she's looking at a stranger. She pulls her legs up on the chair and wraps her arms around them in an odd defensive posture.

'Okay, just relax, I'm thinking,' I say, 'I've never ever lied to you about anything important, Kim. Maybe when you were younger, I had to tell you things to make you feel better about why I lived here and you lived there, you didn't understand why you had two dads. You didn't understand the situation. It was that sort of thing.'

'Okay?' What else?' she asks.

I really don't like where this is going.

I can't tell you who I am, can never tell you what I've done, you can't know that. You just can't.

She speaks first.

'I don't know anything about you. I don't know anything about where you grew up. Where my grandparents are, where you went to school. Nothing,' she says.

'I told you your grandparents aren't with us anymore,' I say.

I feel heat against my face. I see a raging fire. I control the image. Force it back into that dark place.

'Is that a lie?' she says.

'No,' I say, 'and I told you I grew up in a tiny town nobody's ever heard of, so what does it matter?'

'Because,' she says, 'it matters. It's weird that you've never had a girlfriend for longer than a year, it's weird that the second I was born, you just shipped me off and it's just weird that you're this rich and so alone.'

That one hurt.

'Jesus, I'm taking a pounding today, huh?' I say, 'not everyone can do the family thing, Kimmy, not everyone is able to have the relationships that you're used to.'

She gives me a suspicious look.

'What spooked you today?' she says.

'What?' I say.

'You got spooked by something,' she says.

I think very carefully about the next things that come out of my mouth.

'Yes, I did.'

'Well, what was it?'

I lean back as she folds her arms and glares at me. There are only two options, to lie to her or not. She's not ready for this. I'm not ready for this.

'We're being sued,' I say.

A horrible knot in my stomach makes me nauseous, and all of a sudden, I feel the urge to vomit.

'You're being sued?' she says.

'Yeah, it's a big one, It could take away all of this?' I say, waving a finger around the penthouse.

She sighs and picks up her knife and fork again, and she begins to eat. We sit in silence for a while before she looks up.

'Can I put some music on?' she says, holding up her phone.

'Please do,' I say.

She links her phone to the top-of-the range sound system and begins a play list of classical music. I'm a little surprised.

'What?' she says.

'I didn't know you liked classical music?' I say.

'There's a lot you don't know about me,' she says.

I reach for my wine and take another sip.

Ditto.

## Chapter
# FIFTEEN

After dinner, we're sitting on the sofa, next to the open fire. Kim is under a large cushion, and I have my feet stretched out on a futon. We're listening to The Well - Tempered Clavier by Bach as the flames cast their flicker over the walls. I'm watching the light through a half-full wine glass, my third of the evening.

'This isn't going to work, is it?' Kim says.

I turn to her.

'What isn't,' I say.

'You don't want this,' she says, wriggling her hand between me and her, 'to be a full-time Dad. I can see it in your eyes. You're having an internal meltdown because you don't know what to do here and it's freaking you out.'

I smile at her.

'I adore you,' I say, 'and that's bullshit. Just because something is complicated doesn't mean it can't work. But...'

'Here we go,' she says.

I turn to her.

'No, listen to me here,' I say, 'you have a life in England, you have friends, a school, relatives, grandparents the works. I have an empty penthouse on top of a cold building and a helicopter on the roof. I have no wife, no family. That's no life for a 12 year old'

'I'm sorry, what?' she says.

'What?' I say.

'You have a helicopter on the roof?' she says.

I can't help but laugh.

'Yep,' I say.

'That's obnoxious,' she says.

I laugh.

'Yeah, well for someone who has a fear of flying, it's a nightmare, but I need it to get around fast for meetings.'

'Hang on,' she says, 'you told me you have a pilot's license.'

'I do,' I say.

'But you're afraid to fly?' she says.

'I wasn't always,' I say, 'leaning my head against the sofa.'

'Did you crash or something?' she says.

I shake my head.

'No, which is odd,' I say, swirling the wine in my glass, 'I never had a fear of flying before taking a trip to Denver about twelve years ago.'

I see her smush her face into the cushion, loving the fact that she's about to learn something new. There's a real fascination in her, a desperate sense of wanting to connect and belong, that she's too afraid to tell me about. She's vulnerable right now, lost, we're both vulnerable, and I have to be so careful.

'So, I'm on a Boeing 737 from New York to Denver right,' I say, 'it's all going fine, I've never given a second thought to being in the air. I've flown in the worst weather imaginable, and it's never fazed me, ever, except this flight.'

I can feel my pulse quicken.

'So, we're flying over the mountains when all of a sudden the plane drops like a rock,' I say, making an exaggerated drop motion with my hand.

Kim's eyes are fixated on my movement.

'This wasn't any normal turbulence, I've never felt anything like it, but even so, planes don't crash because of turbulence. They just don't, I know that much, but something about that feeling flipped a switch and short circuited my brain.'

I glance at her.

'The plane dropped for a full minute, in free fall. There were people screaming, bags were falling out of bins, and the guy next to me was in tears and texting his wife or whatever even though there was no signal. It was chaos.'

I look back at the fire, remembering the panic, fear, and blind belief that we were all going to die.

'It takes a lot to rattle me, it really does, and to this day I don't know why I lost all my objectivity. Like, entirely, but I truly believed that I was going to die in that moment,' I say, feeling a sense of shame wash over me.

'It's so strange,' I say, 'to have certainty stripped away from you. The brain is a weird organ.'

'Gosh,' says Kim.

'By the way, you'll never crash because of turbulence,' I say, 'ever.'

'What do you think it was?' she says.

'The fear?' I say.

She nods.

'I honestly don't know,' I say.

My phone suddenly vibrates. I take it out, frowning at the sender's name.

'Jean Rose'

I click on the message.

'I just wanted to apologise if I was rude in front of your daughter today. It wasn't my intention.'

'Who's that?' Kim says, 'you're making a weird face.'

I look up at her. I don't think I've received a text from Jean Rose in over a year.

'It's Jean,' I say, 'she's saying sorry for being rude to me in front of you.'

Kim perks up and gives me a large smile.

'What?' I say.

'I told you,' she says.

'Told me what?' I say.

'She likes you,' she says.

I scrunch my face up.

'What? The woman hates my guts,' I say.

I begin to text back.

'Stop!' Kim is leaning forward.

I freeze, a little shocked at her excitement.

'Stop what?' I say.

'What are you replying?' she says.

I blow out a long breath.

'Kim, stop it,' I say, beginning a text back.

'Show me the text,' she says.

I can't help but laugh.

'No!' I say, 'this is ridiculous, stop being ridiculous, she works for me. I can assure you that she has absolutely no interest in me that way.'

'You know absolutely nothing about women, and I mean zero, less than zero. As in, you're actively losing information on a daily basis about the opposite sex.'

I raise both eyebrows at her.

'You're twelve,' I say.

'And?'

'And what do you know about anything?'

'Clearly more than you do," she says, holding out her hand, 'which is concerning. Give it to me.'

'I'm sorry, what?' I say.

'Your phone, give it to me?'

'Absolutely not,' I say.

'Give it here,' she says, 'I want to see, I won't touch it.'

I shake my head but hand it to her. She reads the text.

'She definitely likes you,' she says, lowering the screen.

'Okay, let's use base reasoning here,' I say, 'you don't know this woman. You don't know anything about her, she could be married, have kids be very happy, oh, and she hates me.'

'You're projecting,' she says.

I laugh.

'I'm what?'

'Is she married?' she says.

I actually have to stop and think.

'I ...'

'You don't know if she's married?' she says.

For a moment, I'm a little stunned.

'No,' I say, 'that's not my job, and it's inappropriate for me to ask. You can be sued for even asking.'

'You're telling me you don't know if she's married because you're afraid of being sued?' she says.

'Okay, maybe not, I don't get personal with business associates,' I say.

'God, this lying thing is really bad, isn't it?' she says, 'how many children does Marge have?'

I give her a large smile.

'Three boys,' I say.

'Three boys,' she says matter-of-factly.

'Why don't you know anything about this woman, you bought her company,' she says.

'It's just never come up,' I say.

'Well, it's about to,' she says, and she starts texting.

I leap forward, spilling my wine on my suit. By the time I can get over to her, she's off the couch and running.

'Don't!' I shout at her, 'Jesus Christ, are you insane!'

She's laughing hysterically and running through the hallway.

'Kim!' I shout at her, it's hard not to laugh, and I have to admit that it's both funny and terrifying.

She stops suddenly, holding the phone up in the air.

'DONE!' she says, throwing it back to me.

My heart is pounding, and I have no idea why. I look at her in horror before looking at the screen.

Not at all, I can be a jackass sometimes, she took no offense; it's me who should be sorry, make it up to you over a drink?

I look up at her. My jaw drops open. She breaks into a wonderful laughter that infects every fibre of my being.

'WHAT.. .DID..YOU..JUST..DO?!' I say to her.

The laughter subsides as Kim casually walks past me back to the sofa, burying herself under the cushion again. I stare down at the phone in disbelief.

'I can't believe you just did that,' I say.

There's now anger brewing in my stomach. A loss of control has annoyed me. An exposure I didn't ask for.

'Kim,' I say.

'Oh, would you ever relax,' she says.

I move over to the sofa and see the wine stain. I sit back down.

'Don't ever do that again. That was not cool, do you hear me?'

Her face meets mine in defiance. She's itching for a fight; I can sense it. The phone vibrates.

'Oh shit,' I say, putting my face on my head.

Kim leaps up and joins me, pressing her head against my arm. She's excited and I just give in. I look at her, then at the text.

'Read it!' she says.

'If she sues me for this, I'll never forgive you,' I say, clicking on the message.

Okay? As long as this isn't a public execution!

'Gosh, Dad, what did you do to this woman?' Kim says.

'Nothing!' I say.

'Grow a pair,' she says.

'Excuse me?' I say

'Sorry,'

'You're damn right, sorry, watch it young lady,' I say.

I lean back and wonder why I'm getting so riled up about all this. I shouldn't really care, but for some reason I do.

Odd.

I look at the phone again, then at Kim.

'Screw it,' I say, 'what now?'

She smiles at me.

'May I?' she says.

I give her the phone.

'Have at it,' I say, 'If I'm going down in flames, maybe I can blame you anyway.'

'Excellent,' she says, taking the phone, 'eh... right.'

I move over her shoulder and watch her type.

No Execution, just a drink, I promise.

I throw my head back.

'Christ!'

'Relax,' she says, 'sent.'

We sit in silence, Kim holds the phone for a few minutes, after which my eyes drift towards its inactive screen. I turn to Kim.

'Now what?' I say to her.

'She's thinking,' she says.

'We're not children, Kim, this is New York,' I say, wondering what this strange feeling of butterflies is doing in my stomach.

I look down at the screen again.

'This is bad,' I say, 'this is very, very bad.'

'Be patient,' Kim says.

The phone vibrates. Kim reads out the message.

Okay? But if this is an execution, I'm coming armed with a metal clutch that'll do damage.

There's an odd excitement in me now. I smile at the message.

'Boom!' Kim says, dropping the phone into my hand, 'I'm good. Set a time and day, and let's do this thing.'

Kim is now bouncing on the sofa. I can't help but laugh.

'You're nuts,' I tell her.

I take the phone.

Tomorrow night? 8 o'clock, O'Sullivans?

She texts back.

Let the battle commence.

I shake my head and look at Kim.

'You're trouble,' I say.

'I'm trouble,' she says, smiling and flicking her hair.

## Chapter
# SIXTEEN

I'm in the back of the car, looking out at the streetlights and pavement. I'm four blocks away. I picked O'Sullivan's because, at a crunch, I can pass this off as a quick chat about strategy in a casual setting, and worst-case scenario, it gives us both an out. The truth is that I have no idea what I'm doing here. I'm not interested in Jean Rose. I've never been interested in Jean Rose, and she's not remotely interested in me. I know when a woman is attracted to me, that much is certain, and of all the women I've met who've shown interest, Jean Rose does not.

That's also part of the reason I followed through, simple curiosity. Perhaps a distraction from the responsibility of now having a full-time daughter in my life, perhaps a distraction from the piece of paper that's been circling in my inside pocket for two days.

Either way, I need a drink, with an adult.

More than that, though, I'm curious as to why Jean agreed so quickly to it. Part of me doesn't really care. Even when she gives me an earful for fucking her department, it's still a distraction. Roger is taking a strange delight in this whole thing. He's been giving me raised eyebrows in the mirror, begging me to engage in conversation. I meet his eyes again. He's almost jumping out of them.

'Okay, what is it?' I say, before he bursts.

'Nothing,' he replies.

'She told you,' I say.

'Sir, I don't know what you could be talking about,' he says.

I shake my head.

'That girl is gonna cause chaos,' I say.

'And what's so wrong with that?' Roger says.

'I don't like chaos, Roger,' I say.

'Like a butterfly flapping its wings in Beijing?' he says.

'Like a butterfly flapping its wings in Beijing,' I say.

'I know chaos, sir, it ain't always such a bad thing,' he says.

'Why's that?' I say.

'It trims the fat,' he says.

'It what?'

'Trims the fat,' he says, 'the mind and body get lazy, set in their ways, and after a while, you start taking your foot off the gas, your focus gets a little off track, your belt notches start to go up, and you forget about the mission.'

I lean my head back and look at him.

'My mission is my work, Roger, and you of all people know that,' I say.

'Is it?' he says.

There's something in his tone that I can't quite put my finger on. Is it anger?

'And obviously my daughter,' I say, getting an odd paternal scolding that remains unsaid, but I see it in his eyes.

'I don't doubt that for a second,' he says.

There's a quietness in the car as we pull up outside O'Sullivan's. I look forward to seeing him again.

'Roger, you didn't see anyone suspicious in the parking lot yesterday morning, did you? Someone who seemed out of place?'

He furrows his brow.

'Not that I can recall,' he says.

'Okay, keep alert, will you, and let me know if someone seems out of place around the building or the house,' I say, putting my hand on the door handle.

'What's going on?' he says, a genuine protective concern radiating from his burly voice.

I smile at him.

'Probably nothing,' I say.

'Doesn't sound like probably nothing,' he says.

'I can't go into it right now,' I say.

'Eyes open sir,' he says, 'you get into anything, I'm your first call.'

I smile at him.

'Well, this could be over in fifteen minutes, so just do a lap before you head off,' I say.

'Oh, I doubt that very much, sir,' he says.

I give a light laugh and open the door.

'Goodnight, Roger,' I say

'I sincerely hope so, sir,' he says.

# Chapter
# SEVENTEEN

I'm sitting at the end of the bar in O'Sullivans. It's one of the most popular Irish bars in New York, run and owned by Paul O'Sullivan and his two sons, Seamus and Connell. There's a girl playing the violin in the corner, flanked on either side by two men with long white beards. I'm not that much of a regular, but I'm partial to it as it was the first place I came to when I moved here. There's just something homely about it. It's warm and friendly, and there's no pretence.

Behind the bar is Paul, a thirty-something guy who's working hard filling people's orders. I've known him properly for about eight years. He's a big guy, a boxer, and there are photos of him in the ring pummeling various assortments of poor souls he's conquered over the years. He has a soft voice, but he's the opposite physically.

'Well, what'll it be?' he says, catching my eye.

'Bourbon on the rocks,' I say.

He nods and fetches it, placing it on a coaster.

I'm not waiting long when I see Jean push the door open and make her way inside. I've never seen her out of her business suit. She's wearing tan fitted trousers, a white shirt, and a dark fitted jacket. There's an odd flicker in my chest as she catches my eye.

That was weird.

Her hair is different, it's curled at the edges, and her makeup has changed too. She gives me a wave and comes over. I've saved a stool. There's no two ways about it, she looks beautiful.

I stand and pull out the stool for her, which elicits a slightly raised eyebrow from her. I catch myself looking at her thighs. I move my eyes quickly up to meet hers. There's a little smile brewing out of the corner of her mouth.

'Well, well, an actual gentleman' she says, 'classy joint.'

I smile at her.

'Well, at least if we get into a bar brawl, there's stuff we can throw at each other,' I say.

She looks at Paul.

'Or I can take him home,' she says.

I look at Paul, who hears her. Her face flushes red, she puts her hands up.

'Sorry, I didn't mean that,' she says, showing a moment of genuine embarrassment.

It's endearing. Paul looks at me.

'No pressure so,' he says.

I chuckle.

'What'll ye have? It's on the house,' Paul says to her.

Jean laughs.

'Chardonnay,' she says.

Paul smiles at me. Jean meets my glance.

'So,' she says.

'So,' I say.

She has blue eyes, how have I never seen that before?

There's an odd silence as Paul places her drink next to mine. He winks at me.

'There really was no need, thank you,' she says.

'Any friend of Mr. Page,' he says.

'Oh we're not friends,' she says smiling.

'In that case, your second is on me too,' he says, laughing.

'Jesus,' I say, mockingly.

He chuckles and walks away.

'Your reputation precedes you, huh?' she says, crossing her legs.

I sigh, there's an oddly comfortable silence between us. She leans back a little.

'What am I doing here, Carter?' She says, 'lay it on me, I can take it.'

'Why do you always assume I have an ulterior motive?' I say.

'Because you do,' she says.

'Not this time,' I say.

'So you're trying to tell me this is an actual casual out-of-office drink?' she says.

'Yep,' I say.

She raises her eyebrows and looks to her glass. She fiddles with it and I notice how perfectly done her nails are. For a brief moment, her expression becomes sullen.

'I'm very sorry to hear about your ex-wife, by the way,' she says, 'it can't have been easy.'

I look at her, slightly taken aback by the bluntness of the comment. I hesitate before giving an answer, feeling a knock at my first wall of defense.

'No, it hasn't been,' I say, 'how did you find that out?'

'How does anyone find out anything?' she says

'Marge,' I say.

'You've got a strong ally in her, she's an exceptional human being, and she really cares about you,' she says.

'Yeah,' I say.

'She doesn't call me a Demon,' she says, 'why is it when a woman asserts herself, she is labelled as the antichrist?'

'I've never done that,' I say.

'Hmm,' she says.

There's a moment of silence before she looks up at me again.

'This was Kim's idea, wasn't it?' she says.

I look at her. Meeting her eyes, a little smile forms uncontrollably. She slaps the bar with both hands and laughs.

'I knew it!' she said, 'she's a smart girl, I could see it in her eyes.'

I can't help but join in the laughter, and it feels good.

'Hang on a second, I didn't confirm that.'

'You just did,' she said, 'you think I don't know how you operate?'

'Christ, I'm being ambushed on all sides here,' I say.

'Let me guess, she grabbed your phone?' she says, 'she replied back, didn't she'

She puts her hand on mine for a second, and it sends a wave of something through my chest. She laughs.

'I'm kidding, it's totally fine,' she says, 'I have nieces who try that all the time. You're not used to dealing with daughters, are you? or women, by the sounds of it.'

She winks at me.

'No,' I say, raising the glass to my lips.

'You know what, I'm glad she did,' she says.

'You are?'

'Carter, we can't go on being at each other's throats anyway, we should have talked years ago. It's not healthy.'

'I'm not hard to talk to,' I say.

'Are you kidding?' she says, 'it's like dealing with a bullheaded ox. You're the most stubborn man I've ever met in my life.'

'Well, don't hold back,' I say.

She sighs and begins twirling her glass.

I think about what she's said and can already feel a defence mechanism kick in. I try something new.

'Here's what I can't figure out,' I say.

She meets my gaze.

'What are you still doing here?'

She glances out of the window at the passing cars in the street.

'At any point, you could have sold your interest and walked away with enough money to never work another day in your life. You keep threatening to do it and yet, you never do.'

She nods.

'Guilty,' she says.

'Why?'

She pauses, glancing around at the paraphernalia on the walls of the bar. The old photos and newspaper articles are from Irish and American papers.

'Because stories are important,' she says, 'look at all this. Dead writers' words on the walls of some bar in New York City. They had something to say. They thought their words mattered to someone. Maybe they didn't and never will, but without them, maybe we'd never even know they existed.'

I don't respond. She hesitates for a second.

'Carter, I started this in my backyard, you know that, right?' she says.

I nod.

'You don't need to prove your passion to me Jean,' I say.

'I'm not proving anything, I'm just…'

She pauses and looks away.

'I don't know why I do that,' she says, looking back at me.

'How about we don't talk shop,' I say.

She inhales deeply.

'Oh shit,' she says, 'what, you mean we actually get to know each other?'

'Why the hell not?' I say.

She gets her glass of wine and downs the whole thing, motioning to Paul to refill it.

I laugh.

'Jesus, I'm not that scary, am I?' I say.

Paul refills her drink as I down mine, and he does the same for me. Jean looks back at me, hesitating for a moment.

'Is this a…' she comes to a halt.

'A what?' I say.

'Like this isn't a …'

She wiggles her finger back and forth between us.

'A what?' I say.

'Like a… thing.' She says.

'I don't know what you're talking about,' I say, knowing exactly what she's talking about but cruelly relishing how uncomfortable she's becoming.

'Fuck off,' she says, looking away down the bar.

'Not exactly something I've heard from a date so early,' I say, taking the plunge, because, why not.

She looks back at me, tilting her head.

'This isn't a date,' she says.

'Okay,' I say.

'You don't date,' she says.

'What is that supposed to mean?' I say, 'you don't know anything about me?'

Nor will you

'I know that I'm not your type,' she says.

'Well, as far as I can tell, I'm not your type either,' I say.

'Then it's agreed,' she says.

'But for argument's sake, let's say I didn't know what my type was. What would that be exactly,' I say.

'Super models,' she says, 'mostly without much going on upstairs.'

I can't help but burst into laughter.

'That's nonsense!' I say, 'my god, is that what people think?'

'I'm just saying,' she says.

'What other revelations are there,' I say.

'That you don't let anyone near you, and when you do, it's curtains,' she says.

I pause and look down at my drink.

'You got me there,' I say, in a rare bout of honesty that I wasn't expecting, 'I'm guessing you have a similar thing, I don't see a wedding ring either.'

'Men are children, and I don't have time to raise one,' she says.

I grab my chest. She smiles.

'That's a bullshit excuse if ever I heard it,' I say.

'Oh?' she says.

'You could have any man in this city, and you're telling me it's only children? Come on, Jean, that's a cop out,' I say.

'Daddy issues,' she says.

Ditto

'That's another cop out, we all have that,' I say.

'Not to this extent,' she says, pointing at her head.

If you only knew

There's another silence, not uncomfortable, as if we've both just dived into a memory.

'You mind me making an observation?' I say.

'Oh, this should be good,' she says, leaning her head on her hand.

'You always expect a fight,' I say

She shakes her head as her eyes drift around the room.

'Three times the bullshit, three times the fight,' she says.

'What do you mean?' I say.

'I'm not going to sit here, Carter, and explain to you why it's harder for me than it is for you. You're a smart guy, I'm sure you can figure it out,' her eyes drift down to her breasts.

'Oh, come on,' I say, 'it's more than that; give me a break; stop hiding behind that shit.'

'Excuse me?' she says.

'I know all about how hard it is for women is this city to make it over men, I'm not going down that rabbit hole thanks very much,' I say, 'I'm talking about something else.'

'Okay, well, please, Mr. MAN,' she pauses, 'EXPLAIN it to me.'

I sigh.

'See, this is what I'm talking about. Yeah, maybe I was tough on you the last few years, but Christine Waits was a fuckup that nearly sank the whole damn place, and you know it. It had nothing to do with your breasts, regardless of how impressive they are,' I say.

Her eyes go wide, and we both burst into laughter. It's hearty and real. It's like a 10-year release and seems to open up something else. She has a gorgeous laugh.

Shit. Dammit Kim, what have you done.

She finally speaks.

'Have you any idea how many HR regulations you just broke?' she says, with tears in her eyes.

'All of them?' I burst out laughing.

'And please, for the love of god, don't say the word breasts again!' she says.

The laughter subsides, and she glances at me.

'Okay, maybe you're right,' she says, 'you want to know what my chip is?'

'I took your company,' I say.

'You took my control,' she says, 'I'm not twelve Carter, but this thing...'

She pauses.

'This really matters,' she says.

'I know that,' I say, 'it's still yours, Jean, I've never wanted to take it away from you.'

'Is it?' she says.

I lean back in my chair and think about Kim at home by herself. She was reading a book by the fire when I left. She gave me only one piece of advice before leaving.

Be nice.

'I thought we weren't going to talk shop?' I say.

'Sorry,' she says.

I turn to her.

'Fuck it,' I say.

'What?' she says.

'You want her back?' I say, 'total control?'

She seems taken aback. Her face goes dead serious.

'Don't fuck with me, Carter,' she says.

'I'm not,' I say, 'I'll give you back the majority shareholding, I'll even pay for it, and she's all yours.'

Her eyes are locked on mine.

'Why would you do that?' she says, 'we're still in litigation.'

'Ah, that's old news; they're tying up loose ends with nonsense," I say.

'You're offering me back full control of my company?' she says.

'Yep,' I say, 'I can't think of a single person more capable of running it anyway.'

Her eyes are wide, her mouth slightly ajar. She's on high alert. I can see it in her body language. She's tense, unsure of what just happened.

'What's the catch?' she says.

'The catch is that we stop talking about work,' I say, raising my glass.

Her mouth is open. She hesitates for a second, but her glass meets mine.

'Why?' she asks, 'why now?'

'Jean, you know how to run the place, you don't need me anywhere near it. You never have,' I say.

'It didn't seem that way,' she says.

'That wasn't anything to do with you, the markets do what they do, and sometimes people get fucked. You're miserable, and I'm miserable listening to it. We've gotten through the rough patch, and we're both in different places.' I say.

'I don't know what to say,' she says in one of the most earnest tones I've ever heard.

'Nothing,' I say, raising my glass to meet hers.

'Can we now stop talking about work?'

'You realise a clinking glass is bounding agreement,' she says.

'Yes, I do,' I say.

We clink, then sip. Her eyes are now completely focused on mine. The sound of a fire engine speeding past the bar drowns out the music for a moment.

'You're not on drugs that are going to make you forget this tomorrow, are you?' she says.

I laugh.

'No,' I say.

'Just checking,' she says, her voice still in shock.

There's another silence. The music being played in the corner is an old, soft Irish ballad. She turns to me as I take another drink.

'So, you think my breasts are impressive, huh?' she says smiling.

I actually snort my bourbon through my nose. We burst into laughter again. I scramble for a napkin to clean up my face, which is now burning red.

'I didn't mean...' I start to say.

She slaps the side of my arm.

'Shut up, Carter,' she says, 'I'm allowed to say that now because I don't work for you anymore.'

I beam at her.

'See!, Now you can tell me exactly what you think of me,' I say.

She interlinks her fingers and stretches them out.

'You asked for it,' she says.

There's mischief in her eyes.

'So why did Claire dump you?' she says, smiling.

I lean my head back and look at the ceiling.

'Come on, Carter, that wasn't exactly a secret, she was one of my authors for Christ's sake,' she says.

I clench my teeth for a second.

'We had a difference of opinion,' I say.

'I see,' she says.

'She obviously told you everything?' I say.

'Honestly?' she says, 'she said you were a great guy. Which I was surprised about.'

'Easy,' I say.

'You guys were never going to work, and you know it,' she says.

'Oh?' I say, 'what other dirty little secrets did she tell you?'

'Ah, the usual nonsense Carter, girl talk, you hurt her,' she says.

'Funny,' I say, 'figured it was the other way around.'

'That's the thing about relationships,' she says, 'everyone remembers it in whatever way makes them heal quickest. I didn't get deep into it, I don't delve and it's none of my business.'

'Bullshit,' I say.

She smiles.

'Okay, I may have delved a little bit, but you never get the full picture. Not when there's pain and anger.'

'That's true,' I say, 'I don't kiss and tell anyway, it just didn't work.'

'Admirable,' she says.

'You think so?' I say.

'It's easy to shit on ex-boyfriends," she admits, "and maybe it's healthy."It's simple self-preservation.'

'She wanted something I couldn't give her,' I say.

The truth?

'Sanity?' she says, smiling.

'Perhaps,' I say, 'what about you and that fisherman?'

She laughs.

'What fisherman?' she says.

'You were seeing some fishermen?" I say.

She gives another hearty laugh.

'What the hell are you talking about, Carter?'

'Marge told me you seeing a fisherman!' I say.

'Christ, do you mean the Carpenter?' she says

'That's the one,' I say, knowing full well who he was, and what he did for a living. Marge was always suspiciously keeping me up to date with Jean's personal life for some mysterious reason.

'Thanks for taking such a keen interest in my life, we've only known each other for nine years,' she says.

'So what happened with the fisherman?" I say.

She sighs.

'We were engaged,' she says, 'when I found out he was having an affair.'

'Ouch,' I say.

'Ouch,' she says.

'Cut and dry, huh?' I say.

'Cut and dry,' she says, 'it's a tough city.'

She says it with a practised strength, but I can see in her eyes that it really hurt her.

'Fuck him,' I say.

She turns and raises her glass again.

'Fuck her!' she says, 'maybe people like us aren't meant to find it.'

'And what are people like us?' I say.

'Damaged,' she says.

'Everyone's damaged, Jean, I didn't take you for a cynic.'

'Hey, I'm not a cynic,' she says, 'I'm a realist.'

She looks down, and I see sadness in her eyes.

'You ever think you're just too angry, that maybe this place is just eating you up alive?' she says.

I lean forward and put my head in my hands.

'Yeah, but then I catch the little things that aren't part of the life con,' I say.

'The life con?' she says.

'Yeah, there's a list,' I say.

'Tell me more,' she says.

'I have a list of life cons,' I say, 'bullshit things you're led to believe growing up.'

'And you say I'm cynical?' she says.

'Oh, it's not cynical,' I say, 'how many people fall into life cons, like 2.4 kids and marriage when they barely know who they are as people? Why do they do it?'

'Hope and love Carter,' she says.

'Is it?' I say, 'are your parents still married?'

She frowns.

'No,' she says, 'well, to be more accurate, I don't know, I haven't spoken to either of them in twenty-two years.'

There's a sudden spark between us, like an unbreakable electrical circuit that's just formed, drawing us closer to each other. She seems to sense it too. For a moment, I think I noticed her move an inch closer to me. She looks into my eyes.

'What is it?' she says.

'What?' I say.

'You're looking at me funny,' she says.

'No, it's just that..I didn't know that,' I say.

'Well, you can put that in the box marked 'Things I don't know about Jean Rose' and put it in the same warehouse where Indiana Jones keeps all his archaeological findings.'

I laugh.

'Beautifully put,' I say, 'what's inside the Ark of the Covenant?'

'You remember what happened to the dudes who took a peek?' she says.

'Their faces melted off?' I say.

'Exactly,' she says.

'Oh, come on can't be that bad,' I say.

'What about you?' she says, flipping it nicely.

'No, my parents died when I was very young,' I say.

She goes soft in the eye.

'I didn't know that,' she says.

'I wonder if we share the same warehouse?' I say.

'Well, just keep away from my stuff,' she says, taking a drink,

'You won't find it anyway; have you seen how big this place is? 'I say.

She smiles.

## Chapter
# EIGHTEEN

It's 1am, and Jean and I are strolling down the street towards Carlucios for a slice. I told Roger to take the evening off. It's warm, and the sidewalk is quiet. I can hear Jean's heels on the pavement as we slowly meander after talking nonstop for the whole night. There's a strange comfort here. It wasn't what I was expecting at all. We're both a little drunk, but not so much as to be completely out of control. I can tell she's mulling things over in her head. This is about that time when she's making up her mind about whether or not to come home with me. There's a spark here, it's undeniable. What is that spark? I have no idea. I haven't trusted my judgement in matters of the heart for a very long time, which is why I tend to be led.

'I'm not going to sleep with you, Carter,' she says, out of nowhere.

I stop walking and stare at her, it's hard not to laugh.

'Eh, excuse me,' I say, '(A) that's a little presumptuous (B) I've never once indicated that I was at all in any way interested in you romantically'

Her smile widens.

'And (C)?' she says softly, taking a step towards me.

'And (C), I don't put out on a first date,' I say.

'I see,' she says, taking another small step towards me, 'so what I'm hearing you say, is that this was a date.'

I catch my breath for a moment.

'It would appear that I offered that as a factual statement,' I say, meeting her eyes.

She nods, frowning like a lawyer hearing testimony from a witness on the stand. She then turns away from me and continues walking. She places her hands behind her back. I follow her. The hatch for Carlucios is on the corner. We head up and order two slices of pizza and go across the street to a nearby bench, where we sit and eat quietly.

'I really shouldn't be doing this at this hour, I've got a figure to maintain,' Jean says, with a half full mouth.

'So do I,' I say.

'God, it's so good though,' she says.

I nod. She looks at me.

'You look like her,' she says.

'Who?' I say.

'Kim,' she says, 'she's really gorgeous.'

'Yeah, she's something else,' I say, feeling a profound sense of sadness that Jean notices on my face.

I don't know where it's coming from.

'Is she going to stay here in New York?' she says.

I shake my head.

'I don't know, Olivia's brother has offered to take her in as she's got friends and grandparents and school and a life there, you know?' I say.

'I don't think that's going to matter,' she says.

'Oh?'

'I'm sorry, I don't mean to interfere,' she says.

'Please,' I say, motioning for her to continue.

'You're her dad, Carter, and she's lost,' she says.

I see tears form in her eyes suddenly, and I realise that this has nothing to do with Kim.

'You can't fight that bond, and right now she's probably on the edge of exploding,' she says.

'I don't know how to be a father,' I say, 'or a mother, and now I'm both.'

'You're not bad, Carter,' she says.

'I'm not?' I say.

'No, I think you like to pretend to be every now and then, and I think we're more alike than you think.'

'I don't have to sit here and be insulted,' I say, giving her a big smile.

She slaps my arm.

'Jerk!' she says.

'I'm kidding,' I say.

'People like us can make it work if we need to,' she says.

'Oh yeah? And how's that working out?' I say.

'You're scared, aren't you?' she says.

I look up at a streetlight, and a flash of overwhelming honesty bursts out of me.

'I don't think I've ever been this scared in my entire life,' I say.

I feel her move close to me. I feel her lips on my cheek as she kisses me. My muscles go weak. I turn to her, she pulls back and looks away, tucking back into her pizza.

'What was that for?' I say.

'It looked like you needed it,' she says.

We sit in silence as the feeling of her gesture cements itself in my mind. I'm disarmed, vulnerable. I think I could sit on this bench forever. My attention is drawn to a scent in the wind. I look to Jean, whose head is turned, looking behind her.

'Something's burning,' she says.

I nod and look to the tops of the trees in Central Park. I can see the wisps of black smoke flowing over them. In the distance, I hear another siren. Jean stands up and walks over to the corner. I stay on the bench. She turns to me suddenly, her eyes filled with horror.

'Carter!' she shouts from the corner.

I get up and move quickly over to her, sensing something is very wrong. As I move past the trees, the skyline opens up, and I see.

It's the BMX building. The top floors are completely engulfed in flames.

# Chapter
# NINETEEN

### 1987
### Thomas

It's pouring rain as I cycle my bike home from school. I'm taking my time because there's no point in rushing. I've reached peak soakage, and it makes very little difference at this stage when I get home. Besides, there's something peaceful about hurtling down the hill on Grove Street with the thick raindrops pounding against my face. I close my eyes, just for a second, to feel the rush of emptiness and danger as the water pours through my wet hair and down my face. I open my eyes and see the front wheel of my bike spinning across the pavement. It feels good to feel free. I reach the bottom of the hill and check my watch. As I pass the forest on my right, I realise I still have a half hour before I have to be home. It's enough time for a detour to Alpha Base. I turn off the road and into the trees, down a thin dirt road that breaks off into a dozen or so trails, but the one I take hasn't been followed for years. As far as I know, I'm the only person who's ever ventured down this path. I found it when I was much younger, by accident. I'd run away for a night when I was six or seven. A last act of defiance I'd spend a year paying for. In the end, it would be worth it. Nobody knew about Alpha Base.

The rain begins to ease. The thick leaves overhead, catching the water and feeding themselves with it. The ground is muddy, but my thick tyres have a good grip on the soil as I speed over humps and bumps. Silence descends all around me, apart from the sound of water droplets hitting the leaves above.

I continue on as the foliage becomes thick. The track dips down, that's how I know I'm close. I pull the brakes at the large boulder, which marks the end of the trail. I'd slammed straight into it the first time I'd been down here, but now I know the exact moment to slow my approach. My wheels skid a little in the mud but still come up short of the giant rock. I get off my bike and wheel it around the back. There's a drop off directly behind it where the small cave is located. I jump down, then reach up and take my bike with me. The cave itself is recessed into the rock and well-hidden with dense leaves and bushes. I move in behind it, being careful not to disturb the natural camouflage, until I come to the wooden door.

It's not so much a door as it is two large planks of wood that I'd dragged down and placed in front of the entrance, which is only a few feet wide. I've painted them green and covered them with moss and branches, so it's impossible to see from the outside.

There's a small chain threaded through two holes that I've punched and clamped with a heavy padlock. I don't have the key on me, there's no way to hide such a thing at home without her finding it. She finds everything, there's no secrets in that house, only the one handcuffed in the basement from time to time, and the other dark things I don't like to think about.

The key is under a rock I found years ago and hidden in a crevice to the right of the door. There's a little indent under the base of it which fitted it perfectly. I reach for it and remove it, doing one final check around me before unlocking the door and climbing inside. The entrance opens up into a relatively large space, about ten feet square. There's a little hole near the back wall that leads all the way to the top, which lets air and some light inside when it's bright out. It's dark at the moment, but there's an oil lamp that I stole from a local hardware store. I've written down the cost of it in my 'stuff' ledger so that I can pay back the owner, a lovely sixty-year-old man named Chuck, whenever I get a job.

It made me sick to my stomach to have to do it and I remember actually vomiting after I'd snuck out of the store, imagining the police on my tail all the way here.

My "stuff" ledger is a small notebook that I keep here with a list of names and shops from which I've purchased items over the years. As of this moment, I owe $74.35; I've made an oath to pay back twice that amount to those people when I make it big. The price of the oil lamp was $12.50.

I pick up a box of matches from a ledge and light the lamp, taking a seat on a small orange cushion that I have wrapped in black plastic to keep it dry. There's a small wooden crate with comic books, notepaper, pens, and an assortment of other bits that I've collected.

The lamp casts an orange glow around the walls as I check another wooden container that holds the food. I've been collecting canned goods for over a year now and there's a healthy stock building up. I have a small number of tools, plastic knives and forks, a spool of rope, and thread. There's a book on top of the magazines. It's an old nature survival book that was given to me on my birthday by him. I don't think he bought it as the edges were torn and the pages look old. It wasn't even wrapped when he gave it to me, but I pretended to be overjoyed at the gift. Something he probably begrudgingly gave away, has actually become one of the most useful things I own, but more than that, it's about to become my long-term bible. I place the box of matches back on the holder, making sure to count them before I do. There's only nine left, so I remind myself to take a trip to the store before the week is out. Nobody ever misses a box of matches.

I sit on the cushion and lay my head against the rocky interior. I reach over to another metal container and open its lid. I reach inside and take out a large bundle of papers wrapped in a rubber band. I sit back again and remove the plastic wrapping. I keep them in there, so they stay dry. I lean back again and reach over, pulling the light a little closer as I try and find the last page I worked on. I also stole this notebook, which is what I feel most guilty about because of what's inside; my stories. I figured there must be some sort of nasty energy around creating something on paper that never belonged to the writer, so every time I take this notebook out, I say sorry to it. I ask it for forgiveness, and I promise to pay the money that I owe whenever I have it.

I open up the pages to the last sentence.

'Captain Starfinder locked his helmet into place and waited for the sound of air in his spacesuit. He then took out his ray gun, opened the hatch, and floated outside to face him'

I smile at the image of my hero, his thick, dark, and wavy hair slicked back. The silver streak of grey running around its edge. His chiselled jaw and muscular body, hardened by all the space battles. Also, if I sell the rights and make a billion dollars like in Star Wars, it would make an excellent action figure. I take a step back and pick up the tip of my pen. I already know what's going to happen in this part of my story. I've been thinking about it for a week. Captain Starfinder is about to face off with his nemesis, Gro-Gon, from the planet Yirius. Gro-Gon killed Starfinder's whole family when he blew the Earth up, and he's spent his whole life searching the galaxy for revenge. This is their first encounter. Gro-Gon has just damaged Starfinder's engines. Just when he is about to blow up his ship, and with only fifteen minutes of air left, Starfinder is going to attack Gro-gon's ship in a blind rage with the only weapon he has left, his hand-held ray gun. Gro-Gon, seeing that Starfinder is pretty much on a suicide mission, decides to leave his ship and face him with his own hand-held weapon in an old-fashioned type of duel, but in space. I begin to write.

'Starfinder pressed his rear suit thrusters, which pushed him away from his burning ship towards Gro-gon's battle cruiser. He pointed his ray gun at the massive ship and pulled the trigger. Blue beams of light shot out towards the ship as Starfinder screamed at it.

'Come out and face me, you coward!' he shouted in his helmet.

I smile at the image of my gallant hero blasting away at this mighty vessel in space. My smile begins to drop as I begin to feel his anger. I press my pen a little harder against the page.

'Come out and face me, you bastard!' said Starfinder, 'You're nothing! You can't hide in there from me. Come out and play fair! One-on-one, just like real men. Stop hiding behind your ship you coward!'

Starfinder began firing his ray gun again, over and over, he pulled the trigger. The beams of light, just bouncing off the giant ship. He wasn't going to make a dent in it. It was too big, too strong. He watched as the huge ship pointed its cannons at him, ready to vaporise him into a million little bits. He didn't care. He kept firing. He was so angry. He pressed his thrusters again and moved closer to the ship. He saw a door open on its side and stopped shooting. He saw a figure float out into the nothingness. It was Gro-Gon. Starfinder pressed his forward thrusters and stopped moving. He lowered his ray gun as Gro-Go approached. His huge size, almost four times that of Starfinder, came closer. He heard his radio buzz.

'Starfinder,' growled Gro-Gon, 'you can't win, you're small, so small, so weak.'

I can feel my teeth clench as I write.

'You think your size matters to me?' shouted Starfinder.

'It should,' said Gro-Gon as he floated closer.

The movement of my pen slows as I lean into the page. I continue.

Starfinder raised his ray gun and pointed at Gro-Gon's huge head. The alien smiled, bearing his vicious, shark-like teeth. Row after row of flesh-eating bone glared down at Starfinder.

'When I'm through with you, I'm going to feast on your blood,' said Gro-Gon.

'It's not over yet,' shouted Starfinder.

My pen cuts through the page, and I realise that my eyes are watering. I stop writing for a moment as I press down on the torn bit of paper to try and fix it. I wipe my face and look at my fingers, wondering where that came from. I can feel my heart beating fast. I want to finish this scene, but I suddenly close the notebook and lay it on my lap for a moment. I close my eyes and try to think of Captain Starfinder and Gro-Gon, floating in space, their weapons aimed at each other, ready to kill each other, and I smile. I don't think I've smiled all day.

I love it here. It's peaceful, and above all else, it's safe. Nobody will find me here, not when it's time. I think about the nine matches left in the box. I'm going to need more, a lot more. I reach out and get my 'Stuff' ledger. It says :'Property of Thomas Keeling' in bold marker on the front. I open it up and begin making a list.

## Chapter

# TWENTY

### 2021
### Carter

I suddenly feel very sober as Jean and I get out of the taxi and rush up to the barrier of fire trucks a block away from the BMX building. There's a wooden barrier with a couple of cops guarding it. I look up to see plumes of black smoke billowing out of the windows on the top floors. My office seems to be glowing in red flames, and there's flickers of soot and ash falling onto the street below. I can taste it.

'Move back, sir,' One of the cops says.

'That's my building,' I say to him in a strangely calm tone of disbelief.

'Oh right, you're going to want to see the marshal,' he says, pointing to a uniformed fireman who's perched next to a car.

I turn to Jean.

'You can go if you want; you don't have to stay around,' I say.

Her eyebrow goes up.

'What? Carter I'm staying as long as you need me to stay, Jesus Christ,' she says.

I smile at her, there's a support there that I hadn't expected. I turn back and head towards the marshal. He's in his fifties and has a pot belly and a white mustache. He's on the radio and giving orders as I wave at him to get his attention.

'What,' he says, seeming hassled.

I point to the flames over my shoulder.

'That's my building,' I say.

He looks up at the flames and then back down to me. He moves towards me.

'You're going to have to clear the area, sir,' he says.

'No, as in I own that building!' I say.

He looks at me funny. I don't look like someone who should own a building in New York City. I take out a business card and ID and hand it to him. He looks it over.

'No shit,' he says.

'What happened?' I say, as he hands me back my ID, after taking the details of it in a little notebook.

'Is anybody hurt?'

'We don't know,' he says, 'eyewitnesses say they heard a pop and explosion, so it could be a gas main.'

My heart stops. I feel the muscles in my face drop, and I feel cold as the last remnants of alcohol seem to evaporate into the night, leaving only the cold sober reality.

'A gas main?' I say.

'Well, we don't know yet, we've got it under control at the top four floors,' he says, 'look we've got some work to do, but people are going to want to talk to you, so give your details to the officer and we'll be in touch. Please, there's nothing you can do right now, best if you head home.'

I just nod at him and look to Jean, who's standing there with her arms folded.

'Here's my card,' he says, 'call me.'

I take it and wave it at him as a 'thank you' before turning and walking back to Jean.

'What the hell happened?' she says.

'They don't know. He says it's under control,' I say.

We both look up at the flames high above as they lick and curl upwards.

'It doesn't look under control,' she says.

I shake my head. An ever-present feeling of heaviness presses down on my chest, and I have an overwhelming urge to get back to Kim. I turn to Jean.

'I better get home,' I say.

'I'll come with you," she says.

'You don't have to do that,' I say.

She smiles at me.

'Your world is on fire. I'm just offering some team support. I'll cook you breakfast in the morning. I presume you have a spare room in Wayne Manor?'

I smile and nod at her.

'Too many,' I say.

Jean links my arm and turns me away from the commotion. It's a surreal moment that seems disconnected from the rest of reality, and I suddenly feel like a man in a small boat staring at a dark cloud on the horizon.

# Chapter
# TWENTY-ONE

The sounds of talking wake me up the next morning. My mouth is dry. Images of a dream are fading fast. I can't quite remember what it was about, but there was something about wet pavement and bare feet running. I reach across to touch my chest. I'm still wearing the shirt from the night before. It's soaked with sweat. I touch my face and my hair and see they're equally wet. I take off my covers and reach for the glass of water on my nightstand. There's a Tylenol beside it to help with my headache. I can smell something coming from the kitchen. I strip off and get into the shower. I'm still in a daze. There's a fog surrounding me as the memory of my building in flames comes crashing back. I look at myself in the mirror, making sure not to turn around. Something is happening to me, and I don't know what it is.

Come on, Carter, get a grip.

I put the thought out of my head. It's not possible. It's not.

I turn the shower on to ice cold, take a breath, and plunge under the water. The intensity of the freezing water shocks the fog out of my mind. My muscles tense up. A sharp pain runs down my back as my mind focuses. I can hear my phone ring on my side table. That'll be Marge. Today will be chaos. I have to try and keep it together. I can feel the rocking wooden boat beneath me as the waves begin to swell. I hear my phone again, ignore it as I wait for my mind to clear.

A few minutes later, I shut off the shower and look at my reflection in the mirror. There are dark circles under my eyes and a shadow forming on my cheeks. I run hot water and splash it on my face as I take a few minutes to shave.

Afterwards, I find a new, unopened white shirt and a fresh black suit and put them on. My phone continues to ring. I pick up a pair of antique gold flat cufflinks and delicately put them on. I put on a new pair of black shoes. I look at myself in the mirror and take pride in the only thing I can control.

If I'm going down in flames, I'm going to look good doing it.

I look at my phone; there are twelve missed calls.

I just put it on silent and make my bed. I then open the bedroom door, take a breath, and move into the hallway. I look over the railing and see Jean and Kim sitting at the table. Something smells good.

'Good morning,' I say from above them.

Jean looks up and nods. She looks refreshed. The guest bedroom she stayed in is well stocked with an assortment of women's and men's grooming products, and it certainly looks like she took advantage of them. Her hair looks washed. She's still dressed in the same clothes she was wearing the night before, but there's no sign of a hangover on her face. She smiles and nods at me.

'Oh my god Dad!' Kim says, leaping up, 'what happened! The fire! It's all over the news.'

I move down the stairs and over to Kim. I reach around her and give her a massive hug.

'We'll figure it out, these things happen,' I say.

I look up at Jean.

'How did you sleep?' I say.

'Well, it's pretty much the best hotel I've ever stayed at to be honest. Someone knows what they're doing!' She says it in an almost accusatory way.

'The housekeeper sorts all that, I have no idea what's in the rooms,' I say, almost embarrassed.

'Uh Huh,' she says.

'Something smells amazing,' I say, looking at the spread.

'Well, Kimmy here said that she was missing her English breakfasts. I know what she means from when I lived there, so I whipped up what I could from your extremely well stocked fridge.'

'Again, the housekeeper...'

'Keeps every food known to man in your kitchen,' she says, 'seems a little overkill for a man living alone.'

I put on a posh English accent.

'Well, one doesn't know when one will have company,' I say.

Kim laughs.

'Oh gosh, please don't do that again, you sound like a weird horse,' she says.

'Help yourself,' Jean says.

I take a seat and serve myself some scrambled eggs and toast. I look at Jean.

'Thanks for sticking around last night; you didn't have to,' I say.

Jean looks at Kim, who gives her a smile as if there's an inside joke I don't know about. I give Kim a curious look.

'Did you know Jean writes children's books?' Kim says.

I look at Jean, who's coughing as if to signal Kim not to tell me.

'No?' I say, looking at Jean.

'It's not important,' Jean says as she pours herself coffee.

'You really should get to know people,' Kim says.

I laugh.

'Excuse me?' I say.

'Well, you don't,' Kim says.

'Why do I have the feeling I should have arrived here earlier this morning?' I say, 'and what else did I miss?'

'Nothing from the fire department?' Jean says.

'I've about a billion missed calls, but I thought I'd eat first before I listen to what sort of damage control I have to do today.'

'You're remarkably calm, Dad,' Kim says.

'Am I?' I say.

'I'd be going mental,' she says.

'Why?' I say, 'the building was empty, nobody was hurt, it's just a thing, Kim, things can be replaced.'

'You are remarkably calm,' Jean says.

No, I'm not.

My phone vibrates again in my pocket. I look at it. It's a call from Marge.

'Carter, answer the phone for the love of God,' Jean says.

I nod at her and click the answer button.

'Holy God, you're there! I thought you might have been working late or God knows what. Where the hell are you, Carter? What happened? Was anyone hurt? What do you want me to do?' she says, at a thousand miles an hour.

'Slow down, Marge, slow down,' I say.

I can hear her almost hyperventilating.

'I'm fine, we're all fine, I was there last night, they think there's a gas line or something, don't worry about it. I'm going to head down this morning to take a look,' I say.

'I'm here already, Carter, they won't let anyone in the building?' she says.

I look at Jean and Kim, then around the penthouse.

'Might as well use the space for something, huh?' I say.

'What?' Marge says.

'Marge, come over to my place, I'll have Roger pick you up, and we can run control from here today. Get a hold of Daniel and get him over here as well,' I say, 'and Marge, try and be calm.'

'All right,' she says.

I hang up and put my phone back in my pocket.

'I should probably go and let you get on with this,' Jean says suddenly.

A flicker of panic grips my chest for a moment.

'Jean, you can't get into your office,' I say, 'they're not letting anyone into the building.'

'Oh shit,' she says, looking for a moment to Kim, 'sorry.'

'Oh, don't be silly, we're well past that nonsense,' Kim says.

'Fair enough,' Jean says.

'This has been, like, the craziest month of ever,' Kim says looking at me.

'I know,' I say, 'I'm sorry,'

The table goes quiet as we all finish breakfast. It's an odd moment, but in a way, there's something comforting about it. I can't put my finger on it. Kim breaks the silence.

'So,' she says, 'how'd the date go?'

Jean beams at her and then looks at me. My face is burning.

'So, it WAS a date,' she says, playfully.

'Kim, I swear to god,' I say, trying hard no to laugh.

'What? ' she says, 'there's tension here, and it's always best to cut straight through it.'

Jean stands up and begins clearing the plates away.

'I'll let your father tell you all about it,' Jean says as she moves towards the kitchen, laughing gently to herself.

I lean back as Kim puts her hand up to her face to hide her face. She makes a motion with her mouth.

I LOVE HER!

I silently mouth back to her.

SHUT UP!

Kim giggles and takes a drink of orange juice. Her smile is like a warm blanket.

## Chapter
# TWENTY-TWO

'It wasn't a gas main, and it wasn't an accident.'

The words come at me like a shotgun blast to the chest. I'm sitting downtown in a police precinct on East 51st Street. Opposite me is the enormous figure of Detective Jim Crown. He's a bald, African American from the Bronx with hands the size of small boats. He's twirling a plastic pen around his fingers with dexterity and smooth, effortless skill, which for some reason I'm finding oddly relaxing.

'The main computer server was destroyed in the basement,' he says.

'What?' I say.

'It looks like an accelerant was used to start the fire, which originated in your office,' he says in a monotone voice that I can't get a read on.

He gazes at me with that typical cop stare, reading every muscle movement in your face to get a read on how many lies you're about to tell. This time, he gets the truth.

'I was in a bar,' I say, 'before you ask.'

'I know that Mr. Page,' he says, 'that all checks out. What I want to know is what kind of enemies you have.'

'You say that like I should have many,' I say, folding my hands together.

'You don't get to the top without em sir,' he says.

'Can't argue with that,' I say, 'but I don't know of anyone who'd pull this.'

Do I?

'Is that right?' he says.

'What accelerant?' I say.

'Gasoline, by the looks of it,' he says, 'but as you now know, whoever it was, put in a call to the fire department, which probably saved the whole building from going up. They didn't want the whole thing burned down, by the looks of it, and the suppression system inside the building took up a lot of the slack.'

I look at the clock on the wall. The sounds of the second hand seem far louder than they should be.

'I believe you lost your ex-wife a month ago?' he says, 'that right?'

I take a breath, seeing her smiling face in a photograph of the two of us on a sandy beach.

'Yes,' I say.

'I'm sorry to hear that, that's tough,' he says emphatically, 'your security systems are all cloud-based, right?'

'Yeah, they're handled by Gold Star,' I say.

'Hmm,' he says.

'Hmm, what?' I say.

'Well, seems they had a major server outage last night,' he says.

'What?' I say.

'Yeah, some sort of electrical surge took it out,' he says.

'You're kidding me,' I say.

'No, I'm not. Odd coincidence, don't you think?' he says.

I don't answer. My mind begins to form the worst-case scenario.

It can't be.

'I don't have any mortal enemies, I've never received death threats, and as far as I know, other than business acquaintances who'd like to see my company go under, they play the same game I do,' I say.

'The same game?' he says.

'I know people, Detective, like you know people,' I say, 'we don't play like this. I'm not a gangster.'

'I see,' he says, writing something down in a notebook.

He looks back up at me, meeting my eyes as if to bore a hole into my brain.

'You're from New York originally, are you?' he says.

There's a little flicker in my heart. I don't like where this is going.

He knows something.

'No, not originally,' I say.

'Uh huh,' he says, taking a pause, waiting for me to fill in the blanks.

'I grew up in the Midwest,' I say.

'Well, you got rid of the accent pretty quick huh?' he says smiling.

'Did I?' I say, trying to sound calm.

He leans back.

'Look, I'm just trying to help Mr. Page, Someone torched your office on purpose, you've got a little girl here, and I think it's prudent that we go over a full list of anyone who you might think holds a grudge. Seems reasonable, no?' he says.

'I couldn't agree more, detective, but I swear to god I can't think of a single person who'd do such a crazy thing,' I say.

Oh, but I do.

'Ok, well, we need to talk to everyone in the building,' he says.

'I'll make sure everyone is available,' I say.

'Thank you,' he says, 'just one more thing, I hope you don't take this the wrong way, but we'd appreciate it if you didn't leave town.'

'I understand, Detective,' I say.

He stops for a minute.

'I hesitate to ask you this one last thing,' he says.

I already know what's coming.

'My little girl is obsessed with that band, the Lucid Dreams, you guys handle their tours here, right?' he says, 'they're playing Madison Square this weekend and well...'

'Let me know how many tickets you need, and I'll have them sent to your office this afternoon,' I say.

He seems generously grateful.

'Really, oh, that would just mean the world to her,' he says.

'Consider it done,' I say.

'Thank you, Mr. Page,' he says.

'Please call me Carter,' I say.

There's something that reminds me of an old TV detective I used to watch growing up: Columbo. His ability to form connections with those he was investigating was a way to make them feel at ease. In a sense, it makes me nervous, but I follow along like one of the celebrity killers that he's about to bring down. I consider the connections he might have to me, the threads he could pull at, but I have always covered my bases.

ALWAYS.

There was no way he could find it. I still make a note to go over what happened very carefully. I'm in danger here. I can feel it. I make no sudden facial movements.

'Will that be all, Detective?' I say.

'Yes, thank you. If you think of anything at all, please give me a call,' he says, handing me his card.

'My personal cell is on that, day or night,' he says.

Thank you. I get up to leave.

'Oh, before you go,' he says.

Columbo is it then. I turn to face him.

'If you wouldn't mind providing me with your old home in the Midlands, just for my records.'

*Fuck.*

'Of course,' I say.

I pause for a moment. I've always been ready for that.

1444 Oak Road, Minneapolis.

'Thank you,' he says, smiling at me in a way that shows me I've got a serious problem on my hands.

## Chapter
# TWENTY-THREE

Daniel is waiting for me outside on the steps of the station, smoking a cigarette. I walk over to him and tap him on the shoulder, taking a seat next to him on the step. It's a beautiful day outside as the traffic passes us both. Daniel gives me a smile and places his hand on my back.

'This is so fucked,' he says, offering me a smoke.

I turn it down initially, then hesitate.

'You know what, give it to me,' I say.

He hands it over, and I light it up. When you quit smoking, you never really quit. That's the insidious nature of the little white sticks. As soon as you spark one up again, it makes you question your sanity as to why you gave them up in the first place. I inhale deeply and let the sweet nicotine filter through my veins. It's the best feeling I've had in days.

'Jesus Christ,' I say, closing my eyes.

'You're only having one,' Daniel says.

'One is enough,' I say, already knowing that I'm buying a pack the second I get down the street.

'I've leased a building in Soho, so we'll be back up and running by the end of the week,' Daniel says.

'Okay,' I say quietly, 'thanks for taking care of that.'

'What did they say to you?' he says, 'they grilled me pretty hard, legal are having a shitfit that you went in there alone.'

'I've got nothing to hide, Dan,' I say.

'It doesn't matter, and you know it, please tell me you didn't say anything,' he says.

'Like what? My building burned down, what the hell else is there to say?' I say.

'You think Mattis would have...' he says.

'Nah,' I say, 'not his style, besides we settled that IP; there's no conflict. Whoever did this, it was personal.'

'At least we've got a tight arson policy, so that'll help the clearing up,' Daniel says.

'Is money all you care about?' I say.

'No!' he says, 'but it's my job to do the dirty work.'

I give him a look.

'Don't look at me like that,' he says, 'you're the one who went on a date with the Demon.'

I turn to him.

'You didn't think that wouldn't get around. I had to hear it from a fucking cop, Carter! A cop!' he says, looking hurt, 'why didn't you tell me?'

'Because I knew you'd blow a blood vessel, and it wasn't a date,' I say.

'Did you ....' he says, smiling.

'No,' I say.

He begins to laugh.

'So, you didn't get laid and your building burns down on the same night?' he says.

I can't help but laugh.

'What a shitty night!' he says, laughing again.

I can't help but join in.

'You know what?' I say, 'It was actually a really good night.'

He turns to me, sparking up another cigarette as two patrol officers stroll by.

'I want to know every last detail,' he says, 'nobody dates the demon, nobody.'

'It wasn't a date,' I say.

'Bull....shit!' he says, 'what the hell happened? Come on, man, my office is in cinders, give me something here.'

I lean back.

'This probably isn't the best place to be talking about this,' I say.

'What are they going to arrest us for talking about romance?' he says.

'There's no romance,' he says.

'Come on man, you've been wallowing for a woman who treated you like shit, throw me a bone here.'

I look up at the blue sky.

'She's not what I expected,' I say.

'Oh?' he says.

'Yeah, she's ... just not.' I say.

'Oh oh,' he says.

'What?' I say.

'You've got that look,' he says.

'Shut up,' I say, 'Absolutely not. She slept in the guest room, nothing happened.'

Daniel straightens up his back.

'She spent the night at your place in a separate bedroom!' he says.

'Oh, Christ, here we go,' he says.

'I also gave her back control of Pepper, majority shareholdings,' I say.

His eyes go wide.

'You did what?' he says, his eyes wide.

'Yep,' I say.

He begins to belly laugh this time.

'Don't start with me,' I say.

'Look, you're the boss, and you know how I feel about Pepper anyway, that was always your baby, but fuck me, you might as well have proposed to her there and then.'

I can't help but laugh. Extreme life events have a way of making you let go and surrender to the madness, about being completely out of control.

'Give me another smoke,' I say.

He hands it to me without hesitation.

'You remember what happened with Katie?' he says.

'I have a feeling you're about to remind me,' I say.

'You gave her everything, everything, you go all in, all your markers on red 32 and you roll the dice over and over again because you think that's going to make a blind bit of difference.'

'Dan, nothing happened,' I say.

'Everything happened!' he says, 'look, you're my boss, but I'm also your best friend, your only friend actually, and even though you could technically fire me for this, I'm just asking you to watch your fucking back and stop trying to live a movie. It doesn't exist. It's a fucking chemical reaction that lasts a year.'

'I know that,' I reply.

'Hmm,' he grumbles, 'it's just an office Carter. The insurance will have the place spick and span in no time. A date with Jean Rose, that's not something that's going to be spick and span. That's gonna be all spick, no span,' he says.

'That makes about as much sense as that tie you're wearing,' I say.

He looks down and flicks it. It's a horrid, speckled brown colour.

'Yeah, ok, you got me there,' he says, removing it and scrunching it into a ball. He then proceeds to throw it with perfect precision into a nearby trashcan.

He looks at me and we both laugh.

'You're not all there, are you, Dan?' I say.

'It's what makes me the big bucks,' he says.

I lean back and let the sun hit my face.

'Oh man, this has trouble written all over it,' he says, 'what happened the next morning?'

'Nothing,' I say, 'my phone blew up with cops and firemen and shareholders and lawyers and she made me and Kim breakfast and I came down here to be grilled.'

I pause, his eyes are locked onto mine as if I just told him where the treasure of the Sierra Madre is buried.

'She made you and Kim breakfast?' he says, raising both eyebrows before closing his eyes and turning his face towards the sky.

I shake my head, bewildered.

'Yeah, and?' I say.

'You're fucked,' he says.

## Chapter
# TWENTY-FOUR

### 1987
### Thomas

I'm cycling as fast as I can down the street. The rain has picked up again, but this time the wind has come with it. There's a storm on the horizon, and it's sweeping in fast. I'm late. I accidentally fell asleep while reading a book. It wasn't a long nap. It could have only been fifteen minutes, but at this rate, I'll be nine or ten minutes late. If he's home before I get there, there'll be hell to pay. I can't be late, ever. Not unless I've been hit by a car or had a flat tyre, and even then, there's no telling what his reaction will be. It's not far now, my clothes are soaked through. I round the bend in my street and pull the brakes hard. My wheels come to a halt. My heart freezes as I check my watch, rubbing the face of it with my thumb.

Eleven minutes late, only eleven.

I look up and see his beat-up Chevy sitting outside the main gate. I can see the lights in the living room are on. The rain pours down my face as my hands begin to shake. It's cold, but this is different. This is real fear, not the kind most boys and girls get when they get scolded. I think about turning my bike around and heading back to Alpha Base to wait it out until the next day, but that would only make things worse. I've never not returned home. That would be suicide. Eleven minutes turn into twelve. I look down at my tyres and instantly jump off my bike. I take my school bag off and frantically search for my metal pencil case. I crack it open, find the protractor we were using today in math, and with one hard stab, I plunge it into my back wheel.

The tyre pops, as the sound of whooshing air comes billowing out. I place the protractor back in my bag and sling it over my back as I walk up the street towards my house. The back wheel feels clumpy as the loose rubber drags along the pavement.

I'm about fifty feet away now and in story mode. I have a thousand permutations as to when this happened, and then it hits me. I stop short of my gate and look through the living room window. The blinds aren't drawn, which is strange as it's dark now, and she always pulls the blinds down when the sun starts going down. I see a shadow drift past the window, and I look down at my hand. I move past the gate and jab the back of my hand against the corner of the stone pillar. A fresh cut forms. I take the pain of it without even flinching as droplets of blood make their way through my fingertips. I close the gate behind me. The rust of the metal is enough to bring his dark figure to the window. I can't see his face, just the dark outline of his muscular body. I bow my head and move around the back of the house, placing my bike in the shed, before covering my hand with the sleeve of my school shirt. The kitchen light turns on.

My legs are beginning to shake. I feel numb. There's something in the air, I can sense it. I can feel the danger as if I were stranded in a murky swamp with alligators biding their time to take a chunk of flesh. This time, there may be no stopping it. I walk nervously down the path in the garden towards the rear kitchen door, praying that I'll simply be led into the basement. Somehow, looking at the pair of dark shadows looming through the brightly lit window, I don't think I'll be so lucky.

The wooden door to the kitchen creaks open, and I take several terrified steps up and inside. They're both there. Glaring down at me, an endless pool of water forms under my body on the floor. They don't seem to care that I'm cold and wet. They just glare. He has his arms folded as she takes a seat at the kitchen table and smiles sweetly at me. I look into vacant eyes and know that there's nobody there. Or more accurately, something inhuman—something from the dark place that's taken control of them. Behind her smile is a sea of whatever chemicals she's flooded her bloodstream with this evening. His eyes are different. They're razor sharp. Clear. Focused. Determined.

He grins at me with his perfect teeth, which he spent all my birthday presents on. His leathery skin has a tinge of artificial yellow, and his phoney hairline likely cost more than his

Hollywood smile. His hair, thick and slicked back, is revolting in every sense of the word.

He's got a college football ring on one hand. He always told me he won it, but there's no evidence in the house that he ever even played. I'm certain that it was stolen. A fake, like everything else in his life. Fake hair, fake teeth, fake skin, fake suits, fake wife, fake house, fake son.

I've looked at these people's faces for years and never seen even a passing resemblance. Our eyes are different, as are the shapes of our hands, our noses, our ears, our hair, our eyebrows, our jaws, our smiles—everything. There's nothing of me in these two. I know it deep down; I just know it.

As they stare at me, the dripping water from my jacket and droplets of blood bounce off the ground. I lower my head, averting my gaze away from him. Despite his size, he's a relatively soft-spoken man, but his words are lethal, like those star things that samurai throw at their enemies.

'Thirteen minutes,' he says quietly.

'I'm sorry,' I respond.

There's a slight slur in his speech, which lets me know he's had a drink. Not enough for him to be completely out of control, but enough to make a difference.

'Why?' he says, taking a half step towards me.

The shark is circling.

'My bike,' I say.

'Speak up,' he says.

'My bike,' I say, 'the tyre went flat?'

'The tyre went flat,' he says.

'Yes, sir,' I say.

'How?'

'Must have been a nail or a stone or something, it was dark,' I say, 'I had to walk it back.'

I meet his eyes, just for a second. They're unmoving, unblinking.

'Show me,' he says, moving past me and opening the door to the pouring rain outside.

My heart is beating so fast, it's hard to take breaths. He moves past me and walks into the rain. He's wearing a white shirt and black trousers. He doesn't care about the rain. He already knows I'm lying and wants the punishment to fit the crime. I've made him go outside. I've made him get soaking wet. He wants to see how far I take it, how far he can push what he's about to do to me. He wants to see when I'll crack.

For a brief moment, I don't care. I make the choice to go all the way. Take it as far as it will go. Maybe he'll go through with it this time. Maybe he'll just murder me and be done with it, but maybe before he does, I'll get that final moment of courage and tell him exactly what I think of him. Maybe I'll get a strike in, maybe.

It's just a fantasy. It's not real. I know that. The fear is too old. Too entrenched.

We walk down the path towards the shed, the rain now pouring so heavily that everything appears to be washing away. He pulls back the rusted bolt lock and slowly opens the wooden door, stepping back and holding it open, motioning for me to enter first. He's soaked now, calm. His eyes track my little self as I move past him, stepping up onto the wooden slats. I feel him move in behind me. Closing the door and flipping on the soft white light bulb that's suspended on the ceiling. He glares down at me.

'Show me,' he says.

I look down at the bike, already knowing that it doesn't matter what happens next. We're in the shed, and the door is closed. I flick my eyes upward at the walls for a second. I know he sees me do it, but he doesn't care. This is no ordinary shed. Behind the hanging garden tools, the shelves with wooden boxes that hold the normal things that people keep, is something very different. It's all over the walls, all over the ceiling, and all over the inside of the wooden door.

Sound proofing.

Like the kind you find when you see musicians recording in studios, grey foam padding with triangular cutout shapes. The same kind he has in the basement, so nobody can hear me scream.

I point to the tire. Lift the bike up with shaky hands and spin the wheel so he can see. He takes a step towards me, kneels, and begins examining the slice. It's clean. He looks up at me.

'And you say a rock did this?' he says softly.

'Maybe,' I say.

There are tears now pouring down my face. They've betrayed me, but my body doesn't know how to keep secrets in the shed. He looks at me and gently smiles.

'Tell me you're lying, or it'll be worse,' he says.

My voice is shaking now. A dam breaks within as I place the wheel back down.

'You did this, didn't you?' he says.

I can't speak. My eyes are blurry now as the flood merges with terror. I nod.

'What did you use?' he says, standing back up.

'A protractor,' I whisper.

He puts his hand on my shoulder. It feels cold.

'Thank you,' he says, 'you just saved your life, you should take pride in that.'

He moves to the side of the wall, and I see him lift a three-pronged hand rake from a small peg. He then moves to a set of golf clubs and removes one of them. He hands it to me, grip first.

'Because you came clean, you can bite down on this,' he says.

He then removes a red first aid box from the shelf and opens it. He removes a roll of white bandage and lays it out on the shelf.

My whole body is shaking. I want to beg him not to do it. I want to plead with him. I want to scream as loud as I can and run as far as my legs can carry me but I'm too small. Too slow. He'll catch me. He always does, so I just take the club.

'Take your shirt off,' he says.

I unbutton my shirt. It takes me a while because my fingers are cold and numb from the rain.

'Now lean against your saddle,' he says.

I lean my hands on the saddle, take the grip of the golf club, and bite down hard. I close my eyes and try to go to that place.

I wait.

He does it fast, like a bear attacking a deer in the forest with its claws. The prongs of the rake tear into my flesh as he rips it from my shoulder to the base of my back.

Blistering, unheard screams howl through my clenched jaw. I bite down so hard that I hear one of my teeth crack as the flesh on my back is torn open. I feel the warmth of the blood as it seeps down onto my trousers. I wail, I beg, the club drops from my mouth onto the ground as my crying intensifies, and then it's over. I collapse onto the cold, sodden wood of the shed as he kneels down, cradling me, telling me everything is going to be OK.

The world is spinning, I feel weak, and lightheaded. I feel his hands on my back as he applies the bandages around the wounds before the light begins to fade and the pain fades away. I drift into oblivion, wondering if I'll ever wake up again.

Not really caring.

# Chapter
# TWENTY-FIVE

## 2021
### Carter

It's been two weeks since the fire. The evidence has been taken, and clean-up and reconstruction crews are moving through the building, taking photographs, measurements, and structural assessments. I've finally been allowed in. The black and charred remains of my office are laid out in front of me as I step over the crunchy floor. There's not much furniture left. My desk is a pile of ash, and my art is all completely destroyed. There are wooden and metal panels where the windows blew out, so the light coming into the space is patchy and uneven. There's a strange feeling in the room, as if someone is watching me. I move across the floor towards the corner of what used to be the drinks cabinet and pull back the melted remains of the mirror.

The hinges on the right side are nearly completely melted and snap the moment they come loose. The whole thing drops, falling to the floor and smashing. The noise bounces off the eerily quiet space, and for a second, I think I hear someone laughing down the corridor. A laugh I haven't heard in years. It only lasts a fraction of a second, and I dismiss it straight away as the mind playing one of its sick little games. I turn back to the wall where the mirror was hanging and look at the door to the safe. It's fireproof, but I'm still wondering if its contents have been able to withstand the heat.

I enter the twelve-digit code, and it clicks open. The door swings open with ease. I take a step towards what should be an interior full of contracts, personal items, and a rather large collection of gold Krugerrand coins. I'd always believed in having gold to hand. It stemmed from another part of my survival, though. I kept a part of it deep inside in a dark place that nobody knew about. There was something else missing, something I'd hoped survived at least the fire, but it was gone. My heart breaks as the ghost of what was is nowhere to be seen. It had been the only real thing left. The only reminder of a hope that I'd held onto. A dream that was. Now, it's gone.

It's gone.

I feel my eyes begin to well up as I briefly look down at the charred floor. Someone took it. I try to make sense of what is happening, but there is just no way to describe how I feel.

I peer closer into the open safe and see the corner of a white, folded piece of paper. I reach inside and lift it up. I bring it closer and see that it's sealed by a piece of tape. I check the safe again, padding it down with my hand.

Nothing.

I look behind me to the open door and make sure that Marge isn't there. She was down at reception but said she'd follow me up.

I look down again at the folded paper. It's crisp, clean, and completely unharmed by the flames that had engulfed the place. I break the seal and open it. I stop breathing. I don't know for how long. My blood runs cold, and I can feel a distinct constriction in my chest as every muscle in my body tightens in preparation for the flight.

The inked lettering is steady and meticulous, clearly written by hand. The letters are blocky with no real identifying characteristics.

I lower the hand holding the letter and walk towards a gap between the two metal sheets, where the windows overlooking the park used to be. I can see the sunlight through the trees below as I hear footsteps behind me.

'Well, would you look at that,' Marge says.

I turn to her, folding the letter in half in my hand.

'What's that?' I say through a cracking voice.

'There's a piece of carpet over there, untouched,' she says, pointing in the corner.

I follow her finger. She's right. I look back at her, and she gives me a look of concern.

'It's just a lick of paint,' she says.

'Not always,' I say.

'No, not always, but it's a good place to start,' she says.

'You've got a two-o'clock with Hanson,' she says.

I nod. Our temporary offices are ten blocks from here, so I'll have to go soon.

She turns to leave, casting a momentary glance at the trembling paper in my hand. I hadn't noticed its shaking until now. I look down at it once more, bringing it up to my eye line and opening the page. The message hits me again like a .22 caliber to the chest.

NO MORE HIDING

# Chapter
# TWENTY-SIX

My head is spinning as I walk down 32nd Street. I've given Roger the night off because I can't face anyone at the moment and need to breathe. My pace is brisk, but I'm still taking detours—an extra block here or there—doubling back on myself and checking behind me every now and then to see if anyone is following me. Every face I see seems to glance at me, and my chest is constricting to the point where I'm having to consciously remember to inhale and exhale. The smell of ash lingers all around me, and it feels like the world is burning. In my mind, I'm walking down a flame filled street. Empty burnt out cars line each side, the leaves on the trees, long incinerated and charred corpses from some apocalyptic event, lay neatly on the pavement like broken dolls. The sound of an ambulance blaring by the street junction ahead brings me back to reality, where pedestrians go about their business. There's a cool breeze moving its way in the opposite direction. I can hear voices in the wind. I don't know what they're saying, but there's something too familiar about their tone before one makes its way through.

*No more hiding.*

I stop mid-stride.

'No,' I say aloud.

There's no response. A single leaf falls from a tree and rests next to my shoe. I glance down at it as its tip graces the leather. My pocket vibrates. I reach inside and pull out my phone. It's Jean. I look back at the leaf as a light breeze breaks its touch. I'm about to reject the call when something tells me not to. I answer.

'Hello?' I say.

'Well, this is an absolute shit storm,' Jean says, 'where the hell have you put the editorial department?'

'What?' I say, turning for a moment to look behind me.

There's silence for a moment on the line.

'Editorial, Carter,' she says, 'they're all standing around an empty corridor with no desks.'

'I... I ... don't know, I'll speak to Marge,' I say.

There's another pause.

'Carter?' she says.

'What?'

'Carter where are you?' she says.

'I'm on, I dunno, 34th and something why?' I say, beginning to walk again.

'You sound off,' she says.

I take a long breath and try to form words. I should have hung up by now and told her to just sort it out but I'm keeping her on the phone. I don't know why.

'I always sound off,' I say.

'Carter, I've known you long enough to know you should have hung up by now,' she says.

There's something in her voice. I can't quite put my finger on it but she's lingering. The defensiveness is gone from her tone.

'I …' I start but words fail me.

'Sound like you need a drink?' she says.

'Should really be getting back to Kim,' I say.

'It's early yet,' she says, 'how about you meet me in the Plaza for a quick something.'

I look to the sky, about to reject the offer, but my instinct tells me otherwise.

'Why not,' I say.

'Great I'll be thirty minutes,' she says.

I text Marge and tell her to cancel my 11 o'clock.

I arrive at the steps leading to the plaza, suddenly aware that I've forgotten how I arrived here. I step inside and am instantly greeted by one of the bell boys. His name is Joe. He's in his early twenties and going to NYU to study anthropology. He's originally from Denver and lives with his boyfriend somewhere in Hoboken. I always make it my business to get to know anyone in the service business, especially when they go that extra mile. There's a hope in their eyes and a thirst for life, especially in New York, that I connect with. They're not defeated by it, yet. People of a certain age have a strange glassy look if they've lived in this city for a long time and haven't made it or have had life take a chunk out of their soul. It's more accurate to say that it happens to all of us, but you see it in major cities most of all. Having a dream isn't enough. Joe comes straight over to me and puts his hand on his hip.

'Mr. Page, it's always a pleasure,' he says, 'you look particularly dapper today.'

I smile at him. He cocks his head as he looks into my eyes.

'Tough day at the office, huh? I heard about the fire, are you all right, sir?' he says.

I nod at him as he extends his hand for me to shake. I take it. He grips it with friendship and warmth.

I give him an earnest nod of my head before removing my hand.

'It's just a building, Joe, we'll paint it up and get back to work in a couple of weeks,' I say.

'Nothing in this city is just a building, sir; of all the places in the world, you know that much,' he says.

He's right. After 9/11, it's like every structure here now has its own heart, its own name, and its own personality. The bricks and mortar have become family.

'Well said,' I say to him.

'I have a way with words,' he says playfully, 'so what brings you to our little palace today?'

'I'm meeting a friend for a drink,' I say.

'Well, that's just an excellent idea; the bar is half empty. Come on I'll show you to your seat,' he says.

'You don't have to,' I say.

'Nonsense,' he says, turning and leading the way.

We talk a little through the grand lobby. He tells me about the troubles he's having at school and fills me in on intimate details of his love life, which I really have no business listening to, but he's just that type. An open heart, with all the pages of his book available to read by all. I find it refreshing to listen to, even though deep down I wonder how long a person like that can last. I've never opened my book to anyone. Most people get the blurb on the back. A skim through will entice the reader to get close, except the fiction inside doesn't match the cover.

We reach the cocktail bar, a plush oval in the centre of marble floors, gold leaf, and adorned with fresh flowers. He pulls out a stool at the bar.

'Can I take your coat?' he says.

'No thanks, Joe, I won't be here that long,' I say.

He nods to the bartender, and there's a silence between us that I suddenly find I can't fill. I feel tightness in my chest again. He puts his hand on my shoulder.

'Keep up the good fight,' he says.

I smile at him.

'Thanks, Joe, and don't let that man of yours treat you like that, if he won't step up to the plate, you've got to bench him,' I say.

Joe laughs.

'Oh, you better believe it,' he says, winking at me and moving away.

I take off my coat and place it on the hook under the bar before sitting down and ordering a whiskey. Before the drink arrives, I feel a tap on my shoulder. I turn to see Jean smiling at me.

# Chapter
# TWENTY-SEVEN

### 1988
### Thomas

I always sit in the back left corner of the classroom. There's something about knowing that the wall is behind me and nobody can see my scars that I find comforting. It's kind of silly because there's no way anyone would see them anyway. I don't play sports, so I never use the showers in the school gym. I don't even go swimming. I have a doctor's note about having ear problems or something that I had to present to the principal to get me out of that. I don't know where she got the doctor's note. I'm pretty sure it's just a good fake, but regardless, I am under strict instructions never to take my clothes off unless they're both with me. I don't want to anyway. It's been over eight months since the shed incident, and it still hurts a little when I stretch or move my shoulders the wrong way.

It's a few minutes before class is due to start when a paper ball gets flung across the classroom and hits me on the head. I don't even look up. I hear giggling and the usual taunts from Billy Strauss at the front. He usually greets me by calling me a freak. He's not a typical bully, he's never started a physical fight with me because, as it so happens, I'm bigger than him, and he probably knows he wouldn't last long in a fight.

The laughter stops when the teacher, Mr. Hastings, comes in. It's math first this morning. I hate math. It's not that I'm not able to do it, it's just that it takes me a lot longer than anyone else to grasp the concepts. I'm always behind. I seem to see things differently than everyone else. When he puts up numbers and problems on the board, it just doesn't make any sense. It's like trying to learn a foreign language every day. It's hard to explain, but the only way I'm eventually able to solve the problems is by making visual patterns in my head. Like paintings or something. My brain doesn't seem to work with numbers the same way it does with other subjects like English or history. I think it has something to do with left or right brains or something. I haven't been able to concentrate on math in any way for several months. I haven't been able to focus on anything. There's a strange fog over everything. It descended after the attack. The memory of the whole thing seems to be coming from someone else. Like my brain has been put in a glass box to be observed like an act in a torture circus. I was kept out of school for two weeks, again with some sort of doctor's note, and left in the basement wrapped up in bandages. It wasn't so bad. I think she was actually angry with him for doing it, as he backed off me for months and has even been talking to me differently. There's still that look of a predator in his eyes, but he hasn't touched me since. My body remembers it, though. My muscles are freezing up every time he comes home, and I'm not able to really look at him. I know it's starting to bother him. He thinks I'm gonna tell someone. They both do.

I'm not allowed to cycle home from school anymore. She picks me up every day outside the gates, so it's been a while since I've been to the Alamo. I haven't been able to work on my story or my preparations.

I'm staring out the window when a hand is placed on my desk. It's Carla. She normally sits in front of me. She places a note on the desk and turns back around, meeting my eyes for just a second before she faces the board again. She has the biggest blue eyes I've ever seen. We don't talk that much. She's only said hi to me a few times since she transferred in from Wayland High School in Virginia. She's soft-spoken and always wears a baseball cap turned backwards and baggy jeans. She has a soft face, and I've caught her looking my way a few times. I don't know why. I think there must be something off with the way my hair is parted or something wrong with my face. I look down at the folded piece of paper and open it up.

It reads: 'Fuck those guys'

She turns back and gives me a smile. I smile back, take my pen, write a reply to the note, and hand it back.

It reads: Thanks

She takes the note and nods at me. The class goes on as I try to get my head around this simple act of kindness. I'm tense for the rest of the class, and it doesn't feel good. I don't know why she did that, and now I don't know what I'm supposed to do. After class, I'm putting some books away in my locker when I feel a tap on my shoulder. I flinch away from it, and jump in a gross overreaction. It's Carla. She begins to laugh as I grab my chest.

'Please don't sneak up on me like that,' I say.

'Jeez sorry, grandpa,' she says.

I turn my face away from her for a moment and adjust the books I've placed on a shelf, but also to try and hide the fact that my face is burning up with embarrassment.

'Wanna eat lunch with me outside on the grass?' I hear from behind me.

I turn to see her eyes beaming at me.

'Eh..' I think for a moment about how easily it could be seen from the street.

'A girl just asked you to have lunch with her, you're supposed to be happy about that,' she says.

Carla has a big personality. She's not shy, and she's really pretty. She gets a lot of attention from the older boys, but she seems to have no time for anyone. She dresses in denim coats, Converse sneakers, skinny jeans, brown rimmed glasses, and a wool hat. She doesn't seem to be interested in boys, which has me wondering why she's talking to me.

'Okay then,' I say, breaking eye contact.

'Great,' she says, 'my mom made me the best roast beef sandwich, and I'm hungry, so let's go.'

I close my locker, and we move down the hallway to the exit. I can hear someone say my name in the crowd, but I ignore it. We go outside and sit on an empty bench by a tree in the courtyard. Carla sits on the table and puts her feet on the bench, and I sit below her. She takes out her lunch and begins to unwrap it.

'What do you have?' she says.

'Oh, I already had a big breakfast,' I say.

'You ain't got any lunch?' she says.

'I'm okay,' I say.

She frowns at me, breaks off half her sandwich, and hands it to me.

'Oh, that's okay, I don't....'

'Take it, trust me, this is something holy,' she says.

I take it out of her hands, our fingers touch.

'Thanks,' I say, trying to hide the fact that I'm actually starving and haven't eaten since the previous night.

I take half of the sandwich, which is served on rye bread that is soft but thick and filled with tender meat. I waste no time in tucking into it. I think it may be the best thing I've ever tasted in my life.

We sit in silence as we eat. I watch the courtyard where kids are playing and walk past them to a row of trees next to the fence, which looks out onto the street. I scan up and down the sidewalk, an annoying habit, but I don't see anyone staring back at me, at least not today. I savour the taste of the meat and pickles in my mouth, and for a moment I feel like a warm blanket. Before long, the whole thing is gone, and I'm wiping my hands and brushing some of the crumbs off my trousers. I look back up at Carla and realise that she's only halfway through hers.

'Wow,' she says, 'I don't think I've ever seen anyone inhale food that quickly in my life.'

For the second time, I look away, embarrassed, but manage a nervous laugh.

'Sorry, it was just so good,' I say.

'That's okay, my mom will be chuffed. I'll send your compliments to the chef.'

I smile at her.

'Well, you're going to have to sit there and watch me finish mine then,' she says.

'That's okay,' I say.

We sit quietly. I look down at my feet and realise that the sole on the bottom of my right shoe is coming apart at the toe. I pull it back under my other leg to hide it and quickly check the other one. It looks okay for now, but the stitching looks like it's about to give way as well.

'You know my dad could probably fix that,' she says.

I look up at her, embarrassed.

'Really,' she says, 'he's a cobbler, has a shop on Duke Street.'

'It's fine,' I say.

'Okay, but you're going to trip over it when it comes off properly?' she says.

I look down at my shoe again.

'It's my only pair,' I say to her.

She smiles at me, and my heart feels like it's gonna explode.

'What size are you, a nine?' she says.

I nod.

'I'll bring you a spare pair tomorrow, my brother is the same size, you give me yours, and I'll get 'em fixed up right,' she says.

I've never been offered kindness, I don't know how to respond, but I can suddenly feel the onset of tears. I get up from the bench.

'I gotta go, I'll talk to you later,' I manage to say before walking away from her at speed.

'Hey!' she says as I move faster.

She says something else, but I can't hear it. I'm trying to hide my face in my sweater so that nobody else can see me.

# Chapter
# TWENTY-EIGHT

### 2021
### Carter

'You look like shit,' Jean says to me as she sips her drink.

I raise my glass to her. She has her hair tied back and over one shoulder. She's wearing a black business suit with a white shirt open and a little gold necklace.

'Thanks,' I say.

'How are you, Carter?' she says.

I look away for a moment as my phone pings in my pocket. I take it out and read the text. It's from Kim.

WHERE ARE YOU?

I text her back.

JUST HAVING A DRINK, WILL BE HOME IN A WHILE, EVERYTHING OKAY?

WHO YOU HAVING A DRINK WITH?

I look up at Jean and smile, shaking my head.

'That Kim?' she says.

I nod.

'Yeah, she spent the day with Daniel's kids down at the park,' I say.

'Daniel Foster has kids?' she says.

'You didn't know?' I say.

She blows air out of her mouth in shock. I text Kim back.

JEAN, I WON'T BE LONG, DID YOU HAVE FUN TODAY?

There's a momentary pause before I get a response.

TAKE....YOUR...TIME.... PLAY IT COOL OLD MAN. I'M JUST WATCHING A MOVIE. XX P.S. A PACKAGE ARRIVED FOR YOU.

I smile.

THANKS FOR THE TIP. SEE YOU LATER X

I put my phone back in my pocket.

'Sorry,' I say, taking another sip of my drink.

'That's okay,' she says.

Why are you so surprised Daniel has kids? I say.

'Eh..'

'Oh, come on he's not that bad, you and he would get along if you just gave him a chance,' I say.

'I'll take your word for it,' she says.

'He's good at what he does, Jean, and he's loyal,' I say.

'Donkeys are loyal if you feed them carrots,' she says.

I laugh.

'That's a good one,' I say.

She smiles at me.

'Did you find editorial?' I say.

'Yes, thanks for putting us in the damn basement,' she says.

'Don't look at me, Marge has taken over all of that, and it won't be for long. A couple of months and we'll be back inside,' I say.

'It's fine,' Jean says, 'Do they know what happened?'

I look away from her, at the faces around the bar. It's mostly full of professionals, lawyers, businessmen, and women, all suited and all deep in their own little worlds. I have a feeling someone in here is looking at me. I shake my head at Jean.

'I don't know Jean,' I say.

'You don't know, or they don't know?' she says.

'You're sharp,' I say.

'That's why you used to pay me the big bucks,' she says.

'Can we talk about something else?' I say.

'Sure,' she says, 'can I ask you something?'

I nod.

'Did you really make your first billion at thirty-two?' she says.

I raise my eyebrows and laugh.

'What?' I say.

'I was just curious because you were so young,'' she says.

I look down at my glass and swirl the ice around.

'Thirty-three,' I say.

'You don't have to tell me about it, it's really none of my business, and I don't care about the money Carter,' she says.

'You want to know why I did what I did?' I say.

She nods.

'So it's true,' she says.

I nod.

'You gave it all away,' she says.

'Not all of it,' I say, 'why do you ask?'

'Well, the truth is, I don't know that much about you, Carter,' she says, 'that was very noble.'

'There was nothing noble about it Jean,' I say, remembering the day I wrote the check.

She pauses and looks away before meeting my eyes again.

'It's just that...' she says before pausing.

'It's just that what?' I say.

'It's who you gave it to,' she says.

I don't like where this is going. If there's one thing I've learned about Jean over the years, it's that she could have been a homicide detective with her attention to detail.

'I don't really like to talk about it Jean,' I say.

'I understand,' she says, 'I'm sorry for asking.'

I look at her face, and it seems to be going red. I think I've embarrassed her. It's hard to know and track back to try and remember if the tone I used was rude. She sits quietly. I look at her soft face, the lines under her eyes showing a past that's filled with something I can't quite get a read on. There's pain in there somewhere. The silence isn't awkward. There's a strange comfort between us that I haven't felt in a long time as I notice a crack opening up and a sudden desire to let her in, just a little.

'I didn't deserve it Jean,' I say.

'What?' she says.

'That money,' I say, 'I got lucky with a tech patent that took off. I didn't even invent the thing; I only bankrolled the development of a piece of software that some clever kid came to me with. He was smart, came from a shitty family in the Midwest and had that hunger. He came to me with the idea and needed a year to get it off the ground. I believed in him, so I took a slice. I had no idea it was going to transform finance. To be honest I wasn't even that interested in it. I didn't do the work, so I took what I thought was enough to get BMX off the ground, made sure he was set up and gave the rest away.'

I take another sip of my drink.

'In hindsight, it was probably crazy, I nearly lost everything in the first two years of BMX. I couldn't pay rent, there were weeks where I lived on rice,' I say.

'You didn't give yourself a nest egg?' she says.

'Nope,' I say, 'every penny went into the business.'

'Well, that's crazy,' she says.

I laugh.

'Yep,' I say.

'There's gotta be something else though?' she says.

'What do you mean?' I say.

'You're the most unusual person, you know that?' she says.

'How so?' I say.

'I didn't like you when we met, you know that?' she says.

'Yes,' I say, straightening my back, 'you weren't exactly shy about that Jean.'

'No, I wasn't,' she says, 'but let's not talk about that anymore.'

I smile.

'What do you want to talk about?' I say.

'Oh, I don't know,' she says, 'maybe we don't have to talk at all. Maybe we just sit here all day and drink to the mayhem.'

I look away for a moment, then back at my drink.

'So is Daniel, like, married?' she says.

I laugh.

'Okay, seriously, what did he do to you?' I say.

'He thinks books are stupid, and hasn't read anything, ever,' she says, 'I just don't understand people like that. And he gave me a nickname because he's an insecure man child who thinks I'm just riding on your coattails when he hasn't so much as run a lemonade stand.'

'That's actually not true,' I say, 'he respects the hell out of you.'

'No, he doesn't,' she scoffs.

'And I think he's more of a movie buff anyway,' I say.

'Look, he's your right-hand guy and I get that, but I'm just saying he's got issues with me,' she says.

'Maybe he's in love with you,' I say.

'Yes, that's it, you've nailed it on the head. He's in love with me, and he's just pulling my pigtails in the yard,' she says, smiling. 'Well, you'll have to let him down lightly as he's not my type.'

'Oh? And what's your type?' I say.

'The broken,' she says.

I lock eyes with her and raise my glass.

'You've come to the right place, welcome to my emporium,' I say.

'Are you broken, Carter?' she says.

I clench my jaw and shake my head.

'Who isn't,' I say.

'There's levels,' she says.

'Levels?' I say.

'There's broken and then there's broken,' she says.

'Okay, you'll have to be more specific,' I say.

'Well, you can't be calling yourself broken because you own one of the biggest multimedia companies in the world, which requires compos mentis to at least some degree,' she says.

'Thanks for that,' I say.

'You're welcome,' she says, 'that may be the nicest thing I've ever said to anyone.'

'I'd hate to hear what you've called me when I'm not around,' I say.

'Oh, that's between me my bathroom mirror,' she says.

That makes me laugh.

'To be a fly on that wall,' I say.

'Never gonna happen,' she says, with a wry smile.

'That's the second time you've gone out of your way to make sure I don't hit on you,' I say.

'Well, where there's smoke there's fire,' she says.

'So, you're saying there's smoke?' I say.

She raises her eyes to heaven and looks down at her drink, flicking her hair away from her neck. There's a moment's silence as I let my gaze rest on hers. Her eyes meet mine, and she gives me the smile that says nothing and everything.

We sit there, and I let the moment linger as a spark ignites between us. It takes me a little by surprise, as Jean has always been, well, just there, and all of a sudden, I'm wondering why this is the second time we've met up like this in a matter of weeks.

I decide to be direct.

'What's this about Jean?' I say.

'What's what about?' she says.

'The sudden...,' I gesture with my hand towards her and back to me.

'Ah,' she says, 'you think I've suddenly come to my senses and seen you for the charming misunderstood man that your previous conquests have and I want a slice?'

'You have a very strange perception of me,' I say.

'I think most people do Carter,' she says, 'but to answer your question.'

She leans back in her chair.

'I'm really just making sure you're okay,' she says, 'I've seen that look of absence before, and quite frankly, I can't have you go off the rails right now.'

'So, this is an investment protection friendship?' I say, admittedly a little taken aback by her answer.

She smiles again.

'Of course.'

'Ah,' I say, 'well. you don't need me anymore.'

'That's not entirely accurate,' she says.

'Oh?'

'You're still my largest creditor,' she says, 'regardless of the control you give me, I still gotta pay you back.'

'Jean,' I say, 'can we leave that to the accounts department and the Lawyers?'

She lowers her head.

'I'm sorry I'm shit at this,' she grits her teeth, 'this is my way of saying thank you.'

She pauses.

'That store really mattered to me,' she says, and what seems like a lump is forming in her throat.

'I used to love it,' she continues, 'coming in on winter mornings. Taking out the small padlock keys that were frozen and rattling the old bolt on the shutter, watching it come up. Turning on the lights and putting out the stock and having that first coffee before people started to come in and browse.'

I listen intently. My focus entirely on her eyes.

'Talking to customers about titles and the day and the little things.'

She stops and starts spinning the liquid in her drink.

'Now it's this...'

She trails off.

'This what?' I say.

'This monster of a thing, wrapped in quarterly reports and corporate mergers and acquisitions and shareholder lawsuits, and YOU,' she points at me and widens her eyes, smiling, 'and just grey bullshit.'

She leans back and takes a breath.

'But above all that,' she says softly, 'I never said thank you.'

There's a long silence.

'I'm not a very good business person.'

'You could have fooled me,' I say.

'That's not what I mean,' she says, 'I don't like it. I did it for the love of stories, which is why that plagiarism thing hit me so hard. I just didn't think it was possible. It took away the magic, and I'm not sure it's coming back.'

'There's always magic,' I say softly.

'What?' she says.

I realise that I've said it so softly that she hasn't heard me.

'I said there's always magic.'

'Carter Page, thinks there's still magic in the world, as it burns all around him,' she says.

'This is when it's there the most,' I say.

'Who the hell are you?' she says, genuine bafflement in her tone.

I don't answer.

There's another text coming in on my phone. I look at it. It's a media file. I frown as it downloads. My jaw falls open as my head begins to spin around.

'Carter?' says Jean, a million miles away.

I scan the room, looking at every face.

'Carter!' Jean says.

I snap to her.

'Sorry,' I say, 'I have to go Jean.'

'What?' she says.

'I look back down at my phone. At the photo of the two of us sitting at the bar taken moments ago.

'I'm sorry Jean,' I say, getting up and taking my jacket from the chair.

'Carter, you look pale, what's going on?' she says.

I don't answer her. I open my wallet and put down some cash.

'I'll call you later ok?' I say.

She nods, a look in her eye of complete confusion.

'Sorry Jean,' I say.

'Go,' she says.

My back is turned by the time she says it, and I'm moving fast towards the exit.

# Chapter
# TWENTY-NINE

## 1988
### Thomas

I'm sitting at home watching TV. It's Sunday, so I'm allowed an hour in the afternoon while they're upstairs. There's only one thing on Sundays that I like at this time of day, The A-Team. It's awesome. The stunts, explosions, and plans they come up with to save all these small towns, always filled with helpless villagers defending against some evil drug kingpin or dictator. Over the years, I've noticed that loads of the action shots are reused, but I don't care. Murdoch is my favorite. He comes off as crazy, but I think he's the smartest of them. BA, played by Mr. T, is currently bringing some steel beams around the black van they use to toughen it up in preparation for the finale stunt. I begin to hear noises from upstairs. I look up at the ceiling and move over to the TV, turning the volume dial up a notch, scooting back to the floor with my back against the sofa.

I have a half-eaten bowl of cornflakes and a glass of orange juice beside me. I pick up the bowl and finish eating as the explosions start to go off on the TV. There's a loud thump on the floor, my signal to lower it, which I do with haste. My heart begins to race as I watch and wait to see if anyone will come down the stairs. They don't. I sit there, occasionally looking out the main front window to the street, watching as passersby go about their business, oblivious to what's going on behind the bricks and mortar. It's strange how close people can appear to be, yet be light years apart. We're all just wandering around in our own little bubbles of the universe.

I see a bike begin to pull up the street.

It's Carla!

She has a little backpack on and is riding her yellow racer. My heart begins to pound. She's been to my house once, a few years ago, when her mom dropped me off. She pulls up outside my front gate, and I hear the noises upstairs stop. I leap up, almost throwing my bowl on the ground, and run to the window, hiding behind the curtains as she opens the front gate and starts walking up the driveway.

'Oh shit,' I say, my chest going nuclear.

I hear footsteps on the stairs.

'Oh no!'

I don't know what to do, so I run to the living room door, but before I can make it, I hear the bell ring. I open the door, see my father standing there in his robe, his large bare feet slapping firmly on the ground. He looks back at me in a way that tells me not to move a muscle.

'Hi there, is Thomas in, I'm Carla,' comes her voice from behind the door.

'Well, hello there Carla,' comes my father's charming and practiced tone, 'I don't think I've ever met you before.'

'Oh, I'm a friend from school, my mom dropped Thomas off here, but I've never visited,' she says sweetly in return.

There's an odd, elongated pause as I try and figure out what he's going to do. Then he calls out to me as if I were miles away.

'Thomas?' he asks, 'a friend for you at the door.'

He looks back.

'You'll have to excuse my attire, Carla, I wasn't quite ready for the day to start today.'

'Oh, that's quite all right, it's Sunday,' she says.

'That's right, it is,' he responds.

I move quickly to the door and look around.

'Nice to meet you, Carla, I'll leave you to it,' he says as he moves back upstairs.

I look at Carla, who shows me something odd in her eye. As if she knows, like she's scared.

'Sorry, I was in the neighbourhood and wondered if you wanted to go for a bike ride; I'm so bored, and it's such a nice day out,' she says.

'Eh,' I say, 'sure thing. Give me a minute to pull my bike around.'

'Okay, great,' she says.

I shut the front door and look up at the top of the stairs, where he is waiting for me.

'Is it okay if I take my bike out for an hour,' I say.

He glares at me.

'One hour,' he says, in a rare gift of freedom granted when he had OTHER things to do.

I just nod and move quickly to the rear of the house, to the bike shed, and take out my bike. I race it around the side, scraping the handles on the brick walls because I'm in that much of a hurry. She's at the gate already, on her own, as she smiles at me. We pull away. She turns to me.

'So where are we going?' she says.

'This was your idea,' I say.

'I know, but you know this place better than I do, anything worth seeing?' she says.

I think about it for just a second. A fleeting thought that only lasts as long as it takes for me to dismiss it.

Don't be stupid, not there, absolutely not!

'Well, there's the old salt mine about two miles south, which is sort of cool,' I say.

'Let's go!' she says, picking up the pace.

I look back at the house, and for a moment, the curtains of the upstairs bedroom pull back momentarily as a pair of eyes glare out. About a half hour later, both our bikes are perched on the ridge of a concave outcropping overlooking the valley below. Circular tracks made from large excavators spiral down into the giant hole in the ground.

'Wow, how have I never seen this?' she says, 'looks like a giant ice cream scoop.'

'Sure does,' I say, 'come on, you can cycle down to the bottom; the hard part is getting back up.'

'Lead on, Ranger,' she says.

We cycle down the rocky roads to the basin, where I pull up to the now sealed off entrance to the mine shaft. I get off my bike as Carla skids to a halt and joins me. The entrance is boarded up and has a large painted wooden board warning people, kids in particular, to stay out.

'Wow!' says Carla, 'okay, there's definitely a dead body in there.'

'I've checked,' I say, 'there isn't'

'How far in have you gone?' she says.

'Quite a ways,' I say, 'wanna see?'

She looks into the darkness and hesitates. I can see she looks nervous.

'Or not, I mean, there's nothing really in there but empty rock, I just thought it would be cool to show it to you.'

She smiles at me.

'That's the most romantic thing a boy has ever done for me,' she says.

My face flushes instantly as I look at my shoes.

'I'm joking, you dolt,' she says, punching me in the arm, 'let's take a look'

'You sure?' I say.

She nods while placing her bike on the ground and adjusting her backpack. We move over to a gap in the wooden boards and move under.

'I can't see a thing,' she says.

I take a small torch out of my pocket. I always have one in case it's too dark in the Alamo. I turn it on and hear a gasp as the light catches the long caverns' edges and flows away into the depths.

'My god, it's so deep,' she says.

'Yeah, I think it goes down a half a mile, watch your step,' I say, instinctively reaching out my hand for her to take. There are two planks of wood covering a water filled hole. She takes my hand and steps over. For a moment, I feel something. Connection. Physical touch that's not followed by intense pain. I let go of her hand, feeling uncomfortable with it. It's too close.

She steps over and smiles back.

'Much obliged, young sir,' she says, mock tipping a cap.

I shine my light around as we peer into the nothingness.

'There's not much else down here, and it gets a little slippery down there,' I say, turning to her.

She's looking at me in an odd way. Her eyes were looking at mine intently. She leans in. I freeze, and she kisses me on the lips. I can feel my hands start to shake, not so much at the enormity of the fact that this is my first kiss, as at how tender it is.

*Is this what it's like?*

A warm blanket descends around me, and the world implodes, leaving the pair of us floating in the nothingness. It seems to last for hours.

She places one of her hands gently on my cheek.

I recoil.

She stops, a look of disappointment and sadness crosses her eyes, and a look of embarrassment follows.

'Sorry, did I hurt you?' she says.

'Sorry,' I say, as memories of metal on skin burst through my mind, 'that took me a little by surprise.'

'A good surprise?' she asks.

'Well, of course, I ... eh..'

'Relax, Thomas, I don't bite,' she says with a smile that's so genuine I can feel my eyes begin to water.

I lower the flashlight, in case she sees it but I'm too late. I feel a finger across my cheek, wiping away a falling tear. I have no words.

'What's happening to you?' she says.

I shake my head in the darkness, unable to respond when I feel her lips on mine again. She reaches down and turns off the flashlight, leaving us in the darkness. She unbuttons my shirt and slides her hands around my waist. For a moment, I tense, and she releases.

'It's okay,' she whispers.

I relax my body as the heat grows. I'm lost now. Lost in her forever as we unclothe each other.

I don't remember how long we were there, naked in the dark. I know it was late at night when I got home. I know that I spent the next week in the basement. I know that being locked to the radiator for that time was the closest to happiness I have ever felt.

## Chapter
# THIRTY

### 2021
### Carter

A switch has been flipped. My senses are honed as I move past the entrance to the hotel, clocking every face, every car, and every shadow under every streetlight. For a moment, I think I catch the sight of a little boy's face looking across the street at me. On second glance, there's nothing there. I reach for my phone and dial Roger. He's only two blocks away. I ask him to pick me up right away and hang up before he can ask about the strain in my voice.

A few minutes later, I'm in the back of the limo, en route back to the penthouse. Roger is moving fast. I'm glaring down at the photo from the unknown number. I think about sending a message back, but my instincts say no. I know what it's like to be threatened, know it all too well. The isolation, the fear, the universe's bubble you've found yourself in, where all eyes seem to be locked on you. You become primal. Mostly, it's just angry business associates or random lunatics who think you owe them something, but this is different. This is familiar. This is moving itself up and down my spine like a centipede, telling me something is very, very wrong.

'Sit rep?' Roger says from the front seat.

I look at him. I think he's been staring at me for some time.

'I don't know Roger,' I say.

'Your eyes say different,' he says.

This time, I feel a real concern coming from the front seat. I think about it for a moment. Think about what to let in, who to let in.

'Don't worry about it, Roger, I'll let you know if I need reinforcements,' I say, trying to convey a sense of calm.

'Say the word,' he says.

I nod, smiling at him, when my phone buzzes again. It's another message, from the same number. My eyes dart down as the traffic moves again. Roger is putting the foot down now. The message begins to download as streetlights flash past the windows at the speed of light. As the image resolves and the light from my screen feeds the information to my senses, I feel my heart stop.

Not flutter, not increase, just stop. My stomach seems to drop into a black hole, and I feel suddenly sick. I can't breathe. It's as if I'm suspended, weightless, in another dimension where there's nothing but darkness, nothing but pain. I don't blink. I'm frozen at the photo. It's my penthouse. It's my living room table. It's the back of Kim's head as she looks into a large box. There's a message beneath it.

NOT A WORD.

They're in my house!

They've got her!

Roger has already seen the reaction. My eyes must be red as I glare at him through the rearview mirror.

'Roger, MOVE IT!' I shout at him.

He doesn't hesitate. We're now breaking every law in the book. Car horns explode as Roger kicks it into full emergency mode, his skill and training matching any manoeuvre a seasoned NYPD officer on the road can handle. He mounts the sidewalk and pulls off some crazy turns to break traffic. I hear sirens in the background. I take hold of the handhold while glaring down at the screen. I call Kim.

No answer.

I call again.

And again.

And again. We pull up outside the main entrance. I'm already out of the car and running for the door. The sirens from the following police car coat the building in blue and red as they approach fast. Roger says something to me. I don't hear what it is. I'm already inside. I look for the concierge, but there's nobody there. I've never seen the desk unmanned. I get to the elevator, press the button. I look at the stairwell and think about running, but I know I'll be faster in the lift. The wait is torture. The metal doors slide open, and I rush in, pressing the top floor and the door close buttons multiple times. The elevator is swift. I hold my breath, hoping nobody else presses the floor button. I'm lucky. The doors swing open, and I see the front door to my penthouse.

It's ajar.

I don't think about it. I run straight for it, bursting it open with my shoulder. I enter.

'Kim!' I shout.

The living room is empty. I see a large open box on the table.

'Kimmy!' I shout, running to her room.

Her bed is neatly made, and clothes are folded on the dresser. I spin around and begin looking in all the other rooms. I hear the door close.

'Kim!' I shout again as I move to the living room to see a uniformed officer standing in the doorway.

I ignore him and look at my phone again. He looks at me, clearly recognising something is wrong. I call her number. Not even a ring. It cuts straight off.

'Sir?' the officer says, calmly.

I look at him, then at the table with the large open box. I rush over to it. There is a small note in a little envelope inside. I take it and conceal it in my jacket with a light hand, so the cop doesn't notice. I turn to him.

'Sorry officer,' I say, 'My daughter is being a pain in the ass, she's not allowed out after dark and she went out with friends.'

I look at my phone.

'There she is now,' I say.

I pretend to read a message.

'Typical,' I say, trying to control my exploding heart, 'I'm so sorry for the trouble.'

'You live here?' the officer says.

'Yes, I do,' I say, 'I know we broke a few lights, but I got panicked, it's her first time in New York, and I haven't seen her in a year. Her mother died a few weeks back, and I've just been all over the place.'

I hand him my ID. He scrutinises it as he's joined by a colleague.

'Really, I am very sorry,' I say.

The officer looks at me.

'I'll have to write you up, you can't be driving like that sir,' he says.

'Thank you, officer,' I say, grateful I'm not in cuffs, 'really, I'm so embarrassed.'

He writes me a stiff ticket, takes all the details, and finally leaves after a few more questions. This will get back to Detective Crown, of that I'm certain. I close the door after they leave, thanking them profusely before collapsing on the floor behind the door.

I start to cry. My head in my hands feels like a bowling ball.

'Oh god. what have I done Kimmy!'

I catch my breath, wipe my face, and get up. I move to the open box and close the lid, looking at the handwritten address on the front of it. Nothing resembles anything; it's done in block capitals. I take out the note from inside my coat and open it up. It says two words.

Silk pillowcases?

I look to my bedroom, manage to gather myself, and move inside the room. It's neatly made up, as the cleaner usually does. I look at the pillowcases and see what the note is referring to. It's a small voice recorder. I pause. Looking at it before taking a tissue off the nightstand and picking it up carefully. I press "play."

I hear breathing. A raspy breath as if it's struggling for air. Then a voice, electronic, distorted, soft.

'Carter Page,' says the voice, taking a moment to pause for a wheezing, strained breath of air.

'You have quite the fancy place here, quite the fancy place indeed.'

I lean into the recorder, trying to discern anything that might give away the identity of the strange alien voice, but there's nothing. And yet, I know this voice. That small part of my brain that's locked behind a fortress knows this voice.

'I'm going to make it simple, easy. Easy enough for even you to understand.'

There's something in the inflection. Something there raises the hairs on the back of my neck.

'You've made me a believer again. If you can make all this happen, if you can do all the things you've done, with your little brain, then there really is hope for us all. Maybe that's a conceit, I don't really know anymore.'

Another long inhale of a breath that seems to be a struggle.

'I've wandered, you know. I wandered the earth in search of you, and here you are hiding in plain sight the whole time. Right in front of my very eyes. A bold move. A bold move, but not entirely unexpected. You think you've got the smarts, don't you?'

A raspy breath follows, almost as if it's aided by some mechanism. There is something very familiar about this voice. As if I can see it staring up at me through the thin surface of a dark lake.

'Well, you can't hide, not from me. And you can't hide your little girl.'

I feel a stabbing pain in my chest.

'She's mine now. And soon you'll be mine too,' says the evil.

'I want to show you something. I want to show you what pain truly is. Your nightstand has an envelope with an address on it. I'll see you there in two days. I want you to bring your lady friend too, but that is all. Tell no one or she will die. If you do as I say, I may let her go. I may not.'

I look at an envelope on my nightstand.

'I want them to see you for who you really are, for what you've done. For what I am going to do to you. I'm watching you.'

There's a long pause. The voice has shakiness now, as if it is riled with emotion, with rage.

'Carter... Page. I wonder why you picked that name. It's so mundane, but then again, so are you.'

The recording ends. I move my arm, as if dreaming, to the side table and open the envelope. There's an address written on it.

It falls from my hands, gently hitting the floor as my world falls apart. There's no escaping this. There's no way around it. No way to see it any other way.

My life, as I've known it, is over.

# Chapter
# THIRTY-ONE

## 1988
### Thomas

Something very strange has been happening over the last few weeks. Since my release, they've been different. Not in a subtle or nuanced way that could be barely noticeable. Not in a way you could dismiss as them just having a good day or whatever. They've changed. He's being nice to me. Again, there have been times where he's barely even noticed I existed. Normally I'd consider this as being nice, but this new behaviour has me on edge. He's buying me presents. He's coming home from wherever he goes during the day and giving me books, toys, and candy from the local store that sells them in big bell bottom jars, which means you have to pick them out individually by hand. It's been going on daily now. She made me an apple pie yesterday and served it up to me on the sofa. I'm never allowed to eat in the living room, except for breakfast when they're upstairs making noise. It was a good one, too. She handed it to me on one of the good plates. It had little cookie bits on top, and the ice cream was cold and smooth.

It's strange because there's been something else different in the last week. Carla hasn't been in school. I haven't seen her since last week, and I figured she'd just caught something in the cold and was maybe sick. It's been nerve-wracking going in every day, as I don't know what to do now. I've never been in this situation. It's terrifying, and my mind is racing with things that I've done wrong. Is she that embarrassed about what happened? Is she so humiliated that she can't face me? Has she transferred schools to another state? What's she telling her friends? I've been keeping a close eye on a group she hangs out with, but other than the usual odd glances, there's nothing that indicates she's said anything to them. I'm trying to keep my brain from torturing me with the laughing faces of strangers. The kind that tells me I'm a joke, a useless sack of flesh that belongs in the basement for the rest of my life because who on Earth could love a face like this. The sides of my fingers are scabbed over with the nervous pulling of skin. My chest feels tight all the time, and something isn't sitting right. I noticed some hair fall out near the back of my head a few days ago, but I don't recall pulling at it.

Everything is calm, as if I'm treading water in the ocean with a thousand unseen eyes looking up from the darkness. All of them attached themselves to things with sharp teeth, slowly making their way up to my unsuspecting and defenceless body.

It's Sunday today. They're usually home all day in the living room drinking, but he left early this morning and hasn't been back since. I didn't hear them arguing about anything, and he didn't slam the door on his way out. It was quite the opposite. I only heard it because I was awake anyway. I'd had a strange dream, which I can't remember, but I know that it had woken me up just after five a.m. He hasn't been back since. She's in the living room watching some wildlife documentary about elephants or something, and I'm in my room, reading a book. I usually stay up here on Sundays either reading, studying for school, or doing homework. My room, that is to say, my normal room, not the basement, is another one of my sanctuaries when I'm allowed to use it. The bed is at least comfortable, and I have a little desk and chair where I can do my school work. There are bookshelves full to the brim of my favourites and a nice enough view of the park outside. To anyone who visited, you'd almost think it was the bedroom of a normal teenager. I even have movie posters on my wall.

I've been up here now for a few hours. I can hear the TV downstairs. She's probably fallen asleep watching some rerun of an old gameshow. She sleeps most of the day on Sundays anyway, but today she's been quiet since morning. There's a strangeness about the house. I read a book last year about an old CIA program called MK Ultra, where studies were made into the potentially real phenomenon of ESP. It was amazing to think that some people had the ability to sense things that were either happening or were about to happen often thousands of miles away. Today feels a bit like that. As if some part of my brain has been activated and can sense that there's something not right. Something very bad was about to happen.

I lay on my bed for a while and think about Carla. Think about what had happened between us in the mine. It was my first time. I don't know if I was any good or not because I have nothing to compare it to. It had all been so intense, like being swept up in a tornado to be spat out at the funnel. We'd both cycled home afterwards, laughing, and giggling the whole way. I remember the sun hitting my face as she kissed me goodbye before heading home to her house. I felt as if I were weightless on my cycle home. It was a different kind of freedom. I felt detached, as if not entirely a part of this body.

*Is this what peace is?*

She had looked happy when we parted that day. A cheeky little grin on her face told me we now had a secret together that only we would know for the rest of our lives.

I get out of bed, walk over to my small desk, and open my Chemistry homework. It's a subject I'm not great at and all the equations seem to take me twice as long to work out, but I work hard at it. The leaves outside are rattling in a breeze that's picked up over the last half hour or so. I hear the engine of a car as it rounds the bend at the top of our street.

It's him.

I can tell because of this high-pitched screeching noise the brakes make when his Pontiac Parisienne turns corners. He's never gotten them fixed. Partly because I know he's broke, but mostly because I believe he likes to announce his arrival. The hairs on the back of my neck begin to rise as I arch my neck to peer over the windowsill. The large brown car makes its way slowly down the street like a creeping tiger. I turn away and look back down at my homework as he pulls into the driveway. I hear the engine as it idles. He sits in his car for a few minutes, letting the smell of the carburetor seep in through my window. The engine finally turns off, and the car door closes gently. I can hear the metal tipped boots on the pavement as he approached the front door. He opens it gently. There's a pause. My ears are pricked up. Then I hear the footsteps on the staircase. He doesn't say a word to her as he reaches the landing. My head turns to the bedroom door. Light from the bathroom opposite flickers as he stands outside. A light knock follows.

He NEVER knocks.

I don't respond right away. He knocks again.

'Come in?' I say quietly.

The door opens. He stands there for a moment. His eyes look soft. A strange smile creeps its way across his face.

'May I come in?' he says.

Now I know there's something very wrong. I just nod. He's holding a newspaper in his hand as he steps towards me. My guard is up, my veins are beginning to fill with chemicals telling me to get ready for something.

'Sorry to disturb your studies.' He says as he looks around my room, 'how are you?'

He moves over to my shoulder and looks down at my homework.

'What is this?' he asks.

'Chemistry, sir,' I say.

'Chemistry huh? I never got no Chemistry when I grew up,' he says.

It's the first time he's ever mentioned growing up to me, or anything about him at all, now that you bring it up.

'What's it about?' he says.

'How molecules and chemicals bind to each other, sir,' I say.

'What use is that?' he says.

'I don't know, sir, but we have to know it for midterms,' I say.

'Well,' he says, 'I wouldn't worry too much about that. Not much use in the world out there.'

He reaches down and lays his hand on my desk. It's then that I notice the blood on the cuff of his shirt. There's little on the palm of his hand too which transfers onto the pine on the desk. Now my heart is beating fast. I can smell alcohol on his breath. He leans down towards my ear and whispers.

'I saw your little friend last night.'

I stop breathing.

'You know, the little thing that called to see you a few weeks ago? She's pretty. Nice job.'

My body is frozen, and my eyes turn sideways to catch the side of his face before he leans back up. He throws the newspaper on the desk on top of my homework.

'You must have a curse on you, boy,' he says before moving away towards the bedroom door.

'Best not any more young things come to the house, you got me?'

I can't hear him anymore. My eyes are fixed on the newspaper. It's a large black-and-white photograph of Carla, taking up half the page. The headline reads; MISSING.

I turn my head towards him as he shows his teeth. His eyes are wild now. I glance down at his cuff again, but it's hidden by the big fleece jacket he's wearing. He smiles at me, all knowing, all telling. My heart breaks. For a moment, I see myself making a beeline for the door and ripping his face clean off his head but he slams the door shut. I hear a key as I'm locked in. I whip my head back to the paper, pick it up, and try to read it through increasingly watering eyes.

Carla Winslow was reported missing by her family seventy-two hours ago. She was last seen riding a pink and silver bike near Crickets Park. She was wearing a grey sweatshirt and dark jeans with blue sneakers. If you have any information, please dial the local number below.

I look at the locked door and burst into tears. I take my chemistry book and fling it across the room before jumping onto my bed and closing the world out by placing my hands over my face. It's at that moment that I feel something crack inside me as I turn my face into the pillow and scream. I don't know how long I lay there, but my pillow is soaked with tears. My desperation is replaced with something else, Carla's loving face, her kindness, and her innocence. She couldn't have known. I turn onto my back as a rage unlike anything I've ever felt courses through my veins. My hands begin to shake at the thoughts now spilling into me.

It's at this moment that I decide to finally do it.

This has to end.

This has to all end.

Now.

# Chapter
# THIRTY-TWO

## Carter

It's 2 a.m. and I'm standing outside Jeans' apartment building on the east side. I got a cab from my street and told him to double back a few times, a request that had the driver glancing at me through the rearview mirror like I was going to jump him or something. I told him to pull over at a local news stand, and I picked up a pack of cigarettes. I haven't had one in ten years, but right now, as I inhale the nicotine into my system, it seems to be the only thing holding my cracking shell from breaking apart. I check the street a few times, the only light was coming from the yellow streetlights every few feet. Every shadow I see looks menacing. Every way out of a trap. I look up at her apartment, the lights are off. I stare at the ground for a moment, looking at the scuffs on my shoes, and frown. I hadn't noticed the dirt until now. I polish them nearly every morning before going to work, but for the last few weeks, they've gone unnoticed. I smile for a minute, knowing why Kim's face flashes in front of my eyes. I move to the front steps and climb up. Looking up and down the street once more before I press the buzzer to her apartment.

I wait.

As the weather starts to change, there is a light breeze and little drops of rain. There's no answer from the buzzer, so I try it again. I'm about to call her when there's a sleepy answer.

'Hello?' says Jean.

I pause for just a second, realising my world is about to implode.

'Jean?' I say.

'Yes?' she replies, suspicious.

'It's Carter, I know it's late I'm sorry. Can you let me up?' I say.

There's a pause. I lean my forehead against the buzzer, my brain in a frenzy at what I'm going to say to her.

'Carter? What the hell are you doing here?' she says.

I'm about to respond when the buzzer sounds, unlocking her door. I don't answer, just push it and go inside. I climb the two story staircase to her apartment, the door is already open. She's standing there in her robe, looking remarkably well for a 3 a.m. wake-up call. Her door is half ajar. I look at her for a moment. Her eyes meet mine, but I have no words.

'Come in,' she says, wrapping the belt over her dressing gown.

I enter her apartment as she turns on some side lights.

'Coffee?' she says.

I only nod, rubbing my chin, and marvel at how I can't get the words out.

'Why do I get the feeling I'm about to be up all night?' she says, moving to an open and ample open plan kitchen.

'I eh..' I say, running my fingers through my hair.

'Wait, just sit down, and I'll be with you in a second,' she says.

She has a silver barista coffee maker, like the ones you see in Starbucks.

'Don't judge this, coffee is life,' she says.

'I get it,' I say, feeling the blood flow a little easier in my veins.

Her apartment is elegant and spacious for a New York apartment, with large bay windows, a simple, clean style, and large framed images of some of her most well-known books. She has a small fireplace, and directly over the oak mantle is a framed photo of her standing outside her first store. I can see a beaming smile on her face. Full of hope and excitement at a venture that she doesn't yet know will swallow her whole. She looks happy. I don't think I know the woman in the photo. By the time we met, she was beaten down and tired, and the glow of hope had faded from her eyes. She was still determined, willing to go down with the ship she'd built.

I hear the frothing of milk in the machine as I take my scarf off and pick up my phone.

'I just need to make a quick call,' I say, noticing for the first time that my hands are shaking.

I dial Roger.

He answers within two rings. He's a light sleeper.

'Roger, I'm sorry for calling so late,' I say softly enough that I hope Jean doesn't hear.

'I was up,' he says, a strange tone in his voice catches me off guard. It's as if he was expecting the call.

'I need the jet ready to go in an hour,' I say.

'Done, where we headed?' he says.

'I'll be taking her alone, just have them stand by,' I say.

There's a slight pause.

'Understood, sir,' he says, hanging up.

There's a clink on the glass coffee table as Jean puts down a large cappuccino. She sits in the large single chair opposite me with both hands clasped around her own mug. She glares at me, genuine concern oozing out of her eyes.

I take the cup and let the warm coffee sink in. I look at her, then out at the streetlight outside. There's now a thick shower of rain falling in front of the yellow light. I only know one way to tell someone something, and that's to just come straight out and say the facts. The facts have a way of hiding things in plain sight.

'Carter, what's happened?' she says.

'Jean...'

I stop. I don't know how to say this without scaring her. I'm trying to hold it together, but I can feel my hands shaking. I want to scream at her and beg for help. I can't do this by myself anymore. I'm spiraling into a bottomless hole.

'Take a breath, Carter,' she says, reaching over and touching my knee.

I follow her advice.

'I need you to get dressed and come with me on a jet to the Midwest. Right now,' I say.

She leans back, her eyes widen.

'You want me to what?' she says.

I let a slow, controlled breath out and shake my head. There's no other way to go about this, and I just can't find the words to explain it so I reach into my pocket and take out the note and hand it to her. She frowns suspiciously and begins to read. Her eyes dart up to mine.

'Where's Kim?' she says forcefully.

'She's been kidnapped,' I say.

Jean rises from the sofa quickly. Her eyes dart across the note over and over.

'Jesus Christ, Carter, we have to call the police. Right now, fucking hell!'

She moves over to the phone.

'Jean, stop!' I say.

'Carter what are you talking about and what's happening?'

'I can't get the police involved, not at this stage,'

'Are you out of your fucking mind? Your daughter has been kidnapped!' she barks in a familiar way I'm used to in our meetings.

'I know that, Jean!' I bark back, 'I fucking know that, and I'm going to get her back, which is why we need to leave now!'

She reacts to my tone and tries to calm herself before sitting back down.

'Oh my god, Carter, that poor little girl, oh my god!' she says, putting her head in her hands.

I feel a surge of emotion explode inside me as I picture poor little Kimmy's scared little face. All alone in the dark somewhere. I try desperately to hold back the urge to burst into tears, and it takes everything I have just to keep my eyes open.

'Jean, I'm trying to hold this together,' I say.

'Why do they want me? What the fuck is this about?' she says.

'It's about my past,' I say, 'someone wants a piece of flesh from me, and they're using Kim to draw me out.'

'What do they want from me,' she says.

'Nothing,' I say, 'they've seen the two of us together and just want to fuck with me.'

'Are you out of your mind? Someone wants to kill us?' I say.

'I didn't say that,' I say, knowing full well that this is where all this is headed.

'Carter, what did you do?' She says, 'we have to go to the police.'

'We do that, they'll kill her,' I say.

'Is this about money?' she says.

'I don't think so,' I say.

'You don't think so? There's nothing in the note about money. This has to be about money, it's always about money.'

'Maybe, but maybe not,' I say.

'I swear to God, Carter, you've got to do better than that. If my life is being threatened here, I want to fucking know why!'

I raise my hand to her in a gentle gesture.

'Please just give me a minute Jean,' I say.

She blows a slow calm breath out and sits back in the sofa.

'I think I need a drink,' she says. Suddenly getting up.

'I'll take one of those,' I say.

She doesn't respond. She pours two straight measures of bourbon and hands me a glass.

'I'm sorry for snapping at you Carter this is just ...'

'I know,' I say, downing the drink in one gulp and letting the warmth hit the back of my throat. It helps a little.

'Okay,' I say, looking down at my watch while Jean sits back down.

I take a breath; I have to give her something. We've been through hell together, and while we've never really been where we are right now, there's always been a mutual trust and respect. I look into her eyes, and I see that I can give her even a sliver of what's inside. Not the whole thing, just enough to save Kim's life.

'A long time ago,' I start, looking out the window for just a moment before meeting her eyes again.

'I saved a young boys life.'

# Chapter
# THIRTY-THREE

### 1988
### Thomas

They found Carla's body under a bridge, floating face down at low tide with a blow to the back of her neck. The news said that there was no sign of rape, so at least I took some comfort in the fact that maybe he'd done it quickly. Maybe he hadn't made her suffer, but then again, maybe he had. Whatever had happened, he'd done it quickly. One blow, and she was gone. No longer a problem, no longer a lifeline, a confidant, a friend, or a witness. He took her away from me, and like so many other things, the control was absolute. That one moment when I felt wanted, even loved, was like a drug I'd never experienced before. The pull of it was so strong, and now all I can feel is a searing pain that I can't even describe. It's as if I've swallowed a barrel of tiny blades that have been absorbed into my bloodstream and are now travelling through my body, piercing every scrap of flesh they come into contact with. It's constant. I'm having to force myself to breathe, though part of me doesn't want to. Part of me wishes my lungs would just give out, that my brain would just explode and take me to wherever Carla is now.

I try not to think of her wet, broken body. How kind she was to even notice me. The effort she'd made when so many hadn't. I'll never know why she came to talk to me. Why she thought I was worth hanging out with, kissing, and having physical intimacy with in the dark. I don't know if I'll survive this.

I haven't left my room while I'm at home since. I hear him leave in the very early hours of the morning before the sun comes up, and he doesn't come home until well after midnight. They've told the school that I have the flu this week and to keep an eye on me in case I do something stupid, but they haven't put me in the basement. It doesn't matter. One day I'll go into the shed in the backyard and just not come out again.

I'll have to go back to school tomorrow. Sit at the same desk and look at an empty one. I could run to the police, sure. There's nothing stopping me. I could run straight into a station and tell them everything. Maybe they'll believe me. Maybe. Maybe they will take me into protective custody and arrest them. Find some evidence against him for murder and lock him away.

But what if they don't?

What if they send me home and think I'm just some stupid kid? What if they call them to the station to take me home? What if he gets a chance—just one chance to get near me? The risk is just too great. What if he gets to someone else, decides to go out in a blaze of glory, grabs a gun, and shoots up a shopping mall?

I'm alone. There's no doubt in my mind that there's no other way to get out unless I can think straight. I have to get through this pain and clear my head.

It's too dangerous, there's no way to plan right now. My mind is racing with how I'm going to get out, but I have to be so careful. So precise and Carla's face won't get out of my head.

And so, I wait.

I let the tears flow.

And wait.

## Carter

'He was just a kid,' I say, leaning back and aware that time is ticking down.

Jean is watching me very closely. Her fingers resting on her temples.

I take a deep breath and try to get the story out.

'When I found him, he'd spent a life being tortured. Held captive by two people who claimed to be his parents. They beat him, chained him in a basement, and controlled everything he did, everyone he saw, and everything he thought.'

Her brow furrows.

'How did you find this boy?' she whispers.

'It's a little complicated,' I say.

'Sorry for interrupting, go ahead,' she says.

'Well, I did something that...' I trail off.

It's starting to get warm as the words get stuck in my throat. I shake my head and stand up, walk to the window, and lean against the glass. I take off my coat and place it on the back of a chair, loosening my top shirt button.

'Are you about to tell me you killed someone?' she says.

I don't answer right away. I can't. I look out into the cold New York Street as the shadows of a couple passing by in the rain take my mind to running.

Those bare feet in the rain.

'Three,' I say so quietly that I see her lean forward in the reflection of the glass.

'What did you say?' she says softly.

I can't turn around. I catch my reflection in the glass. I look at my eyes, they seem dark now, full of intense sadness. They're not mine anymore. I recognise those eyes. I haven't seen them in a very, very long time.

'Three people Jean,' I say firmly.

I turn to meet her gaze. She doesn't look stunned, or surprised, but what surprises me the most is that she doesn't look scared anymore. She's giving me an odd look, as if it's something she understands. Something she's familiar with. It's difficult to explain, but I believe Jean Rose is hiding something dark from me at the time.

'I'm listening, Carter, you can tell me, trust me on this, you need to tell me,' she says.

I take a breath and gaze back out the window. I can see Kim's face looking back at me. I turn to Jean.

'Can I explain this on the way? I think one of those people may not have been killed and now wants revenge. It's as simple as that.'

I move over to the sofa and sit back down, letting my coat hang loose. Jean's eyes move down to my torso for a moment before glaring at me.

'Carter, why are you wearing a gun?'

I look down at the Walther PPK in the holster under my jacket. I'd forgotten it was there. I'd always had a gun locked up at home, and it had completely slipped my mind that, in my haste and panic, I'd run to the gun safe and strap it on before coming over.

'Sorry, I should have told you about that before coming in,' I say, raising my hands.

Jean gets up and puts her hands on her hips.

'So, whoever this is just wants me along for the ride to fuck with you. Why me?' she says.

I take out my phone, flick to the photograph, and hold it up so she can see. She frowns.

'For a second there, I actually thought I had a choice,' she says.

'You do Jean, I can't make you do this,' I say.

'Carter,' she says, moving over to a wall and pulling a painting of the city back from the wall, exposing a safe, 'I'm not going to be threatened by anyone, ever again.'

She enters a code into the safe door and unlocks it, taking out a Glock. She checks the chamber and takes out a mag clip, looks at it and slots it in like she knows exactly what she's doing.

'This person is coming after me whether I like it or not, and I'm not going to let anything happen to Kim.'

She looks down at the gun.

'Fuck it,' she says, 'I need fifteen minutes to get dressed.'

She smiles at me, and in that moment, I think I fall in love.

## Chapter
# THIRTY-FOUR

In the last half hour, we haven't said much. Roger pulls up to the airport hangar where the engines of the Bombardier Global 6000 are already running. It's a sleek aircraft. It's white with a blue stripe, and the BMX logo is painted on the tail. The crew rotations are always ready twenty-four hours a day. It's one of the most expensive things to own and run in the world, apart from a ridiculous luxury yacht, but right now it's worth its weight in gold. Roger pulls the car up close to the left wing and gets out to open the door for Jean. She steps onto the tarmac. She's wearing a long, dark coat, short boots over jeans, and a warm top. I've told her where we are going and that at this time of year it's usually snowing, so dress warm.

I meet Roger at the rear of the car, and he hands me a small suitcase.

'What's this?' I ask.

'Just some essentials,' he says.

He then reaches inside his pocket and takes out a money clip with a few hundred folded bills inside it. It's an old habit, a request I made to him years ago when I went on business trips. I don't carry cash on me. I don't like leaving home, even to the next state, without some cash, just in case. Ever since then, either he or Marge had, between them, always made sure I had a few hundred dollars in bills at the airport. The cash is kept safe in a small leather clip wallet. I give him a friendly smile and tap the back of my hand against the wall.

'Sir, you sure you don't need me on this one?' He says, turning to look at Jean before giving me a look that bores straight through me.

He's no fool. He can sense that's I'm in serious trouble here, there's no doubt in my mind. He looks like he's waiting for me to say something, but it's him who speaks first.

'If I don't hear from you in twenty-four hours, I'm coming after you,' he says with tone I've never heard before.

He's no longer speaking to me as an employee. His eyes are sharp, focused. Part of me is comforted by it, but the reality is that I can't have Roger or anyone else near this. I take a step towards him and glare.

'No, you won't,' I say.

There's a strangely tense moment, as if a standoff has just begun. Roger doesn't flinch. His eyes are steady, deadly serious, and not to be fucked with in this moment. I don't think anything I say will make the slightest bit of difference to a man who's faced what he has but doesn't know. He doesn't know that we're more alike than he realises.

A look of clarity seems to dawn on his face as he tilts his head slightly, as if he's trying to look right into my soul, past the person he knows me to be to the person he doesn't. He smiles at me and extends a hand.

I take it, he gives it a firm squeeze and his eyes relax.

'Have a safe trip Sir,' he says.

I take a breath and nod back, smiling. The grip of his hand tells me everything I need to know. He releases it, and I move towards the steps as the engines begin firing up. The door is pulled behind me by the co-pilot, a young Italian man whose name is Edoardo. The captain is an ex-Delta pilot, a 41-year-old by the name of Stan, although he likes me to refer to him by his chosen call sign, 'Bobcat'. I've flown with this pair many times.

Jean herself in one of the large leather chairs, crosses her legs and lays her handbag on the floor. The shape of the butt of her weapon is making a little indent in the black leather. She looks out the window as I take the seat beside her, facing the other way and on the other side of the small isle. She turns to me.

'Roger doesn't look happy about this,' she says.

I nod.

'He doesn't like being kept in the dark,' I say.

'He's a very unusual man,' she says.

Roger has driven Jean on plenty of occasions, and it's just dawned on me that maybe they've talked about more than just business. I raise an eyebrow at her.

'Is that so?' I say.

She smiles at me.

'Did you know he still writes letters to a little boy in Iraq? Every week. Telling him all about New York.'

Roger has never told me that. He's told me very little about his time in the military. I shake my head, surprised that he'd opened up to her.

'Yeah, every week he sits down, and hand writes a letter to him,' she says, turning back and facing the window, 'he's never gotten one back.'

I don't answer as her mind seems to drift away. I turn my head and watch as the plane begins to taxi to the end of the runway. My thoughts turn to Kim, and for the first time, a different type of dread begins to take shape. I know where we're going. I know what I'm about to see again, and the reality begins to grab hold of me.

Kim is in grave danger, and I don't know if I'll be able to save her.

# 1989
## Thomas

It's been a year since Carla. The pain has gotten a little easier to deal with, but there's not an hour that goes by when I don't think about her. The media attention and rewards for information posters are left half torn on the lampposts, and it's not even in the papers anymore. Her desk at school has been filled by another student. It's been strange in the house. I haven't been put in the basement since, but they very rarely even talk to me anymore. It's as if they know they've broken me. The last of the straws, and now it seems like a waiting game. He spends most of his time in the living room watching TV, and she spends it mostly asleep upstairs. I never really hear them anymore, and they don't seem to be speaking to each other. It's become a cold house with three strangers now. He doesn't seem interested in torturing me anymore. He's gotten fat and rarely changes his clothes. Sometimes she comes down the stairs in a robe and runs her hand over my head, looking at me with unfeeling and vacant eyes before grabbing a bottle of something before returning upstairs, sometimes for weeks on end.

I'm in my room now, trying to do some homework. It's Thanksgiving in a few days, and while most of the houses I see outside have a new collection of cars outside their driveways, ours remains empty. It's always empty. I've never seen a relative, nor known if there was one, or that I'm related to these people at all. I've never seen a photo of when I was a child anywhere in the house. The walls bear no evidence of my childhood.

It's a normal evening. He's downstairs, passed out on the sofa, and I haven't heard a thing from her room all day. I'm studying about the American Civil War from an old book, but I'm not really paying attention, just flicking from one page to another and looking at the old drawings of battles and men in wigs and old rifles being fired. I'm trying to understand what they're all fighting for.

Carla's face appears in my mind. I grab a pencil and begin drawing on an open copybook page. I remember her eyes so well, and I'm pretty good at drawing. I begin with the outlines of her pupils and work my way around the page gently, crafting her eyelashes and shading in the light colour and defining the outlines that make them so striking. I continue for a while until something hits me. I remove my pencil from the page and realise that I've drawn just her eyes.

They're sad and seem to scream at me through the page.

'I'm sorry,' I whisper.

I don't want to finish the drawing. I could, but that would be too much, and if they found it, I'd be in trouble.

'Who gives a fuck,' I say out loud.

The words come from nowhere. As if another part of me has just taken over and wants me to shut up and listen. I check the door quickly to see if I've said it too loudly.

'Say it again,' I say to the room.

I shake my head and turn my chair away from the desk, placing my head in my hands. There's a wave of sadness about to burst its way into my chest. I grab it with my palm, as if trying to keep my ribs from bursting open. I catch it, contain it.

'Not yet,' I whisper to the anger, 'it's not time.'

There's a reckoning coming. A big one. But I have to get back to the basement before it can happen. It's always deadbolted and padlocked, the only key is in their room, and before I go down there, to do what I have to do, I need to make sure my supplies are ready. I need to make sure that...

THUMP!

My body snaps upright.

The noise comes from outside. I move towards the door and place my hands on it, leaning forward and placing my ear to the wood. I hear a crashing sound. Then something else happened. It sounds strange, like a fish gurgling water or something. I freeze. There's nothing out there that would make me want to leave this room, not even a fire.

*Oh, the fire will burn soon!*

My eyes are wide open, fixed on the wall of my bedroom, as if trying to see through it to find the source of the strange gurgling sound. Then it goes quiet. So quiet. Nothing but stillness for a minute or two before the footsteps from downstairs began to ascend. They sound slow, cumbersome, and uneven. I'm picturing him grappling onto the handrail, trying to steady himself, and dragging his evil ass up those stairs to see what all the commotion is. I step back from the door and move over to my desk, but when he reaches the top, he doesn't turn towards my door, he moves towards theirs. I can hear him enter the room. It's still so quiet. He closes the door. They're not speaking. The walls aren't very thick, and I can usually hear muttering. I'd expect to hear some sort of argument for making him come all the way up here. Something feels very wrong. As if something has changed in the air. Something very serious has happened. I can feel it. The little hairs on the back of my neck are standing up as if whatever spirits live in this house are warning me of something to come. To be aware. To be ready to run.

*Soon!*

Still quiet. I'm getting nervous now. Edgy. There's something very wrong here. I think about making a dash for the window. I've never done that before, and if he caught me trying to run, that would be the end of me. It's strange that my brain would even try to suggest it, but perhaps it's three steps ahead.

The intuition it's had to develop to keep me alive is now in overdrive. I move towards the bed. I'd have to climb over it to get to the window, and I try to think if there's anything I could quickly grab to take with me. My bag, some clothes. A toothbrush?

The door to their bedroom opens, and I hear his voice.

'Thomas,' he says, softly.

I look to the door. I'm out of time. He's not coming towards my room, so maybe...

'Thomas, come here son,' he says again, this time with a little more strength in his voice.

It's calm, but I know it's on the edge. I better come in the next few seconds or never come at all. I take one more glance at the window, and I remember the plan. I remember why I'm still here. I remember what he did to Carla. I straighten my back and turn from the window.

I'm not going anywhere. Not yet.

I move to the door and open it, stepping outside into the hallway. He's standing there. There's a quiet calm in his face, all but the eyes. The eyes are laser-sharp and locked onto me like a rifle scope. They're awake. There's a little wry smile as he takes a step to one side, leaving their bedroom door slightly ajar.

'Your mother wants to see you,' he says, the smile broadening and revealing his yellow teeth. Since Carla, one of the front ones has been broken. Something I only noticed a few weeks later. I wonder if she got a shot off before he got her for good. If she got in one last clock. His tongue rubs against its jagged edge as I move slowly towards him. He pushes open the door and rests his hand on my shoulder. The touch is gentle, but it's also full of darkness and pure-blooded evil.

He gently pushes me towards the door and opens it slowly. It creaks every so slightly.

The room is cold. The window is open, and there's a breeze blowing the curtains towards the bed. Her head is slumped over the edge, her hair tangled and unkempt, her face buried beneath the sloppy sheets. She's not moving. I already know she's dead. There's a bottle of whisky on the floor, and her bedside table is strewn with empty tablet bottles. I stand there for a moment and try to take in the situation. I'm remarkably calm for a moment before a strange thought enters my head.

I don't think I've ever been in this room.

I look around at the bare walls. There's a single cross with Jesus made of wood hanging over the bed, two small lamps, and bare white walls. The wardrobes have mirrors on them, but they're closed. There's a hole in one of the walls just next to the bed. It's about as large as a fist.

I take a step towards the body, still not really feeling anything.

'Go on,' his voice softly echoes from behind me, 'kiss your mother goodbye.'

There's a stench in the room that becomes more pungent with every step I take, as if she hasn't washed herself or the bedclothes in months. Now I can see a small pool of vomit on the carpet just under her head and some white foamy stuff still oozing from the side of her mouth. I hear a creak and turn my head to the door. The light from the hallway window is casting him almost in silhouette, but his eyes shine through the darkness like a wolf in a forest. He moves away from the door and walks calmly, slowly down the stairs. I keep my head turned to the hallway as I hear the TV volume go up.

He's gone back to watching TV, the sick fucker!

I turn back to the corpse, not really moving any closer, just taking it all in. There's now a feeling of something stirring. I can't put my finger on it just yet, but my curiosity gets the better of me. The stranger who's laying on the bed, the woman who I've known my whole life has ceased to exist. That feeling is bubbling up now, from my stomach to the centre of my chest. I move closer now, kneeling and sitting on the carpet, leaning my back against the bed. It wasn't supposed to end like this for her. It wasn't supposed to end like this for her, in a dream or half-consciousness, high or drunkenness. It wasn't supposed to be this way at all.

I often wondered what it would feel like to be free of her, but it doesn't matter now. It wasn't the freedom of one, it was the freedom of both. One isn't enough, and certainly not this one. This one was just a zombie. She might have been more trapped than I was, a mere follower. I lean over and run my fingers through her hair. It's tangled and dirty. I pull her head back, turning it so I can see her face. She's wearing makeup. I've never seen her wearing makeup. There's lipstick haphazardly applied and spilling over her lips and onto her cheeks. There's blue eye shadow and pink powdery stuff everywhere. Her eyes are open, but she is not looking anywhere. They look like empty glass.

They look almost like they did when she was alive. I start to realise that this woman has been dead for a long time. There's a part of me that feels sorry for her, but a split second later, it's replaced by rage.

Pure, hardened rage. Carla's face appears again, and I realise that the feeling in my chest is just that.

*Rage.*

He's downstairs, watching TV, and has left me here with this device to tell me something. He's seen the hate in my eyes by now. He knows it's only going to grow. Knows I'm going to strike at some point, and he's taking pleasure in this, pleasure in the fact that I wasn't given the satisfaction. Part of me wants to run downstairs right now and attack him, but I know he's got a gun with him now. I know I wouldn't get close.

I look at her body with years of pain and anguish in my eyes then I grab a fistful of her hair, bringing her lifeless eyes as close to mine as possible. I ignore the stench of her foam-filled mouth, I growl as I bare my teeth to her.

'You got off easy you bitch!'

# Chapter
# THIRTY-FIVE

## Carter

Soft clouds pass by the windows as the jet screams through the air. It's been a smooth flight. Jean and I haven't spoken much. She fell asleep for about an hour, and I've just been glaring out at the stars. Something occurs to me as my mind drifts upward. The piece of paper that was in the safe in my office. It's still in the breast pocket of my jacket. I take it out and unfold it.

'What's that?' Jean says, her eyes open.

I look at her and fold up the paper.

'A doodle Kim gave me,' I say.

She doesn't look convinced but doesn't push the matter.

'Where are we?' she says, stretching slightly.

'About thirty minutes out,' I say.

The sky outside turns crimson as the darkness begins to break.

'I'm hungry,' she says.

'Yeah, hang on,' I say, getting up and moving to the pantry at the rear. Usually there's a flight attendant, but not tonight. There's a small galley at the back with some preheated food. I find the drinks cabinet beside it and pull out a bottle of Irish Jameson whisky. I look at Jean.

'Yes,' she says.

I take out two meals and read the labels.

'Chicken? Or beef?' I say.

'Chicken,' she says.

I put both of them in the microwave and pour two shots of whisky into two thick-bottomed glasses. I add a block of ice to both, and when the food is ready, I bring it over. Jean takes the glass. We sit, and she raises her hand to make contact with mine.

'Here's to getting this fucker,' she says.

I don't respond. I just clink her back and try to keep the panic in my chest at bay. We both down the drink in one sitting and begin to eat.

'This isn't half bad,' she says.

I'm trying to eat mine, but my stomach just won't take it. I push it aside.

'Carter, you have to eat something,' she says.

She's right. There's a storm on the horizon, and I need the energy to face it. I give it another shot, forcing myself to swallow a few bites before my body just gives up. She finishes hers and leans back as the sun begins to spill over the horizon. There's a little bell.

'Mr. Page, we're twenty minutes to landing,' comes Bobcat's voice.

I look out and see the flat midlands approaching. It's been a long time since I've been here. I don't even recognise the endless fields and roads.

'Is there any sort of plan at all?' she says. 'Like, have you anything in that strategic mind of yours that you're going to pull out last minute?'

'I wish I did,' I say.

'We're just going to walk straight in and hope for the best,' she says.

I shake my head.

'Jean I don't know, at the moment, that seems to be the way it has to play out for now. I need more information.'

'Okay,' she says, a little too calm for my liking.

'You're handling all this pretty well,' I say.

'Oh what you see and what's actually going on in my head are two very different things,' she says.

'Could have fooled me,' I say trying to muster up a smile.

'Carter I don't have to explain to you what it's like to deal with finance and law "bros" on a daily basis. It's going to spill over, that's just the way it is.

'You don't have to tell me, it's a jungle,' I say.

'Yeah, well sometimes it doesn't matter if you're the smartest in the room, blah blah, feminism something, blah blah, you get the idea,' she says, waving her arms around.

'I get it, and to be honest, I rather enjoy our little fights,' I say.

She smiles.

'Little?' she says.

'Trust me, they're little,' I say, 'but useful.'

She rests her hand on the side of her face.

'How so?' she says.

I take a little breath.

'You know an easy way to tell if someone is full of shit?' I say.

'By assuming most people are?' she says.

'That's cynical,' I say.

'Sorry,' she says, 'go on.'

'They look away, even briefly, when they're telling you something important,' I say.

'Okay?' she says.

'You've never looked away,' I say, 'quite the opposite. You've burned holes through the back of my skull.'

She laughs and throws her head back. She really does have the most beautiful smile. How have I never seen this before?

'Well now that you say it, yes, I do that,' she says, tilting her head.

I think she catches my lingering a little too long. The moment doesn't last. For a second, it was as if we were having a normal moment, but a little jolt of turbulence snaps both of us back to the situation.

'Sorry, this is so fucked up, I shouldn't even be fucking smiling,' she says, getting up abruptly and moving over to her own seat again.

She takes her bag up and opens it, removing the gun again and checking the chamber.

'Where the hell did you get that anyway?' I say.

'I'd ask you the same thing,' she says, lowering it and meeting my eyes, 'this is the last chance Carter, we sure we going into this alone?'

'If he gets a whiff that cops or feds are anywhere near this, he'll kill her.'

There's no room for doubt in my tone. She nods before checking the mag and the safety one more time before she looks back up at me.

'He?' she says.

I turn back to the window to see the airport coming into view.

'Yeah,' I reply softly, 'he.'

## Thomas

The local coroner's office came and went, as did the police. There were odd stares from some of the neighbours for a while, and I got to sit down with the school principal to hear how sorry they were about my... well, you get the idea. There was no service and no funeral. One day she was being zipped up in a black bag and put on a gurney, and the next it was just another day in the house. I don't know what happened to her body. He never mentioned it. I doubted he had the money or the will to bury her, so I always just presumed he'd burned her and done something with the ashes.

He stopped drinking a few weeks ago and started shaving again. He's wearing ironed shirts and suit pants and polished shoes, and he's begun to work out in the garage. There's a weight set in there, and he does a few hours every night. He's starting to look stronger and healthier. There's colour in his cheeks, and his eyes are perking up. Any ordinary person would be happy for someone who decided to turn their life around and pick themselves up after something like this, but I know different. He's preparing for something, training for his rebirth, and I don't think that I'm going to be part of it. Time is now running out. He picks me up from school every day now, so I haven't been to Alpha Base in weeks. I need to get down there if this is going to work. I don't have what I need right now, and he locks all the doors with padlocks as soon as we get home.

I'm in my room again, staring out of the bedroom window, which has been locked from the inside. There's a little key that fits into the latch, but that was the first thing he took. The only way I can get out of here is by breaking a window or just making a run for it on the way to the car in the morning and evening after school. A futile gesture, as he'd probably just run me over and say it was an accident.

He's been in bed for about an hour, and I'm sitting in the dark with only the moonlight coming in through the curtains, which are half ajar. I can't sleep anymore, I barely get five or six hours a night. Every sound I hear could be him. Every moment, I need to be alert, ready.

I need to get to Alpha Base. I'm pacing now, obviously in my socks, so I don't make any sound. I need to think.

In my mind, I'm running through every window in the house. There are only three ways out. The kitchen door, the front door, and the garage, door are totally out of the question because the door sounds like a truck that's grinding its gears when it's opened.

I stop pacing when it hits me.

How the fuck have I never thought about this until now?

'The loft,' I say.

I look up. There's a loft.

WITH A WINDOW!

I shake my head in genuine disbelief that, up until now, it's never even entered my head. All those years are under the ground. I used to think my only escape was up those stairs and through the front door. It never occurred to me to look up. To see past. I've always just been in the basement. It was my world.

I'm positive there's a window in the loft. I've seen it.

I start to think.

*When?*

There's no easy answer to that. There's just no way to know. He could come for me any minute, any second. He could come right now. I look at the alarm clock on the side of my bed. It's 11 p.m. The access to the loft is beside his room. There's a ladder you have to pull down to get to it. I wonder how deeply he is asleep and how loud it would be to get it down. He never comes into my room in the middle of the night. Not since Carla. He thinks he has me broken. He thinks that there's no way I'd attempt something so crazy. I catch a glimpse of my reflection in the mirror.

'Do it,' my reflection says back to me.

I figure it will only be a one hour round trip to Alpha Base and back. I'll be back by 1 a.m. at the latest. I feel my heart rate begin to pick up.

*What if the neighbours spot me?*

I move to the window and look out. The street is asleep. It's a weekday, there won't be anyone looking out their windows or going for a walk at this time of night.

*Jesus am I actually about to do this?*

As I slip off my trainers and pull out a small plastic torch from a drawer in my table, I try to clear my mind of the fear that has begun to creep inside. I reach quietly into my closet and take out a warm jacket, which I slip on. I then put on a woollen hat and stand next to the door, my trainers still in one hand. I breathe out slowly and quietly, and I turn the handle downwards, smoothly in one motion, placing my hand on the door to stop it from swinging open. It's dark in the hallway, but there's enough light coming through the small window at the top of the stairs to give me some help. I pull the door open slightly more and take a quiet step onto the hallway. His door is closed. In my mind, I imagine him standing just behind it, red eyes glaring out from behind him, one hand on the handle, and another holding a bloody axe, waiting for me to make my move. Some sort of zombie monster with growling, froth-dripping fangs waiting to bite. I tell my brain to shut up and take another step outside my room. I look down at my feet.

When you live a life walking on eggshells, you learn very quickly where they are and how easy they are to break.

Every creak in the floorboards is familiar to me. I know which piece of carpet they are under, to the inch. It's a dance, as if the hallway is covered with lasers and tripping even one, means certain death. I delicately move forward, taking every step delicately while listening very carefully for movement inside his room. My heart is racing now, there's no way to control it as I have to breathe shallowly, believing that even the smallest of sounds will trigger an apocalypse, and I haven't even gotten to the hard part yet.

I creep across the landing, surprised at how quiet I am when I reach just beneath the access hatch, right outside his bedroom. I look at the wooden pole that is hanging on the wall. It has a little hook on the end of it to pull down the ladder. This is when I begin to panic. I don't really have any way to know how loud this door is going to be, and I start to feel my palms sweat. I think this is a huge mistake. Then it occurs to me. It doesn't matter if I get caught on the way back. What matters is if I get caught on the way out.

*Fuck it.*

I gently remove the pole from its holder and reach for the brass handle, delicately hooking it on. So far, so good. It's eerily still. A feather falling on the floor would sound like a nuclear weapon right now. I begin to gently pull down. I feel resistance, and then comes the first creak.

I freeze.

My breathing stops. It feels like an old, rusty spring is about to pop. I have it down about a quarter of the way. I look at the door of the bedroom. My face is only inches away from it. I pull it down again. Another creaking sound. There's no way in hell he didn't hear this. My chest is bursting now. Blood is pumping through my ears. My arm is starting to ache as the door pulls against me, wanting to snap back up. I wait there for what seems like months, but still no sound comes from the room. I look up at the door. Furious at its betrayal and give it one good yank. It slides down into position smoothly, barely making any more noise. I gently unhook the wooden stairs and very carefully put it in place.

Still nothing from the room. Either he's the deepest sleeper in the history of humankind or he's waiting until I'm halfway up to grab my legs like the monsters I used to think were hiding under my bed at night.

They never scared me half as much as the basement did. I can't believe I've gotten this far. My socks on the ladder barely make a sound as I scurry up. I reach the loft and take the little torch out, flicking it on for a moment to get my bearings. I then carefully reach down and begin pulling up the wooden ladder, followed by the loft door, which doesn't make a sound coming back up.

*Typical.*

I wait there for a moment in the darkness, making sure the monster is still asleep. By the looks of it, he is. I don't waste any more time and turn on the flashlight. I see the window and make my way across the beams to it. It's not latched and opens up easily. I can't believe my luck. I quickly clamber outside onto the roof, the gradient isn't that bad, and there's a flat section over the garage that I can scooch over to. I lean over it and sink into the back garden. I quickly put on my trainers, make for the shed, which is never locked, and swiftly get my bike.

I'm through the side passage and out into the night in less than a minute.

## Chapter THIRTY-SIX

### Carter

We've been sitting on the tarmac for less than 5 minutes when I get the text. It's an image of the outside of the house. I show it to Jean, who frowns at it. Another message comes in, but this one freezes my soul. It's a photograph of Kim, bound and blindfolded. I'm suddenly filled with blind rage and can't help myself. I scream at the phone.

'Fucking bastard!'

I feel a hand on my shoulder.

'Easy,' Jean says.

I almost don't hear her before she takes my hand and grips it tightly.

'Don't play the game,' she says, 'they're three steps ahead anyway.'

I realise that my jaw is clamped shut. The world is starting to spiral out of control.

'Carter!' she snaps.

I look up at her.

'Yeah,' I reply.

Bobcat and Edoardo emerge from the cockpit at the noise, both looking a little startled.

'Everything all right, Mr. Page? says Bobcat.

I look to them and then to Jean, who quietly responds.

'Let's go,' she says, leading the way forward, then to the pilots she adds, 'deal gone bad.'

The pilots nod, not buying the explanation for a minute but knowing it's not their job to pry into things like this. Edoardo opens the main door and extends the stairs, and we emerge into the morning light. The air is crisp here. It's a small airfield surrounded by acres of green fields and rolling hills. I recognise the fresh, open, forgotten landscape immediately as I look around out of instinct to see if there's anyone watching us. It's a short walk through the small terminal building before we arrive at the waiting car that's been rented for us. I haven't driven anywhere in more than a year. It's a grey Lincoln, unobtrusive, and the keys are in the ignition, ready to go as I take the wheel. I wait for Jean to get in and take a breath.

'You know where you're going?' she says.

I look over to her.

'Never mind,' she says.

I turn the keys, shift the automatic transmission into drive, and tear out of the parking lot at speed. We get onto the open road and head south. It's about an hour away. The road opens up into a long highway that seems to stretch straight into the horizon and is split down the middle by two mountains. I increase my speed to over 120 when I feel a hand on mine.

'Carter, it's not going to do her any good if we're killed,' she says.

She's right. I slowly release the gas. I take a long breath.

'Sorry,' I say.

'One of us has to keep us alive, well, before we're attacked or murdered by whoever this psycho is anyway.'

She leans back and stares out the window. The road falls away beneath us, and the sound of the rubber rumbling across the asphalt fills the air. It's quiet. The road is mainly clear as it's a Saturday just after daybreak. My eyes drift to the countryside.

'It's really beautiful here, I'd almost forgotten,' Jean says quietly.

I turn my head towards her. She's gazing out at the Midwest landscape. The still air and sense of freedom would be unmistakable for someone not used to it, but for me it's exposing, there are eyes everywhere. I love the noise of New York. The vibrant sense that while you're surrounded by millions of people, you can disappear into the noise so easily if you want to.

'You think so?' I say.

'I really do, I've thought about vanishing from the city so many times, but it's just that...' she trails off.

'Yeah, it is,' I respond.

'We both came from this place, didn't we?' she says.

'Well, no not exactly,' I respond.

'I don't mean this exact place, Carter, I mean this life,' she says, 'it does things to people.'

'Yes, it does,' I say.

'Some people can do it, live this life, in peace,' she says.

'Could you?' I say.

'No,' she says, 'I used to think I could be happy somewhere like this, in a little store, knowing my regulars, little family someday.'

'Bullshit,' I say.

She turns to me.

'Rose tinted glasses Jean,' I say, 'you love the adrenaline just as much as I do,' I say, 'vacation here? Sure, put up a fence and pop out some ungrateful little shits with some welder? Come on.'

'Jesus,' she says.

'Sorry,' I say.

We continue onward, and I clip the needle of the speedometer over the threshold every now and again, getting more and more impatient.

'I've just noticed you're not using a GPS,' Jean says.

'I know where I'm going,' I say.

Jean doesn't answer. She just looks outside and glances down at the side mirror.

'That guy is not happy you're going to the limit,' she says.

'What?' I say.

My eyes move to the rearview mirror and see a white truck behind us coming up fast.

'Yeah, well, neither am I,' I say, moving over a few inches so he can make a move to get past.

He doesn't move, so I roll down my window and wave him on. He still doesn't move, but now he's beginning to inch closer to the back of the car. I keep a close eye on him in the rearview mirror.

'What the fuck is this asshole doing?' I say to myself.

The van accelerates suddenly and bumps the rear of the Lincoln. Jean and I lurch forward.

'Jesus Christ! What the hell is this lunatic doing?' she says, turning to look through the rear of the car.

I floor the gas, and the Lincoln takes off. It's clear to me now that we're in trouble here. The van increases its speed, making it very clear that it's coming after us. I'm trying to think if I cut him off earlier at a set of lights. Road rage isn't anything new, and there are seriously crazy people who just snap out of nowhere. Catching the wrong person at the wrong moment in their lives can send a certain type over the edge. In the middle of nowhere, a broken mind is capable of anything, and with most folks in these parts carrying a firearm in their glove compartment, I'm not staying around to find one.

The van comes closer, this time at full speed, I try and swerve out of the way, but it catches the right rear tail and I lose control.

'Fuck!' I shout, as Jean grabs the side of the door.

The car spins to the right and goes off the road. I try to counter the spin to stop it rolling, and I just about cling on as it moves across the slipway and onto the grass. Chunks of dirt, mud, and gravel crash into the glass. The windscreen shatters dead centre and sends glass debris all over the passenger seats. I hear a slight crack, and then Jean screams. The sound of the metal crunching on the driver's side of the door bounces around the cabin. I put my arm over Jean's shoulder and rest it there. There's blood trickling down the side of her face and tears streaming out of her eyes.

'Jean,' I say, feeling the adrenaline pumping, 'are you okay?'

'My wrist,' she manages through gritted teeth.

I look down and see that it's unmistakably broken. It's bent and lifeless, with pools of dark swelling already beginning to blow it up. I undo my seat belt and lean over to check the cut on her forehead. It looks superficial. There's smoke starting to rise from the engine now, pooling out from under the wheelbase.

'Okay, try to relax. We need to get out of here,' I say, glancing back through the rearview mirror to see if there's any sign of pursuit. The glass is mostly covered with mud and dirt, so there's no visibility. I unhook her seatbelt.

'Can you move?' I say.

She nods.

'My legs are fine, I can walk.'

I try to take another look out the back of the car, but I don't see anything. I move to the driver's door and open the latch. It doesn't budge. I try it again and slam my shoulder against it. This time, it bursts open. My body is stiff, and pain is starting to form around my chest as the adrenaline starts to wane. I crawl out of the car and move around to the passenger side, pausing for a moment when I see the large van parked up on the side of the road. I quickly scan the area to see if I can see the driver, but there's nobody.

Alarm bells are in full swing now, this was intentional.

*No shit, Carter!*

I grab the handle of the passenger door and help Jean, taking her gently by the arm. She winces and grits her teeth at the pain in her wrist.

'I'm sorry, are you okay?'

She nods, pulling her hair back over her ear. I can see blood trickling from a head wound under her hairline. She places her good hand on it and looks at it as I continue to scan the horizon for shadows and prying eyes. There's someone out there, watching us.

'Jesus Christ, that's him,' she says, pointing to the van parked up, 'that piece of shit.'

She starts walking towards the van. I pull her back, hurting her wrist in the process. She growls in pain and shoots me a look like she's going to bury me in the ground.

'I'm sorry, I'm sorry,' I say, releasing her immediately.

'What the hell,' she says.

'Jean, we have to get out of here,' I say.

'No shit, Carter, I also think we should have a word with that asshole before--' She pauses and returns her gaze to the white truck parked nearby.

She turns to me before looking around in all directions.

'Oh, shit,' she says, 'you think?'

'Maybe,' I say, 'if so, he's got the upper hand here.'

Jean begins moving back to the car.

'Does your cell phone work?' she says.

'Are you kidding me? There's a reason we're here. It's the world's black hole. The tech only works around population centers, and even then, it's patchy at best. She moves back to the car, her arm held against her chest, and reaches inside for her handbag. She removes her gun first, checking it with her good hand, then gets her cell phone.

'Shit,' she says.

'Yep,' I say.

'Okay so now what,' she says, taking out a scarf and throwing it over her shoulder.

'Let me,' I say, wrapping her arm up in a sling.

'I don't like this,' she says, looking at the van again, 'what the fuck is he doing?'

'Watching,' I say.

'We can't just stand here,' she says.

'I know that Jean, but I have a feeling he's about to make a ...'

There's suddenly a sharp stinging sensation in my neck, followed by another whizzing sound past my right ear. I reach up and feel a metallic object protruding out of the side of my face. I turn to see Jean holding her upper shoulder. There's another metallic rod embedded in her skin. She falls to the ground like a rock. I only have time to see a looming dark figure approach as the world blinks away into nothingness.

# Chapter
# THIRTY-SEVEN

## Thomas

It's a cold night and the wind is starting to pick up. It's almost pitch black on the roads, and the only thing keeping me on track is my little headlamp on the front of my bike. I can hear the tree tops rustling with every new gust, and the little glimmers of moonlight cutting through the thickening clouds tell me there's a storm on the way, fast. I'm nearly at Alpha Base. The wind is starting to pick up now as I reach the turnoff into the dead, still forest. With only the headlamp on my bike to guide me, the narrow, lit mud trails are tricky to navigate. I can't see that far ahead of me, so I try to slow down. Just as I apply pressure to my front brake, my wheel locks up, and I enter a muddy skid. I fall to the left as the bike comes from under me and we both go down hard on the forest floor. I hang onto the handlebars, and after a few feet, we come to a stop. My hands are covered in mud, and the side of my face feels like it's taken a few scrapes and bruises, but I'm still conscious, and nothing seems to be broken. Besides, I don't have time for this. I quickly gather myself up, get back on the saddle, and slowly move off. It occurs to me that I'll have no way to explain away any scrapes or bruises on my face tomorrow. By then it's not going to matter, not after what I've got lined up.

I press on through the darkness. Somewhere off in the distance, I hear something scurrying about on the forest floor. I don't think there's anything dangerous here, although I can't be entirely sure, and my imagination is running wild with images of bears and wolves, but I've never seen one, so I push it aside. I cycle onward, the curves of the muddy pathways now becoming more familiar. Eventually I reach the end of the downward slope that reaches Alpha Base. I throw my bike against a fallen tree stump, then make my way inside. I have to think very carefully about what I bring, but first things first. I open the small tin that contains all my boxes of matches, and I stuff them into my coat pockets, making sure to zip them up to keep them dry. I rummage through the rest of my stuff, taking a rope, a small wrench, and some fishing line, and then I see my notebook. I pick it up and flick through the pages of my adventure story set in space. I think hard about this one, but knowing the plan, I decide to leave it here for safekeeping. It won't survive the event, and maybe I won't either, so maybe someone will find it someday. It's the only part of me I can leave behind. My legacy. Who knows, maybe it'll be published by a stranger and find its way around the world. I know that's nonsense, but it's still fun to think about.

I place it back in its plastic wrap and make sure it's secure in case I never see it again. I grab a tin of beans, some fruit and make my way to the exit. I take one more look around.

'Thank you,' I say.

I'm not sure why, but this place has been my home, my refuge, a sliver of sanity and happiness.

I move through the door and close it up. I grab my bike and begin the trek back up through the forest. I can't have been gone for longer than thirty minutes. That's when the rain starts to fall, hard. The branches shield some of it, but the cloud overhead now is thick, and the wind has picked up something fierce. When I hit the road, I realise that I'll be cycling against it, and it feels like a full-blown storm just landed right on top of me. I'm already soaked to the bone, my head hanging low to try and keep the ferocious mixture of water and debris from getting in my eyes.

Now comes the hard part.

The rain doesn't let up for a second for the entire ride home. I'm starting to get scared that the matches in my pocket have gotten ruined, but there's no time to waste. Every minute I'm not in the house is a minute I could be discovered. The ride takes longer getting back because I'm up against a howling gale. My legs are aching as my bike only has one gear and the ball bearings have been steadily rusting for years. It's a real piece of shit at this point, but it's never let me down, so I try not to let it know in case I hurt its feelings.

Yes, I know it's an inanimate object, but I've learned that you have to speak well of these things, or they will have their revenge without you realising it.

I round the corner to my housing block, thanking the rain. It's coming down so hard that there's no way anyone would be able to see me through the dense downpour, especially if he was looking through his bedroom window. It's the perfect camouflage, not that it will matter if he hears me squelching across the landing or wonders why the carpet is wet in the morning, but I'll deal with that later. One thing at a time.

I approach the house, making sure to stay close to the curb and hug the parked cars, as if trying to blend into my surroundings. I reach the driveway, always keeping an eye on the upstairs window. The curtains are drawn, and the lights are off. I carefully step off my bike and gently wheel it around the side passage and into the garden. I gently open the shed door, then place it inside with finesse.

I haven't made a sound, and I also don't remember breathing. My heart is racing right now. I have only one way back into the house. I look to the roof. The window to the loft is still slightly ajar. I move quickly to the front of the house and hop up on the small wall that boundaries the driveway. From there, it's a few feet to jump to grab onto the roof of the garage. I get up on the wall and instantly slip, falling to the ground. The rain is just too hard and has made it nearly impossible to get a grip on anything. I'm not hurt, but I look at the small ledge where I'll have to hold on and pull myself up onto the garage roof, then to the sloping roof of the house that leads up to the loft window.

*Sloped!*

'Shit,' I whisper to myself.

If I lose my grip on the rooftop, I'm dead, simple as that.

I try again, clear my mind, and get a foothold on the small wall before turning to jump. I don't think, I just do it. One leap, and my hands grab hold of the roof. There's a little lip of wood where my fingers have found a grip, and in one motion, I pull myself up and roll onto it. There's a small pool of water collecting on the surface that soaks through my jeans and trainers. It's as if I've just emerged from the sea, fully clothed. There's just no way I can slip through the hallway if I make it across the roof, so I decide that if I make it back into the loft, I'll take off my clothes, leave them there to dry, and pick them up the next time he leaves the house. If he finds me tonight, I'll be getting caught with my pants down.

I carefully move onto the sloped part of the roof. It's slippery, so I make sure I have some sort of grip by leaning over and using my hands to grab hold of any little crevice in the wood that I can. I begin taking very gentle steps, like a rock climber does, securing each handhold before moving forward. I slip a few times, but I make surprisingly good progress until I reach the window ledge, where both feet give way, and my body slides down the roof. I have a grip on the bottom part of the window ledge, so I'm able to hang onto it. It's at this point that I think I'm in serious trouble here. I can't believe that he hasn't heard anything. There's nothing I can do about that now. I have to get back inside. No matter what happens, I have to get in.

I pull myself up and open the window, crawling my way through and into the loft. The rain is coming down hard now as I gently close the window. It's loud in here. There's no soundproofing, and the insulation is spotty at best, so maybe it's covered my tracks after all. I seal the window shut and stand there in the dark as the pounding of the outside weather screams to get through the glass. I can feel a pool of water forming around my drenched self as I reach down and take off my trainers. My socks and everything else are soaked through as I take the torch out and turn it on. I'm amazed it still works. I point it to the floor and can't believe how much water is dripping through my clothes. I push my hair back and try to squeeze as much water as I can out of it. I take off my jeans and coat and decide to hang them out instead of trying to traverse the hallway naked. It's a simpler plan that I think will work just fine. I started to think that maybe my mind was running away with itself with silly ideas while cycling home in the storm. My jeans are wearable, and so is the sweater vest after I give them a good ringing out, so I put them back on and check on the inside pockets of my jacket. Like I thought, they're dry and waterproof, and the bits I've brought back with me from Alpha Base are all fine. I decide to leave them up here in the loft under a wooden beam just in case, as I won't be needing them just yet, and if I'm caught and searched, that will be the end of that.

I make sure they're all secure before putting back on my damp clothes and moving to the loft door. Before I gently push it, I take a deep breath and listen carefully to see if I can hear anything.

Darkness greets me underneath. There isn't a sound from the door this time. I push it down a little further and use the pole to get it all the way down so that it locks in place. I then begin extending the ladder, using the hook on the end of the pole to gently set it in place. I don't waste any time and move, trainers in hand, down the ladder. Ny heart is pounding in my ears with each step as I creep downwards towards the landing.

It's pitch black. The moonlight is now hidden through the storm clouds, so I have to do everything by touch. I can't remember how many steps there were, so I just keep taking one at a time, hoping to reach the carpet. It's taking forever, and my mind starts to wonder if the steps just go forever, all the way down to hell.

I touch the carpet. I'm down. I glance to my right to see the dark outline of his door, still closed. I waste no time in gently folding back up the ladder and inching the loft door back into place. I turn. It's too dark. I can't see anything, so I reach out my arm to try and feel for the landing handrail for a point of reference. I try to imagine where I am, but I know that one wrong step and an almighty breaking crack from the floorboards will reverberate throughout the house.

I move quickly, knowing that if fate decides that my time is up, there's not a damn thing I can do about it. I see the pathway in my mind and begin to take swift but careful steps, one after another.

*Not a sound.*

I reach the end of the landing, not a single creek, nothing.

I've done it. I enter my bedroom and open the door, darting inside and gently closing the door behind me. I let out a long breath and take several more, my head resting against the closed door. I can't believe I pulled it off.

My bedside lamp turns on.

My eyes go wide, and time freezes. I turn and see him sitting on my chair, his legs up on a history book. He grins at me. I'm still not breathing. My hands start to shake as he reaches towards a pack of cigarettes on the table and lights one up. He slowly blows a ring of smoke above his head.

'I always said we needed to keep a closer eye on you,' he says calmly, pointing to me, 'he's got guts this one.'

He pauses.

'This one's got something in his eyes, and we shouldn't stick around to find out what, but...' He looks up to the ceiling, 'She liked you, and it kept her quiet to keep you around, but I knew. I knew you had a little flame inside you and that one day you'd try to burn us all down.'

He turns his cigarette in circles.

'Where were you?' he asks softly, his eyes wide.

*Think fast!*

'I was upset and needed to get out of the house for a cycle,' I say.

He tilts his head.

'You were upset and decided you wanted to go for a cycle?' he says, starting to laugh, 'by climbing out of the roof?'

His laugh turns into something else, like an imitation of a laugh, there's no real feeling behind it, as if he's trying to pretend that he knows how normal humans are supposed to act. It's a monstrous sound. A dark void of something so broken and evil that it'll swallow the world.

I watch his eyes. I don't think he's even blinking. He takes a deep breath and rises from his chair, like a wrecking ball swinging back and preparing to release.

He reaches under the table and pulls out a lump hammer. I wonder how much longer I have to live. He doesn't swing it, just picks it up and puts it behind his back.

'We both know that at this stage you ain't got much more left in the tank here, but I've got a few things to take care of first, and I can't have you running about the place. Empty your pockets,' he says.

I comply instantly. He's going to go up in the loft, there's no doubt about that now, and I wonder if I've hidden everything well enough. I put the little torch on the ground and show him I've got nothing else. He reached into a drawer and takes out a T-shirt.

'Now wrap this into a line and bite down hard. Trust me when I tell you, you'll be glad I asked you to do it,' he says, as if he's talking to one of his buddies in a bar.

I'm shaking now, hands, legs, arms, teeth. I wonder if he'll make it quick. One blow to the head and you're out, but my experience suggests otherwise. I ask anyone watching down on me to be kind. To make sure that the pain doesn't last long. I wrap the T-shirt into a long rope and put it in my mouth, tying it at the back. I stand there, awaiting what comes next.

'Now get down on your knees and put your hand on the skirting board there, just beside the bottom of the door,' he says, motioning to the floor.

There's a thick wooden beam.

I comply, slowly getting to my knees. I don't understand what he's about to do. I don't get it at all. I place the palm of my hand on the wooden beam and wait. I watch as he reaches into his pocket and takes out a handful of the biggest nails I think I've ever seen. My stomach goes, and a fear I've not felt since I was a young boy reemerges. I can feel tears starting to well in my eyes, but there's no way I'm letting them fall, not for him.

*NEVER FOR HIM!*

He kneels beside me, watching me closely in case I make any movements.

'Be very still, child, and you can have a few more days on this little rock of ours,' he says.

I comply. I want him to do it. I want to show him that nothing he does to me is going to hurt me anymore.

He takes the first nail, lines it up dead centre on the back of my hand and strikes.

At first, it just feels like pressure, but only for a second. The blinding pain of it hits soon after as I look away and bite down hard on the t-shirt. He takes a second nail, lines it up, and strikes again. I can feel bones break, skin tear, and warm blood flow. It's too hard not to cry, my body won't allow it. Tears fall, but I look away. I know what tearing flesh feels like. I know what torture is. I know where to go in my mind when it's happening. He strikes a third nail, this time bending the top of it into an L shape. I almost don't feel the third strike. I'm slumped on the floor now as he moves off. He goes to my desk and opens a tin box, taking out a roll of bandages. He comes back over and dresses the wounds. I can barely move, I'm so cold and wet, and part of me wants to just die there and then.

Why is he bandaging the wounds?

He reaches out a hand and puts it on my face.

'It's the only way I can stop your little wandering legs, little man,' he says, getting up and wiping down the hammer.

He collects his tools of pain and steps over me out into the hall. He looks down at me one more time.

'Look at me,' he growls in a voice that demands compliance or there will be consequences.

My beaten eyes meet his. I know he sees the fury in them. He takes the door and begins to close it over.

'Don't.. Go.. Anywhere.'

He closes the door, leaving me there, nailed to the floor.

The tears are falling now.

They fall forever.

# *Chapter*
# THIRTY-EIGHT

## Carter

I'm awoken by a drop, and then a searing blow that wakes me from my nothingness. I'm disoriented, groggy, and feeling panicked about the strange transition from being next to my car and helping Jean to the flashback jump in time to where I am now.

Jean!

I squint through blurry eyes and see her. Her head slumped over, arms were tied over her head and hanging from hooks, bound tightly with what looks like zip ties. Her sling is missing, and her wrist looks swollen and distorted. It's definitely broken. I look up and see that I'm in the same predicament. The floor is hard and metallic, with ridges and bolt studs burying into my thigh, so I've figured out that we're both in the back of a van. Every bump in the road is felt, and I estimate the suspension on this car is twenty years old based on the sound of its over torqued and struggling engine. There are diesel fumes from the exhaust coming through the back doors, which have a little gap at the top where they don't quite seal properly, so there's a little bit of light coming in.

The front of the van is completely sealed up; I can't see the driver and don't remember anything about the face. My legs are free, so I reach over and try to touch Jean's feet. I give the sole of her shoe a tap. Nothing.

'Jean,' I whisper to her, making sure my voice is low enough to be hidden amongst the grumbling sounds of this piece of shit van.

She doesn't move. I can't say I'm surprised. I feel like a truck has hit me. My neck is killing me. He hit us both with some sort of tranquillizer dart, and the only ones I know of are for game animals, so that explains that. I try to breathe so that I can remain calm. I begin to look around for anything to help me break these binds. There's nothing. What little light seeps in reveals a bare, almost polished surface to the moving cell. I look up and try to break the binds with pressure applied in opposing directions, but they're wrapped with more than one. There must be three or four looped around each other. This asshole is no amateur. There's also a strange smell in the back of the van. Something I can't quite place, but it lingers, like freshly cut grass or old, dry leaves.

Another hiccup in the road, this time a large one, possibly a pothole. It nearly launches me off the floor as the sound of what was an even road turns into something that feels like a dirt road. I can hear the wheels struggling over the surface before we return to a normal section of asphalt. I don't know where we are, or how long I've been unconscious. It could have been hours or days. I don't feel that hungry, so I don't think it's been days. Not the most intuitive deduction, but it's the only thing I have to go on right now.

I hear Jean make a low groaning noise and look at her. Her eyes are starting to flicker open. I quickly touch her foot as she regains consciousness. It looks like she's about to scream in pain, but I tap her foot and whisper to her.

'Don't!'

She's dazed and doesn't fully recognise me. I try to keep eye contact; she slowly starts to come around. I shake my head at her as she winces in agony at her wrist. She whispers back to me.

'What's happening?' I can hear her say it through gritted teeth.

I look to the front of the driver's cabin, then back to Jean. Our predicament quickly dawns on her, and she looks to the bindings on her wrists before scanning the cargo hold herself and leaning her head back against the side panel in defeat. It's hard to really concentrate with whatever shit is still swirling around my blood stream. Suddenly, Jean leans over and vomits.

She wipes her mouth with her upper arm sleeve and flops her head back. The van suddenly jerks forward. Jean can't help but let out a scream through a clenched jaw as the pain of her injury breaks through.

The van comes to a full skidded stop. The driver's door opens, and a pair of heavy-soled boots lands on the ground. Our gazes are drawn to the unseen lumbering thing moving around towards the back of the van. Our eyes meet in unison as the futility of being unable to do a damn thing about our situation lingers. I don't think we're about to be killed. In any case, not right away. Not like this.

The rear doors split open, and the sun blasts straight into the cabin. I get a short glimpse of what looks like a demon, silhouetted by fierce sunlight. Its eyes are red, its features inhuman, and its gaze ferocious as it raises an arm and fires two shots at us. I feel a piercing of the flesh, and I'm out again.

Falling back into hell. There's a space between that moment when you're dreaming and when you wake, a strange transition from what your mind is pretending is real, and what it's convincing you is real.

It doesn't last long. Maybe a few seconds, but in that time, you're living in two worlds and it's nearly impossible to tell one from another. That space for me is full of flames, screaming, pain and running.

Endless running, into an endless night.

The screams sound so real as my eyes drift open. I know they're not Jean's, because as I look up she's not in the van anymore. As I try to regain my sense of reality, this time with much more effort, I can still hear wailing sounds. An ungodly animal like howl that's only heard in unspeakable pain. I know these screams. I know them because I was there. I heard them, made by the devil himself.

People think he lives in the flames, flourishes in them, feeds on them and makes others suffer by their heat. I know differently. I know that he can be consumed by them. I know they are not his ally nor his friend. I know he can be defeated by them. You can't escape the fire. The fire won't let you. It never lets you go. Not until it squeezes every scream out of you. Not until it gives you a taste of damnation.

Those screams fade now, just like the fire. The devil is burned to a crisp.

## Chapter
# THIRTY-NINE

I wake. It's late afternoon. I've been drifting in and out of terrifying worlds. I don't know how long Jean has been gone, but I didn't hear anything. Anger bubbles in my stomach and I explode.

'Come on!'

I suddenly realise how dry my throat is.

I rage and flail my arms, attempting to break the bonds in my wrists.

'Where are you! You fucking bastard!'

This time the scream works, and I feel the metal in the cargo hold shake with its ferocity.

This time it gets a response. I hear footsteps again, coming from a little bit away from the van.

The door swings open again, and the thing stands there, wearing a parka with its face covered. This time I can see it more clearly. It's a large man with his head bowed, so I can't see anything from beneath the grey, dusty hood. He raises a gloved hand this time, holding a gun. It looks like a six shooter, a Smith and Wesson type. He pulls back the trigger and takes aim at my face, by the looks of it, right between the eyes. From under the hood, I see the slight glint of what looks like an eye, glaring at me. It's a strange shape, deformed and bulging. He takes a step up into the cabin, pulls a switchblade from his pocket, and shuffles across towards me, the blade almost touching my eye. I freeze, still trying to get a look at the face, but all I see is blackness. I close my eyes, an involuntary reflex, as he moves the metal closer to my eyeball. He pulls it back and up, slicing my bands before replacing the knife and taking out a black piece of cloth. The muzzle of the gun presses against my forehead.

'Eyes,' the creature whispers, in a crackled breath.

I do as I'm told and blindfold myself. I feel a hand under my arm.

'Move,' the thing exhales once more.

We exit the back of the vehicle and start walking. The sun is warm on my face as I'm led over grass and then a path. His grip is firm on my upper arm as we approach what feels like rough ground. I felt him lean over for a moment, then a creak. A wooden door flops over, and I'm leaned over.

'Stairs, down,' the raspy air says around me.

I lean down and feel the creaky wooden steps and begin slowly descending. The light and warmth from the sun disappear as I continue slowly downwards. I hear muffled gag sounds right away.

'Jean?' I say.

An acknowledged reply is attempted, followed by a sharp blow to the back of my head. Not enough to knock me out, but enough to silence me.

The cellar door, or whatever it is, closes behind me. I reach the ground and take a step forward as the second pair of feet reaches the ground. The muffled noises stop. One of them sounds young. An arm grabs mine again and leads me across the floor. One of my arms is raised up. I feel the cold metal of a handcuff as it is attached. My other arm is brought up—another cuff. There's a deathly silence in this small space. My blindfold is removed, and my heart sinks into the darkest place it's ever been. The small, dark space is lit only by a single oil lamp. My eyes are drawn immediately to Kim, who's hanging by her arms from a pipe. Her mouth is gagged, and her tired and hungry eyes are begging me to save her.

'Kimmy!'

I lurch forward, nearly breaking my own wrists.

I see her start to cry. I turn to the hooded monster before looking to Jean, who's dangling a few feet away from Kim.

'Are you all right?'

She nods, though I can see she's in serious pain. I turn back to Kim.

'You're going to be okay, I promise,' I say to her, trying to hold back my fury.

Our kidnapper is in a corner, busying himself with something. My eyes dart around, assessing the situation and looking for avenues of escape. I try and hide the panic that's growing from the others. I hoped I'd have an upper hand. Some sort of bargaining power would somehow prevail, but this is something different. This is evil. This is about something that...

I pause for a moment and look into Kimmy's eyes again. If there was a way to tear out my heart and give it to this evil bastard so that it would set her free, I'd do it. But it's not only her eyes that I'm looking at. I'm looking at the walls. The charred remains of the walls. There's something about this place. Something so deadly and familiar.

It hits me like a meteor.

I know where I am.

## Chapter
# FORTY

### Thomas

I must have passed out because it's sunset. I'm still on the floor of my bedroom, nailed to the door. Moving even an inch is agony. I'm surrounded by a pool of water and I'm freezing. I look at my hand, blood-soaked bandages cover what's sure to be a mess underneath. I know I don't have much time. There won't be a second shot at this. I'm lightheaded and hungry, but I have to get back up to the loft. I look around the floor for anything I can use, but there's nothing. I can reach the foot of my desk, but that's not really any use to me. I'm shaking from the cold, and I don't feel well. I don't hear the TV on downstairs as I try to move my body around. I have to clench my jaw to stop me from screaming in pain, but I bury it in the years of familiarity. I reach up and gently open by bedroom door. I don't think he's here. In fact, I'm positive he's not here. There's this sense I always have of his presence. I can't quite explain it, but I can always sense when he's in the house. Even when he's asleep in his room. It's like there's a dark unseen cloud that fills this place when he's here. I have to get up to the loft and back to my room before he comes back. I'm surprised he didn't put me in the basement yet. It's unlike him to break such a routine reaction, but maybe he did it so that I know it's over. The years of torture and isolation don't matter anymore because when he gets back after arranging for his escape, the game is over.

That's what he's doing. I can feel it. He's getting ready to leave everything behind and start a new life somewhere else.

To try again.

To do it all again, with some other little soul.

*Not gonna happen!*

I look at my hand again and close my door. I lean down and take off my coat, placing it under my injured hand. I take a deep breath and try to close my fingers into a fist. The pain makes my eyes water.

This is going to hurt, and it's going to hurt a lot. I make a small manoeuvre and feel that one of them may be loose already. The wood around the skirting board is old. I close my eyes and think of the beach. The warm sea laps the shore. The little bucket and spade tapping down the sand to build my sandcastle I try to stay here for as long as I can.

*Stay here, you'll be safe here.*

I pull with all my strength, knowing I only have one shot, or I'll pass out. I bury my mouth into my free arm, wrapping my forearm around my face as I stream, wail, and bite down hard. Tears fall quickly as the agony of the tearing flesh explodes through my brain. The hand doesn't come willingly. I don't stop, I can't. I give it everything I've got, and suddenly it's free. I cry into my arm for a moment. Not wanting to look down. For a minute I lose all hope of ever getting out of here, but eventually I turn to survey the damage. To my surprise, there are still two nails in the wood. They must have gone straight through my hand. The tip of the third, the bent one, is still in my hand. I'd feared that it may have just torn right through, but it looks like that's just come clean out. There's not as much blood as I thought, and I quickly wrap the bandages around the palm to stop what is coming out. The point of the bent nail is sticking there. I consider removing it but pause for a moment as a thought enters my head.

I leave the nail where it is and just take a moment to gather myself. I want to get out of these wet clothes, I'm freezing. I quickly start to undress and clamber through my wardrobe for another pair of trousers. I throw on two t-shirts, one over the other, and then a sweatshirt. I find another pair of old jeans, they have holes in them, but I don't care, they're dry. I grab a towel and rub my head with my good hand. It's hard to dress with one good hand, and every once in a while, I hit the Jesus hand, hard to call it anything else—against something and I get punished for it.

After a minute or so, I have dry clothes and sneakers on. I can't tie my laces, so I just shove them inside. I take a long, deep breath and look around my bedroom again. I run to the window and look outside. His car is missing.

Okay, I have a little time here.

I run back to the doorway and out of the hall. I don't waste time here. I grab the loft door pole and get the door open. I clamber up into the darkness, find where I've hidden my belongings, stuff it into my pockets, and get the hell out of there.

I descend the loft ladder and enter his room. I don't know why, at first, but there might be something useful in here. I don't fuck around and tear the room apart, opening up the wardrobe, throwing boxes open, and rummaging around. I shift the bedside table and throw open the drawer onto the floor, leaving only some used condom wrappers and useless crap. I continue to toss the place, looking everywhere before I see something. I missed the shelf above the clothing rack in the closet. There's a little metal box glistening at me. I move quickly, jumping up and grabbing it, throwing it onto the bed. I scramble to open its rusty lid. I can't help but smile a little at the tightly packed rolls of hundred-dollar bills. I'm not sure how much there is, but it's enough to get me out. Get me far away. I grab the money and stuff it into my pocket before running out of the room and back into mine.

I realise I've forgotten my backpack, which I'll need it. I grab it, throw in some extra clothes, and then walk outside.

I take one last look around the room. I don't really feel anything. It could be that my senses are numbed from the pain in my hand, but it's just a room now. A dark place I could hide. I think I hate it.

I move outside and down the stairs, passing the door to the basement on the way. I look at the simple padlock attached to the locking bolt before going into the kitchen to find a hammer. He always keeps one in the drawer next to the sink. I move quickly, opening it up. Sure enough, there it is. I also spot something else in the drawer beside it. The keys to my handcuffs are in the basement. I snort at the sight of them and take them, shoving them into my pocket. I grip the hammer tightly and move out to the basement padlock, smashing it hard. It doesn't break. I hit it again, over, and over. The urgency of getting back down to my cell growing. The last strike does the trick, and the lock cracks. I drop the hammer and, with my good hand and manoeuvre it out of the latch. I swing the door open, hesitating for a second as I look down into the darkness. It's been a while since I've been down here. Maybe a year, I don't remember. I don't let the fear take control of me, and I clench my injured hand just for a moment to bring my mind into focus.

The action nearly brings me to my knees in pain, but it works. Down I go. I whip out my torch and carefully step down into my old world. I move over to my bed, briefly noticing a pair of handcuffs attached to the radiator.

*Not today, you piece of shit!*

I shine my torch away from them, past my mattress, to the gas boiler. Despite my excruciating pain, my eyes lock onto my target, and I feel my mouth upturn into the slightest little smile.

# Chapter
# FORTY-ONE

### Carter

The monster is sitting in the corner on an old armchair. He's just glaring at me through that strange bulging eye. His gun hasn't left his hand in over an hour. It's been pointed squarely at my head for the whole time. I've tried talking to him and shouting at him while the three of us just dangle here helplessly. I feel useless. Kim's head is down, and her eyes are closed. Jean tried her upmost to try and get through to this thing, but it won't even look at her. His only eye, and I say that because I've only seen the one, is locked on me. Time drags on and the torturous silence, obviously intentional at this point, is driving me nuts. If I could cut my own hands off to get to him, I would. The rage hasn't gone anywhere. The thought of this thing putting his hands on Kimmy is enough to make me lock eyes right back with him.

There's another thing I see in his stare. A familiarity.

He knows me, and he hates me.

This has gone on long enough. I grit my teeth.

'Fucking coward,' I say calmly, allowing as much of my panic to fade as possible to avoid giving him the satisfaction.

I say it casually and with as much contempt as I can muster. He raises his head slightly, and now, for the first time, I get a much better look at his face. It's not a face at all. It's like pieces of a face all patched together with skin, like some sort of clay sculpture that's gone horribly wrong. He pulls what looks like a mouth of some sort back to reveal no teeth at all. Just large, bulbous gums. One of his eyes must be half the size of the other and look like glass. Where there was once a nose, there is now a singular hole, which pulsates in and out with each strenuous breath. He pulls the hood back, and I hear Kimmy scream. My eyes turn to her, then to Jean, who looks on in terror.

There's no hair, just lumps over lumps of skin. As with his nasal passages, there are no ears. A barely breathing lump of clay with fury in his eyes. He rises from the chair and takes a heavy step towards me. I think about grabbing the pipe I'm attached to, to try and strike him hard enough to knock him out, but there's not enough room between the ceiling and the metal to get a grip. He knows this. His eye flicks upward for a moment, as if reading my mind.

'Coward?' he whispers in a strange, ethereal way.

'That's right, you're a coward, who has to kidnap little girls to get my attention. You're pathetic,' I growl at him.

He stops and glares at me, turning to the other two.

'You've made a life,' he says, 'look at that.'

I frown, suddenly feeling a desperate need to refocus his attention on me.

'Look at me, you fucking freak,' I say.

He turns, looking slightly amused, before reaching into his pocket and removing the switchblade again. He flicks it open and approaches. Maybe this is it. One quick stab to the heart, and it's all over.

'Be still,' he says.

He approaches me. I can smell a strange, unwashed musk about him. He's filthy and almost proud of it. He slides the knife between the buttons on my shirt and slices upward. He doesn't cut the skin, just the shirt, like a master sous chef. Because my arms are still restrained, he begins filleting my clothing. It's a strange and surreal moment as he makes his way around my body. Cloth falls on the floor all around me. He finishes, leaving most of my upper body exposed, and moves backwards, pulling his bulbous lips apart once again before pulling out his gun and pointing at Kimmy. Her eyes widen as he glances back at me. With his free hand, he reaches up to undo the handcuffs.

'Move and she dies in an instant,' he breathes into my ear, his breath reeking.

He undoes my binds.

'Turn,' he commands.

I wonder if all he wants to do now is kill them both behind me in some twisted torture porn, maybe rape them first so I can listen. I don't know what to do. I'm not faster than a bullet, so for now, I obey. Every second I can keep him entertained is a second, I can think.

I turn, slowly as he cuffs me again to the pipe. The atmosphere shifts suddenly. Jean and Kim go deathly silent.

He leans into my ear.

'Now they know,' he whispers, 'stay right there, I've forgotten the best part. I'll be right back.'

I hear him shuffle backwards as I catch my shadow cast on the wall by the oil lamp. I look helpless. I hear the cellar door shut, and we're left alone.

'I'll get you both out of here, I fucking promise,' I say, barely able to contain my embarrassment and rage.

'Daddy?' Kim says, so softly that I can hardly hear her.

'Yes baby,' I respond, 'are you okay?'

There's a pause that lingers in the air. I look at their eyes as they stare blankly on. I frown at them both, wondering what it is they're looking at. The mystery doesn't stay hidden that long before it suddenly hits me.

Once again, my world is about to fall to pieces. Kimmy raises her eyes to meet mine. She looks at me with a strange compassion I've never seen from her before.

'What happened to your back?' she asks.

# Chapter
# FORTY-TWO

## Thomas

I am waiting now. Standing in the kitchen with my back against the sink, staring down the hallway towards the front door. I start to feel a little lightheaded, but that's okay. The door to the basement is wide open. The lock was in pieces on the floor. I'm tempted to take the small remnants as a memento, but it's just a passing thought. I don't want a single atom of this place when I leave.

*If I leave.*

I'm not here long—maybe fifteen minutes—when I see the lights creeping through the fading light. In the distance, I hear thunder again. The wind is starting to pick up in the yard behind me, and I can hear little flecks of water droplets pattering on the window. However, none of them are distracting. I'm calm. I'm focused. I'm ready for the end, and part of me feels a sense of euphoria that's very hard to put into words. All my senses are heightened as I watch the lights of his car crawl up the driveway. They pause in front of the door, flooding the entrance hallway. The engine idles outside, the headlights revealing my location with ease. I wonder if he can see me through the glass. I doubt it, but if he could, he'd see eyes red with fury and teeth ready to sink themselves into their unsuspecting prey. He'd see a wounded animal backed into a corner. Ready to strike one last time.

The lights go out, and the engine is killed. I fold my arms and wait in the failing light of the day. There's a pause. I think about how long this will last. Maybe an instant, maybe forever.

I check my pocket again. I'm starting to get a headache now.

*Hold fast.*

'Come on in,' I whisper.

I hear the car door close as a large shadow looms over the frosted glass. It pauses. I hear keys jingling. We can sense each other. I can feel it. He knows there's something wrong, and then it hits me.

I've left the light on in his room.

On any other day, that would be a serious breach and possibly land me in the basement for a whole year, or maybe even dead, for violating that space.

I hear the keys in the lock, and the door turns. It opens slowly but swings all the way to the other side of the wall. His face is clear, and his gaze is drawn to mine almost immediately. As the new rain falls, his hair begins to dampen, giving him an odd look of satisfaction. The trees in the driveway behind him rustle past his dark figure like an onlooker in a Colosseum awaiting the mauling of a man by a great lion.

He steps inside and calmly closes the door behind him, saying nothing. He takes off his coat and hangs it on the hook on the wall, then places his keys in a small dish. He then looks at the open basement door. From here, I can already smell the alcohol on him. Something I am counting on. I'm hoping that he's drowning in stuff, which, by the way he's walking, he is.

He moves past the basement door and gently closes it, moving into the kitchen. He stands, leans against the doorframe, and folds his arms.

'How ye doing, slugger?' his tone a wry but dangerous threat.

He looks down at my hand.

'That must have hurt a lot, I hope,' he says, his teeth clenching.

'Yeah,' I respond casually.

His eyes narrow at the strangely nonchalant way I reply. He looks suspicious now. No, that's not the right.

*Is he afraid?*

I think he might be. I think he sees defiance in me now. I believe he sees something that I haven't seen in my entire life. For starters, it just dawned on me that now we're pretty much the same height, I may be even an inch taller.

How could I have missed that? I've always felt like a little boy.

I think this son of a bitch sees a man in front of him now.

'You've been in my room,' he says.

'I have,' I reply.

'What did you take you little warrior you?' he says, 'money perhaps?'

I don't respond.

'Tell you what,' he says, 'you get yourself downstairs for a little while to think this over, and how about maybe I think about letting all this slide?'

I smile at him.

'Something funny?' he says.

There's real danger in the air now. We're saying words to each other, but each of us is waiting to see who really makes the first move. Before I do, I can't help but ask.

'Why?' I say.

'Why what?' he replies.

'Why did you murder Carla? 'I say, fighting the instinct to lunge.

'Oh, that?' he wonders.

He pulls out a kitchen chair and puts its back against the wall. He slowly sits, making a little groan as he does.

'Thomas, children need to be taught,' he says.

I feel my hand clench.

'She was a distraction for you. You're a smart one. You could go far, but you need discipline. You need focus and that little bit...' he pauses, seeing my head lower and the fury in my eyes daring him to call her what he's about to.

'That girl,' he says, backing down, perhaps realising how dangerous I look, or perhaps just fucking with me.

He starts shaking his head.

'She was no good for our family,' he says.

'What?' I say, seething, 'what family?'

'Thomas, we're a family. Sure, it's never easy or perfect. No family is. It takes work, sacrifice. You have no idea what your mother and I went through to give you everything you have.'

'What did I have?' I say, 'broken shoes? Torn ligaments? Scars?' I growled, taking a step towards him.

'Aw, you think we were hard on you, is that it?' he says, almost gleefully, 'you think your little punishments are something to get your knickers all in a twist about, huh?'

I stop moving towards him. I want to hear what he has to say.

'What did you do to Carla?' I ask.

He moves his hand to the bottom of his dirty little chin and starts to rub.

'Okay, if I tell you how I dealt with that, will you go downstairs to your bed and think about how you've spoken to me tonight?' he says.

I just stare, honestly just baffled at how nonchalant he all seems. It's like a little game he's playing. He almost looks bored by the whole thing. Maybe this act of defiance means so little to him now that it doesn't matter what I do. He takes a breath.

'Okay, so I know all your little routines. I've sat outside that shithole school of yours since you were a little boy, you don't think I know your every goddamn movement by now. It's tedious,' he says, pointing at me, 'but it had to be done. I know you little shits, when you get ideas, you want to run, or hide, or talk to cops, or teachers, or God knows who else, and then who will be responsible for raising you, right? Another foster home, that's who!'

A weight falls from my heart, sinking straight into my stomach.

'Foster,' I say.

'Oh, don't be so naive, we don't look a damn thing alike. It was your mother. She wanted you. Even knowing we hadn't a cent to keep that belly of yours full, or clothes, or anything else, we took you in! We got you from that hole in the ground you came from and gave you a fucking roof over your head! How did you repay us?'

He leans back, displaying genuine anger in his voice as he rests his head against the kitchen wall.

'How did I repay you?' I say, flabbergasted, 'what did you do?'

'I asked her if she wanted a lift home,' he said.

My blood starts to boil.

'She said sure, so we went for a little drive,' he says.

There's a gleeful tone in his voice.

Not yet. Not yet.

I reach into my pocket and take hold of our destruction.

'We went for a drive, talked about her life. Did you know she played piano?' he says.

I remain perfectly still.

'Well, I told her all about you, all about how you're not the best influence on people, how you'd use her and then dump her, and how you told me she wasn't the girl for you.'

My head lowers, like a lion about to pounce.

'She didn't really seem to like that, and to be fair to the little firecracker, she spoke back, and you know what she said?' he smiles, 'she said it really wasn't any of my business. Can you believe that. She had heart, I give her that.'

I take another small step towards him. He doesn't react. He wants me to make a move. He wants me to explode.

He'll get his wish soon enough.

'Well, we didn't speak for a lot of that. I was about to let her go, but then she said something I really couldn't stand for. She said soon you'd be gone. Far away from us. She said she'd take you away from us. Well, I couldn't have that. I couldn't have our little Tommy taken away. I hope you understand. We're a family. You and I.'

He moves his hand to a cup that's on the table and starts to slowly turn it.

'We took a little detour, and, well, she wanted to get out. I couldn't allow that. I'm afraid.'

'How did you kill her,' my voice is starting to crackle.

I start to see red.

'Quickly, if that's any consolation, she didn't feel any pain,' he says, smiling.

'You fucking piece of shit!' I say softly.

That changes his demeanor.

'Well, look at you. I don't care for your tone of voice,' he says, his face changing to one more recognisably his.

There's evil creeping in now. An old bit of programming tells me I'm running out of time here.

'You're clearly about to make a move here, you little shit. You think I'm stupid?'

He rises from the chair and takes a small step towards me. The tension has reached a breaking point.

'You owe me your life, you hear me. You owe me the roof over your head, you owe me the life you took. You killed your mother; do you know that? She could have been happy.'

'She was barely conscious,' I say, through a jaw that's almost locked up in rage.

'You don't know anything, stuck in your books,' he said.

'You're a cruel bastard,' I say.

'That's enough!' he shouts, 'now you got your answers, get in the fucking basement!'

His eyes change suddenly as he starts to notice a difference in the air. His drunken state finally giving way to his senses. He looks behind him to the basement door, which is half ajar. He turns back to me just in time for him to see the matches in my hand. My head is starting to hurt now. Lungs full of leaking gas from the mains.

'What's that smell,' he says, 'what did you do?'

I open the matches and take several out in a clump. Readying them for the strike. His eyes widen.

'Thomas, what did you do?' he says.

'You stole my ice cream,' I say calmly.

'What?' he says.

'You stole my ice cream, you evil, murderous piece of shit,' I say, moving the match closer.

He raises his hand.

'Don't!' he says taking a step back.

'You stole my childhood. You really think I'm going to let you hurt anyone else?' I say.

'She wasn't worth it,' he says, fear creeping into his voice.

'She was to me,' I say.

My mind is clear. Neither of us are getting out of here alive. I've made peace with that, and I don't care. I had planned to try and escape. I had hoped I could run, but it's now or never. We're going to burn. I want to be close to him to watch him burn, even if we burn together.

He lunges for me. I see red eyes. The face of pure evil, his hand raised, and a scream so out of control it was inhuman.

I strike the match.

I remember the sound. A bright flash and then more heat than I've ever felt in my life. A bright white fireball was surrounding us both. His face lighting up and then being part of the fireball. I remember being airborne and the feeling of shattered glass piercing my flesh. I wake up on the wet grass. The rain, pouring down like the sea, was falling from the sky. The wind, now howling all around me. Through blurry eyes and the smell of burnt flesh and blood, I see the house—or rather, what's left of it—encapsulated in an angry flame and strewn with bricks and mortar everywhere. I hear a scream from inside the flames. The sheer force of the explosion must have hurtled me through the kitchen window. He was not so lucky. His charred black body is hanging halfway over the remnants of the windowsill. I can hear gurgling. The torrential rain appears to have extinguished many of the flames that had engulfed his miserable self. The roof of the house is half collapsed, and in the distance, I can hear the faint sounds of sirens. I don't know how long I've been laying on the wet grass.

My head is spinning, and I'm disoriented. I move my body over and feel a sharp pain in my shoulder. The house is in ruins; There's fire everywhere, but it's being tempered by the rain. I look at the charred remains laying in what was the kitchen. I think I see it moving.

I get to my feet and see that my coat and jeans are charred and torn. My hands are black and blistered. The bandage on the wound flayed. I reach inside my pocket and feel the rolled-up notes. They feel intact.

There's blood on my face and glass everywhere. My heart is racing, and my head is pounding. I get to my feet; I'm not going to wait any longer. I take one last look at the flaming ruins of my past, and I start to run.

I move down the side passage and climb over the rubble. The rain is beating down hard, but I don't care. There's a small laneway at the corner of our house that leads down an unseen part of the housing estate. I move quickly as I hear doors opening. Out of the corner of my eye, I can see people emerging from their houses to see what the hell has just happened.

I start to run. Everything hurts, but I don't care. I run fast now. The adrenaline kicks in, and my legs start to carry me off and away from this place. I run away from the flames, away from the dust and fire of my old life. Away from the pain, the murder, and the torture. Away from my captivity and loss and broken self.

The sense of elation is hard to describe as the water and wind seem to be on my back now, carrying me with the storm. My pace increases now as my feet barely touch the ground. I flee from hell, flee into the night.

I'll run until I can't breathe anymore, until I've left all behind me.

Even my name.

# Chapter
# FORTY-THREE

### Carter

It's been quiet for a few moments. I haven't answered Kimmy. I don't know what to say. How do I tell them both who I really am? How do I explain the scars on my back from that night in the shed?

I look at my hand, cuffed above me, and the little scars on the back. Three little holes I'd almost forgotten about. A lie so big and so deep that releasing it would drive me insane. There's so much about a life, about which they know nothing, that wants to spill out all over the floor. I feel like I may be sick. I don't know why the first thing to come out of my mouth is this, but I can't stop myself from saying it.

'This used to be my room,' I say.

'What?' Jean says.

I turn my body around and catch her eyes.

'Right over there, there was a mattress, over there, a little bookshelf,' I say.

They both follow my line of sight and see nothing but scorched earth. I turn enough to see Kim's eyes.

'This is where I grew up. I spent most of my life chained to that radiator behind you,' I say.

Kim turns to see the blackened twisted metal. They both stare at what was once my bedpost before turning back to me. The cellar door opens again as he enters and slowly climbs down the stairs. I turn and see what he's holding in his hand. It's a small garden rake.

He moves towards me. My mind flashes back to the shed. From the scars my little girl has just seen on my back, to the night I tried to lie about why I was late coming from the Alamo. He's gleefully going to do it again, in full view of my family, to humiliate and torture me. This man has gone insane; there's no doubt about it. I should have finished the job when I blew up this wretched house.

He moves over to me, places the rake next to what's left of the handrail, and begins to remove his parka. He reveals what's left of him.

His upper body is unclothed. Part of me takes comfort in the amount of damage that's been done. The burns are extensive, with grafts over grafts. His shoulders are melted into his torso, and he has nothing that resembles a chest. He turns to face the others.

By the sounds of it, his vocal chords were victims, which explains why his voice is so soft. He struggles with each word, but the anger and hatred force enough air through them so that he can make sounds.

'Thomas,' he says, addressing the girls, 'This was my boy. His name is Thomas, not Carter. He murdered me. I bet you didn't know that.'

There's no answer from Jean or Kimmy.

'Murdered his family and went on to get all the riches in the world and you know why?' he says, 'because of me. Because I taught him about the world. About how to survive. Look at how he betrays those who loved him. Cared for him.'

He moves towards Kimmy. I strain against the cuffs.

'That makes me your grandfather,' he says.

'It makes you shit,' I say.

His horrid face turns to me.

'You took my life from me,' he whispers.

'And I'll take it again once I get out of here,' I say.

I have to keep his attention on me.

'Oh, I don't think so,' he says, moving to the rake and picking it up. Without a second's hesitation, he strikes. Clawing over my back. I don't scream. That's the thing of growing up in pain. It's familiar to me. I grind my teeth and hold it in. I'm not letting him hear me scream. Not anymore. I feel the blood trickle along with the screams of Jean and Kimmy. I hear her shout out.

'Leave him alone!' Kim says.

My energy drains for a minute as I let the event wash over me, bringing me back to this place. An old reminder that opens the box of bad memories I thought I had under lock and key. I can't help the tears now. I shake my head as my muscles contract and the piercing agony flows around my body. He stops and takes a step towards me.

'You remember me now, don't you,' he whispers, 'you remember all the good times, you little ungrateful shit.'

He flings the rake to the ground. He turns to the others as I hang my head, trying to get my energy back.

'What are you getting out of this!' says Jean suddenly, 'what are you, some lonely psycho? Some bitter old envious little man.'

'I'm his father,' he says.

'Bullshit,' Jean says.

'Jean, stop,' I say, sounding exhausted.

'No, you're nobodies' father. You're a small, weak man who thinks the world owes you something, so you took your crap out on a small kid who couldn't fight back. It's so unoriginal it's almost boring.'

Jean's anger starts to grow.

'Killing and punching and raping and murdering because poor, fucking you. Did Mommy not tuck you in at night? Did she make fun of your tiny balls!'

I hear a smack.

He's given her a sharp hit to the face. Jean starts laughing. There's a real strength to it.

'Shut up,' he says.

'That's it isn't it?' she chuckles, spitting a pool of blood out of her mouth.

'You think you're original, but Carter was right. You're just a coward. Nothing more. A used-up coward who gave up years ago to cause pain to others.'

'You don't know what pain is, but you will,' he says, moving towards her.

'I know what pain is,' Jean says, 'you wouldn't last five minutes with what I've been through because you're weak, and your small, pathetic little child brain isn't worth shit.'

I hear a smack again. Jean screams before forcing out another half-conscious laugh.

'You can't hurt anyone. You're going to die, and nobody is ever going to know. Nobody is ever going to care.'

She starts to growl at him with a fury that's tapping into some memory of hers. I know that anger. I've felt it.

'You're nothing!'

There's a long pause. I hear Jean coughing and the pulling back of a trigger.

'Don't,' I say, feeling blood pour down my back.

'Shut up, Thomas, your girlfriend is trying to distract me, and doing a pretty good job of it too,' he says.

Jean goes silent.

'That's his name, by the way,' he says, turning to Kim, 'Thomas.'

I lower my head, suddenly beginning to feel my old self emerge from the darkness. He turns to me.

'You know the funny thing? It isn't even Thomas. I can't remember what it was when we picked you up from the agency'.

He turns back to Jean.

'You say I'm nothing?' he points a finger at me and says, 'THAT is nothing, a nameless, faceless little bag of flesh and bones, lucky to be alive and roaming around like a street rat.'

He looks me dead in the eye.

'You owe me,' he says, forcing the words out of his throat, 'you owe me for not killing you, for letting you live after you killed me. You.. Owe... me.'

What's left of his eye is red now, as if it's the last part of his face able to express any sort of emotion.

'Okay,' I say to him, maybe finding a way out, 'let them go and you can have me. You want to me.'

'You think I want you?' he says.

'Money,' I say.

'Money,' he replies, 'you stole three thousand dollars from me.'

It's a strange reaction I have, but part of me is brought back to this room, to being handcuffed and abandoned for months on end. Being devalued and discarded. Worth nothing. Now I know. I'm worth three thousand dollars.

'With interest,' he breathes, '100 million dollars, right now.'

I don't even think about it.

'Done,' I say.

I see the grin forming on his bulbous mouth.

'That easy,' he says.

'That easy,' I reply.

He moves towards me, pulling out a phone in one hand and a piece of paper in the other.

'That account, right now,' he says.

He puts the paper up to my face, then the phone.

'What number,' he says.

I relay the number to my personal banker in New York. He dials. There's initial confusion on the phone and a little suspicion on behalf of the bank, but after putting on my 'get it done' tone, the money is transferred. It's a bank in Panama.

The call is ended. He takes the phone and drops it on the ground before stomping on it, cracking the screen.

'Let them go,' I say.

He pauses, moving across the basement and wistfully waving the gun from one to the other. Kim is crying now. She looks tired and beaten.

'It's not enough,' he says turning to me.

'You have what you want,' I say.

'I thought I would be enough, but it means nothing to you, does it?'

'Let her go,' I say, 'you wanted me, you have me, you wanted money, you're rich.'

'But you are still a disobedient little jerk,' he whispers, 'and now I'm going to hurt you, for the rest of your life.'

He raises the gun and aims it Kimmy's head.

'Don't you fucking do it!' I scream at him, finally losing it, 'Please!'

He turns, cocking the trigger again, and moves the mussel up to her head. She closes her eyes and weeps.

'Now you'll know pain,' he says, as his finger begins applying pressure to the trigger.

'Don't you fucking do it!' Jean screams at him.

There's a gunshot. A flash of light.

'Nooo!!!' I scream, pulling my arms against the impossible restraints. I feel my world crack as I watch Kim's face splattered in blood.

She doesn't fall.

She's cries out in terror.

She cries out!

She's still alive. The monster who once claimed to be my father crumples to the floor. His head flops to the side, a hole in the front of his face surrounded by bone and brain.

Kim continues to cry. Her hands and arms are shaking. With another set of footsteps coming down the stairs, the confusion over what has just happened dissipates.

I have to do a double take.

'Roger?' I say, bewildered.

He's holding a gun and flashlight as he reaches the bottom. He does a quick sweep before moving straight to Kim.

'You're okay little Missy,' he says, taking out a key and removing her cuffs. She leaps on him and hugs him for dear life. He looks around at us.

'Everybody all right?' he says.

He removes a small wipe from what looks like a combat jacket and begins wiping off her face.

'Keep your eyes closed,' he says as he moves Kim over to the stairs, 'I'll be back in a second, just breath.'

He moves to Jean first, setting her free, and then over to me.

'You, okay?' he says, as I drop my feet to the ground.

A painful sharp pain goes up my back. I nod.

'Any other injuries?' he says.

I shake my head and quickly move past him. I run to Kim and scoop her up in my arms. She bawls her eyes out on my shoulder.

'We have to move,' Roger says.

We don't waste time and move quickly out of this hell, out of the charred remains of the house, and into the garden. There's a black Lexus with tinted windows in the driveway.

'There's a first aid kit on the passenger seat, you need to strap that up, sir,' he says, turning to Jean, 'there's a sling there as well and an ice pack, I'll help you when we get some distance from here.'

The whole thing is surreal. We get in the car, and Roger takes a phone out of his pocket. He wastes no time in dialing.

'Isaac? This is Cougar 3, I need a clean-up, sending you coordinates. Make it quick and quite.'

There's a pause.

'Thank you, my friend,' he says, hanging up.

He begins texting information into this phone before placing it in a dash holder. He waits for a minute before a message comes in.

'We're good,' he says, turning on the engine.

The back wheels of the car begin to spin as Roger takes off like the wind.

## Chapter
# FORTY-FOUR

We drive at speed, far from the house. Kim hasn't said anything. She's in shock and covered by a blanket as I run my fingers over her hair to try and calm her down. I lean over to Roger.

'What just happened,' I say, wincing as Jean does her best to apply gauze to my back.

Her arm is in a sling, but she seems to be doing okay.

'It's probably best that you don't know that sir,' Roger says.

'How the hell did you know where I was?' I say.

'Eh...' He says, 'I bugged you.'

'You what?' I say.

'The money clip, sir. I installed a tracker in it.'

My eyes widen.

'Not exactly in the job description, but I know a man in serious trouble when I see it, sir,' he says.

'Who did you call?' I say.

'Again, probably best you don't know about that. Suffice it to say, it's not something you need to worry about.'

'Jesus,' I say, 'you didn't really put those skills on the resume, Roger.'

'No, sir, if you actually saw my resume, you'd probably never sleep again,' he says, smiling and looking back at Kim, 'you okay back there? Just keep warm. There's water in the hold there, drink plenty of it. You'll start to feel better in a little while.'

Roger reaches over to a knapsack and hands it to me.

'There's a running sweater in there, sir, you need to warm yourself up," he says.

I put my hand on his shoulder.

'I don't know what to say,' I say, a crackle forming in my throat.

He smiles.

'Now you know how it feels,' he says, knocking on his prosthetic legs.

I lean back in the seat and remove the shreds of blood-soaked cloth.

'Best I can do for now,' Jean says, taping the last of the bandages.

I take her hand, squeeze it and our eyes meet.

'I'm so sorry,' I say to her, 'I'm so very, very sorry.'

Her eyes water.

'Carter we're alive,' she says, 'not exactly what I had in mind for a second date,' she says softly so Kim can't hear.

I move over to Kim, wrap my arm around her, and let her head fall on my chest. Her gaze seems distant.

'I didn't mean to put you in that danger, Kim, I really didn't,' I whisper.

'Why didn't you ever tell me?' she whispers almost inaudibly.

'I couldn't,' I say.

I look out the window and recognise the road we're on.

'Hang on,' I say to Kim, leaning forward.

'Roger,' I say, 'can we stop up ahead?'

'I wouldn't advise that, sir,' he says.

'I know where you can pull off the road and hide the car, just for a few minutes, Roger, I have to see if it's still there,' I say.

'Carter, I have a broken wrist, and you're seriously injured,' Jean says.

'Please, just for a few minutes,' I say.

'It's okay, I want to see whatever this is,' Kim says.

Jean nods. We drive for a minute or two before I spot it.

'Right here,' I say to Roger, 'you can pull in off that dirt track.'

Roger pulls the car into the forest and pulls over beside a tree.

'Keep the engine running, I won't be long,' I say.

He hands me an umbrella.

'We won't be long,' Jean says.

'I'm coming too,' says Kim.

'I really don't think…' I can't finish the sentence after the look on their faces.

I've put them both through so much, they deserve to know the truth. I nod.

'Okay, come on,' I say.

We exit the car, and I flip on the flashlight Roger has handed me. The dirt path has become overgrown, but the route comes back to me in an instant, as if I were only here yesterday. We move on through the undergrowth.

'What is this place?' Kim says, reaching up to hold my hand.

I take it and smile down to her.

'You'll see,' I say, looking back to Jean, 'you still with us?'

She nods.

'After all this?' she says, 'you owe me a serious drink, Carter.'

'You owe us both a drink Dad,' Kim says.

'That's fair,' I say.

We continue down the track for a few more minutes before the light comes on. I point to the mound.

'That's it,' I say

'That's what?' says Kim.

I lead them around and help Jean over a log before we come to the overgrown entrance. It's still there. The small padlock, rusted, but still in place. I pull back the vines and branches and yank them away, revealing the two wooden pieces I'd used for the door. I open them up and peer inside.

'Welcome to Alpha Base,' I say, turning to them.

'Welcome to what?' Kim says.

I motion for them both to come inside. We crouch down into the little cave, and I move my flashlight around. I'm filled with a strange numb sense of memory as it feels like I've never left.

I smile as I spot the little sealed tins.

'What is this place, Carter?' Jean says.

'My home away from home,' I say, reaching over and picking up one of the old boxes. It's in surprisingly good condition. I open it up and give a light whispered laugh.

'Well, I'll be damned,' I say, removing the notebook.

I turn to Kim.

'This is where I used to hide from them,' I say, 'I'd have a few hours here now and again where I could be here and write my stories.'

'You wrote stories?' Jean says.

I hand her the notebook.

'The adventures of Captain Starfinder?' she says, gazing at me and smiling.

'Yeah, it's not half bad either,' I say.

She flicks open the pages, reads a few lines, and meets my gaze. There are tears forming in her eyes.

'You went through all of this? Alone?' she says.

It's the first time it's really hit me. The first time the sadness of what happened to me as a child comes to the forefront of my mind, I can feel a tear fall down my cheek without even realising it. I turn away from them both and try to regain my composure, wiping my face quickly.

'It was a long time ago,' I say, 'it was another me.'

I feel a little hand take mine. It's Kim. I can't look at her. Memories of running for days through the rain, hitchhiking across the country. Being homeless in LA until finally being taken in by social services and moving from foster home to foster home. Educating myself and working three jobs to put myself through community college. Recognizing that I had learned a very valuable skill through it all: how to adapt, how to survive anything, and how to be creative, not only in my fantasy world but also in business. Seeing opportunities, starting small businesses after small businesses, hustling, and becoming ruthless—all in the name of self-protection.

'Your name is Thomas?' Kim says, snapping me out of my life.

I turn to her, tears still in my eyes.

'Once it was,' I say.

'It's a nice name,' she says.

I kneel and run my fingers through her hair.

'I'm sorry I let you go,' I say, 'I was scared that all of this, somehow transfer to you, that I wasn't able to give you a stable home, that somehow you'd turn out like me.'

She takes both hands and puts them on my face, wiping away another tear.

'That's not such a bad thing,' she says.

'Can I have this?' Jean says, closing the story notebook.

'After all this? Absolutely,' I say.

'Daddy,' Kim says.

'Yeah,' I say.

'I think I'd like to go home now,' she says.

I smile at her, stand up and spot one more thing in a plastic sheath.

'Oh, there it is,' I say.

'What's that?' Jean says.

'I owe some money to someone, I wanted to make sure he got paid,' I say, smiling and putting the debt ledger for the hardware store in my pocket.

We move outside into the dark woods, and I cover up Alpha Base one last time.

'Carter,' says Jean.

Our eyes meet.

'Let him go,' she says, taking my other hand, leaning in, and kissing me on the cheek.

All I can do is nod. She's right. I give the hideaway one more look, and with both hands full of something I've never been able to have in my life, love, we begin our journey away from the past. I leave little Thomas where he is always the happiest.

Until now.

## Chapter
# FORTY-FIVE

### Two weeks later

I don't think many people get the chance to face their past like I did. I believe it is mostly stored in the brain, like an old box in a loft. Sometimes the box leaks out the odd memory that punches its way into the present and fucks up our lives. We have little memories of who we used to be that pop into the present to remind us that something isn't right. We need to have a little chat about that. We're not looking after them, and we need to clear the air. In my case, it was a little too literal and nearly cost me my life and that of my family.

It's been a surreal few weeks. When we returned home, we were introduced to another one of Roger's mysterious acquaintances, an old medic, now a cardiac surgeon from upstate New York. He organised Jean's cast, my bandaging, medical attention, and even a therapist for Kim to talk through what had happened. Someone who was trustworthy and wouldn't go to the cops. Roger, it seems, has an extensive network from his Navy Seals years, and although I never really found out what rank he got in the military, it was hinted that he had some involvement in intelligence before he retired. A dark horse indeed.

Jean's wrist has healed nicely, and Kim seems to be doing better. I, on the other hand, have taken a little longer to come to terms with what's happened.

Jean and I have been spending a lot of time together. She comes over and helps cook for me and Kim, and we even shared a kiss after Kim went to bed the other night. It reminded me of a kiss I'd had once before. Back in that dark cave. It meant something. I don't know how this is going to play out, but it's like my mind is back on the beach again, staring out at the ocean and making sandcastles. As messed up as this sounds, the near-death events have blown open a wound that would never have been able to heal otherwise.

I can almost feel little Thomas sitting beside me here in the limo as Roger takes us both to the new offices of BMX. The investigations haven't led anywhere, and that detective seems to have moved onto more interesting cases. I still get the odd call, but it's just been put down to a random act of arson. The building itself should be back up and running in a month or two.

Roger hasn't talked much about what happened. He's sitting there listening to some old country music, and every time I try and get any sort of information out of him, he deflects it like a pro.

I feel at peace. Thomas and I are finally able to fit into the world. No more secrets.

'Everything all right Sir?' Roger suddenly says from the front.

'Oh, I'm just thinking,' I say.

'Best not to do so much of that,' he says.

'Why's that Roger?' I say.

'Thinking gets ye in trouble. Always look ahead, sir; that's all anyone's got.'

I smile at him.

'You know, I still have no idea what you're doing driving a limo,' I say to him.

'I enjoy it,' he says.

'Why?' I say.

'Keeps me sharp,' he says, 'keeps me in the know. I know everyone in this city, and they know me. At least a part of me. I like keeping my nose close to street.'

'Is that right,' I say.

'Yes Sir.' He says.

'I wish you would stop calling me sir,' I say.

'Sorry, no chance, old habits.' he says.

'Thank you, Roger,' I say, as our eyes meet.

He doesn't respond. His eyes lock on mine, and he gives the slightest of nods.

'Let's stop and get coffee,' I say.

'Yes, sir,' he says as we pull up next to Jessie's stall.

I get out and walk over. It's a beautiful spring day in New York, and the green is starting to creep back into the trees on the sidewalk. I move up to the stall and greet Jessie.

'Well, well,' she says, 'where the hell have you been? Holidays?'

'Not exactly, was tied up with some family stuff,' I reply.

'Families aren't easy,' she says.

I laugh.

'No, they are not,' I say, widening my eyes.

'The usual?' she says.

I nod. She moves away and starts to prepare my coffee. I order one for Marge. I lean against the window and turn, wondering what little selves the passers-by are carrying within. I see little ghostly children walking beside each one of them and wonder what each of them would have to say if they were given a chance to speak.

I feel a tap on the shoulder, and Jessie hands me a cardboard holder with my coffee. I pay her and wish her a good morning.

'Oh,' she says, 'there's one more thing.'

She reaches under the counter and brings out a USB key wrapped in a little red bow.

She places it in the tray. Our eyes meet, and she beams at me.

'Is that what I think it is?' I say.

'It is,' she replies, 'and it's good. Best I've ever done. I'm ready.'

I pick up the demo and look at it and place it inside my jacket pocket. Life goes on.

'I know you are,' I reply.

I move away from the counter feeling a sense of hope. That somehow, I've found peace.

## THE END

\*\*\*

Made in United States
North Haven, CT
03 September 2023